Mothers warn their daughters about men like these....

Gentlemen of Disrepute
Rebellious rule-breakers, ready to wed!

All these men have to do is kiss a woman's hand
and she's breathless with desire!

Dominic Furneaux

Stunned to see that the woman who shattered his heart
has fallen so low, he offers her a way out—
by making her his mistress!

Sebastian Hunter

Nights once spent on the town
are now spent in the dark shadows of Blackloch Hall.
Until Phoebe Allardyce interrupts his brooding…

Be seduced by these disreputable gentlemen in
Margaret McPhee's

UNMASKING THE DUKE'S MISTRESS—December 2011
A DARK AND BROODING GENTLEMAN—January 2012

Author Note

This story was not the one I planned to write.

Indeed, I was writing a different tale altogether when Arabella popped into my head. And once she was there she wouldn't give me peace until I had written her story. So here it is, a little more spicy than my usual, but you can blame that on Arabella.

I really do hope that you enjoy reading about Arabella and how she comes to find her happy-ever-after with Dominic.

Unmasking the Duke's Mistress

MARGARET McPHEE

TORONTO NEW YORK LONDON
AMSTERDAM PARIS SYDNEY HAMBURG
STOCKHOLM ATHENS TOKYO MILAN MADRID
PRAGUE WARSAW BUDAPEST AUCKLAND

ISBN-13: 978-0-373-29669-9

UNMASKING THE DUKE'S MISTRESS

For Patricia—I hope that it's not too saucy for you!

Chapter One

April 1809

Within the large and tastefully decorated drawing room of Mrs Silver's House of Rainbow Pleasures in the St James's district of London, Arabella Marlbrook paced and tried to ignore the feeling of dread that coiled deep in the pit of her stomach.

The black silk dress she was wearing had been made for a thinner woman and clung in an indecent fashion to the curves of her hips and breasts and she was all too aware that she was wearing neither petticoats nor stays. Her skin was like ice to touch, yet she could feel the smear of clamminess upon her palms. And she worried that the black feathers of the mask across her eyes did not obscure her identity well enough.

There were five other women artfully arranged around the drawing room, each one in a different colour and all in attires that made Arabella look positively overdressed.

'Do sit down, Arabella,' Miss Rouge said from where she reclined in her scarlet underwear and stockings upon one of the sofas. 'You are making me quite dizzy. You would do better to save your strength for there'll be gentlemen aplenty and eager tonight. And some of what they'll ask for will be demanding, to say the least.' She gave a sly smile and from behind the bright red feathers of her facemask her eyes looked almost black.

'Leave her be, Alice. Think how you felt on your first night. It is only natural that she is nervous,' said pale pink Miss Rose who was leaning against the mantelpiece so that the flicker of the flames illuminated her legs through the pale pink silk as if she were not wearing a skirt at all. Then she looked across at Arabella. 'You'll be fine, girl. Don't you worry.'

Arabella shot Miss Rose a grateful look, before turning to Miss Rouge, 'Please do not address me by my given name. I thought we were supposed to use the names Mrs Silver told us.' Arabella had no wish for the man she must lie with this night—her stomach turned over again at the thought—to know her true identity. It was vital that not the slightest hint of her shame attach itself to those that she loved.

'It's only a name, Miss Noir, keep your skirt in place!' snapped Miss Rouge.

'Leastways till she gets her gent upstairs!' quipped the small blonde in the armchair who was all in blue. She cackled at the joke and all of the other women, except for Arabella, joined in.

Arabella turned away from them so that they would not see the degree of her humiliation, and moved to stand before the bookcase as if she were perusing the titles upon the shelf. Only when her expression was quite composed did she face the room once more.

Alice, Miss Rouge, was buffing her nails. Ellen, Miss Vert, yawned and closed her eyes to nap upon the day bed. Lizzie, Miss Bleu, and Louisa, Miss Jaune, were engaged in a quiet conversation and Tilly, Miss Rose, was reading a romantic novel.

Arabella studied the décor of the room in an attempt to distract her mind from the prospect of what lay ahead. It was a fine room, she noted, perhaps one of the finest she had seen. The floorboards were polished oak, and covered with a large gold-and-blue-and-ivory Turkey carpet. The walls were a pale duck-egg blue that lent the room a peaceful ambience. In the centre of the ornate plasterwork ceiling was a double-layered crystal-drop chandelier and around the room several matching wall sconces sat against large, elegant looking-glasses so that the light of the candle flames was magnified in glittering excellence. The furniture was mainly oak, all of it finely turned, understated and tasteful.

There were five armchairs, two sofas and a daybed, some of which were upholstered in ivory and duck-egg blue stripes, some in plain ivory and others in a pale gold material that seemed to shimmer beneath the candlelight. On a table in the corner of the room was a vase filled with fresh flowers, the blooms all whites and creams and shades of yellow.

It might have been a drawing room in any respectable wealthy house in London. Arabella marvelled at the contrast between the calm elegance of the décor and the crude reality of what went on within these walls… and was faced once more with the stark truth of what she was here to do.

She dreaded the moment when some gentleman would arrive and buy her 'services.' Indeed, she had to fight every minute not just to walk out the door and keep on walking all the way home. But she knew she could not do that. She knew very well why she was here and the reason she must go through with this.

She closed her eyes and tried to calm the nausea and dread that was prickling a cold sweat upon her forehead and upper lip. A hundred guineas a week, Mrs Silver had promised. A fortune, indeed.

A hundred guineas to sell herself. A hundred guineas to save them all.

Dominic Furneaux, otherwise known as his Grace the Duke of Arlesford, swirled the brandy in his glass while he deliberated over the four cards held in his hand. Then, having made his decision, he drained the contents of the glass in a single gulp and gestured to the banker to deal him another card.

There was an audible intake of air from the smartly dressed men gathered around the Duke's gaming table in White's Gentlemen's Club. The pile of guineas heaped in the centre of the table was high, and most of it had been staked by the Duke himself.

The card was dealt with a flip so that it was placed face up on the green baize before the Duke.

Marcus Henshall, Viscount Stanley, craned his neck to look over the top of the heads of the gentlemen that stood before him.

The Ace of Hearts.

'An omen of love,' someone whispered.

The Duke ignored them. 'Five-card trick. *Vingt-et-*

un.' He smiled lazily as if he cared and laid his cards upon the table for all to see.

'Well, I will be damned, but Arlesford has the very luck of the devil!' someone else exclaimed.

There was laughter and murmurs and the scrape of chairs against the polished wood of the floor as his friends threw in their cards and got to their feet.

'What say you all to finding ourselves some entertainment of a different variety for what remains of the night?' Lord Bullford said.

The suggestion was met with raucous approval.

'I know just the place,' Lord Devlin chipped in. 'An establishment in which the wares are quite delicious enough to satisfy the most exacting of men!'

More laughter, and lewd comments.

Dominic watched as Stanley made his excuses and left, rushing home to his wife and baby. He felt a pang of jealousy and of bitterness. There was no woman or child awaiting Dominic. Indeed, there was nothing in Arlesford House that he wanted, save perhaps the cellar of brandy. But that was the way he wanted it. Women were such faithless creatures.

'Come on, Arlesford,' drawled Sebastian Hunter, only son and heir to a vast fortune. 'We cannot have you celebrating all alone.'

'When have I ever celebrated alone?' Dominic asked with a nonchalant shrug.

'True, old man,' said Bullford, 'But I will warrant the pleasures to be had in the house of paradise to which Devlin will take us will beat that offered by whichever little ladybird you have waiting for you in your bed.'

Dominic's smile was hollow. He had his share of women; indeed, he supposed that he truly did merit the title of rake that London bestowed upon him. But there was no ladybird waiting in his bed; there never had been. Dominic did not bring women home. He visited the beds of those women who understood the game and walked away afterwards. He gave them money and expensive gifts, but never anything of himself, nothing that mattered, nothing that could be hurt. And he was always discreet.

He had no notion to visit the establishment of which Devlin spoke. He glanced around the table, taking in how loud and bawdy and reckless was the mood of his friends. Too foxed and excited to exercise any morsel of discretion, young Northcote more so than the others. As if to prove his point Northcote accepted the bottle of wine that Fallingham offered and drank from its neck, so that some of the ruby-red liquid spilled down his chin to stain the boy's cravat and shirt.

'Arlesford is on his best behaviour. Wants to impress Misbourne and his daughter. Nice little heiress and even nicer big dowry!' shouted young Northcote.

The party hooted and cheered.

'Since you obviously appreciate her merits, Northcote, you may have her. I have no intention of being caught in parson's mousetrap, as well you know.'

Fallingham sniggered. 'Old Misbourne doesn't think so. There is a hundred-guinea stake in the betting book in here that the Duke of A. will be affianced to a certain Miss W. before the Season is over.'

Dominic felt his blood run cold. 'A fool and his money are soon parted. Someone is about to be a hundred guineas lighter in the pocket.'

'Au contraire,' said Bullford. 'Misbourne was overheard discussing it in this very club. He is very deter-

mined to have you marry his daughter. Thinks it is some sort of matter of honour.'

'Then Misbourne has misunderstood both honour and me.' Dominic did not miss the meaningful glance Hunter threw him at Bullford's words. Unlike the others, Hunter knew the truth. He knew what Dominic had come home to find in Amersham almost six years ago, and he understood why Dominic had no wish to marry.

Devlin's eyes flicked to the doorway. 'Speak of the devil! Misbourne and his cronies have just come in, no doubt hoping to engage the prospective son-in-law in a game of cards,' he said with a chuckle.

'Time indeed that we departed for Devlin's house of pleasures,' murmured Hunter.

'And give young Northcote the education that he deserves,' Devlin laughed.

'With the amount Northcote has had to drink I doubt he'll be up for that manner of education,' said Dominic.

'That's monstrous unfair, Arlesford! I'll have you know that my chap is more than capable of standing proud. Indeed, he's stirring even at the thought of it.'

'Prove it,' sniggered Fallingham.

Northcote got to his feet and moved a hand to unfasten the fall on his pantaloons.

'Don't be such a bloody idiot,' snapped Dominic. To which Northcote belched and sat down again.

'You see you'll have to come, Arlesford. Who else is going to stop Northcote making a complete cake of himself?' said Hunter.

'Who indeed?' Dominic arched a brow, but the sarcasm was lost on Hunter.

Northcote was out of his depth in such company,

and dangerously so. Dominic knew he could not just abandon the youngster. He supposed he could endure an evening of flirtation in an upmarket bordello for Northcote's sake.

Dominic followed his friends towards the doorway and walked past Misbourne with only the briefest of nods in the man's direction. As he had told his friends, he had no intention of entering the marriage mart.

Dominic Furneaux had learned his lesson regarding women very well indeed. And so he turned his thoughts away from the past to the rest of the evening that lay ahead.

Mrs Silver gave the women only a few minutes' warning before showing the group of four gentlemen into the room.

Arabella felt the wave of panic go through her. Her stomach revolted and she felt physically sick at the prospect of what she was about to do with one of these men and for money. For one moment the desire to flee was overwhelming. She wanted so much just to run away. But then she remembered why she had to do this. And the memory resolved every trembling nerve in Arabella's body and lent her the strength that she needed. She stilled, took a deep breath and raised her eyes to face the men.

They were all young, not much older than her own four-and-twenty years; all used expensive tailors if their tight-fitting dark coats and pantaloons were anything to go by. Ruddy cheeked and bright eyed, and most definitely the worse for drink, especially the youngest-looking man of the group. She could smell the wine and brandy from where she stood at the farthest side of the room behind the striped sofa, as if the distance and the barrier of the furniture could save her from what lay ahead.

Her eyes began to move over them and she wondered which man would choose her. And the worry struck her that perhaps none of them would and then what would she do? Much as she loathed being here in this awful position, the thought of returning home empty-handed was even worse.

The men looked eager, salivating almost, so that she could not suppress the shudder that rippled through her. She turned her glance to the two taller gentlemen who were only just entering the room to join their friends... and her stomach sank right down to her toes.

It felt to Arabella as if she had just stepped off the edge of a cliff. The breath froze in her throat, her blood turned to ice and her heart hammered so hard and fast that she thought she might faint. She gripped tight to the back of the sofa, oblivious to the fact that her fingernails were digging into the expensive ivory material.

It cannot be. The thought was loud in her mind.

'It cannot be.' The words were barely a whisper upon her lips.

She stared all the harder, sure that she must be mistaken. But there was no mistake. She would have known the tall dark-haired man anywhere, even though she had not seen him in almost six long years.

He had not changed so very much. His shoulders were broader, his body carried more muscle and there were a few more lines of life etched upon his handsome face, but there could be no doubting that the man was most definitely Dominic Furneaux, or the Duke of Arlesford, as he was now.

His expression was one of boredom as he surveyed the room and its inhabitants. He looked as if he had no interest in being here in Mrs Silver's drawing room. His glance passed over her and then shot back to her face.

Please God, do not let Dominic, of all people, recognise her!

Her fingers touched the black feathered mask, checking that it was properly in place, but still he stared at her as if he could see right through it to the face of the woman beneath. His bored expression had vanished to be replaced by one of intense scrutiny.

The pop of the first champagne cork made her jump, but it was not the noise that set the tremor racing throughout her body. She averted her gaze and noticed that Mrs Silver was smiling meaningfully in her direction. Arabella saw the older woman gesture towards the glasses and suddenly remembered that she was supposed to be offering champagne to the gentlemen.

Miss Rouge had already dispensed with the first bottle and one of the men uncorked the second and began to pour. Arabella's hands trembled so much that she feared she would be unable to disguise it, but she knew she could not just stand there staring at Dominic. Perhaps if she busied herself he would stop looking at her with that too-seeing gaze.

She crossed the room towards Mrs Silver and collected two crystal-cut glasses of champagne as she had been told. And all the while her mind was reeling from the impact of seeing Dominic after all this time. She felt panicked, agitated, unable to think straight. She squeezed her eyes shut, trying to marshal her thoughts, struggling to control the shock that was roaring through her veins.

Of all the places to see him again, when she had learned to live with the weight of that which had almost crushed her. Maybe he would fix his attention on one of the other girls. Maybe. But would it be any easier to stand here and watch him take Miss Rouge or Miss Vert or any one of the other women upstairs? Could she feign a smile, pretend a flirtation and go willingly with another man, knowing that he was here? She shook her head in an infinitesimal movement of denial. This night had promised to be the most difficult and degrading of Arabella's life. Dominic's presence made it nigh on impossible.

A hand touched against her sleeve and she opened her eyes to find Mrs Silver looking at her with both warning and concern.

'One hundred guineas a week,' she mouthed almost silently. 'Think of the money.'

Arabella gave a tiny nod at the reminder and reined in her emotions with a will of iron. A deep breath…and then she turned around.

Dominic was standing right before her.

'Miss Noir, I presume.' His gaze swept slowly over the transparent dress before coming back to rest upon her face. 'Arlesford, at your service, ma'am.'

So he did not know her after all. *Thank God!* She breathed a silent sigh of relief at that small mercy and steeled her nerves to play the role of a woman she was not.

'Your Grace.' She forced the words to her lips and curtsied, but she could not bring herself to smile. Every bone in her body felt chilled to the marrow, every inch of her skin cold and bloodless. This was the meeting, albeit not under such circumstances, she had prayed so hard first for and then against. All her beliefs that she was over him, that she no longer cared, had been a delusion. She cared so much that it was as if the air had been knocked clean from her lungs.

They stared at one another and for Arabella it was as if the years had rolled back and she was looking at the man she would never manage to forget no matter how hard she tried. She averted her gaze, lest he see even a grain of her riotous emotions in her eyes, and glanced around the room.

The other women were smiling and conversing in coquettish teasing tones, each paired with a single gentleman. From the corner of the room Mrs Silver was looking at Arabella with a look of exasperation. The older woman gestured with her eyes from Dominic to the two glasses of champagne, that Arabella was still gripping for dear life, and back again.

There was no way out, no room for retreat. Arabella held her head high and forced her gaze back to Dominic. 'Would you care for some champagne?'

He ignored her question and studied her with those dark brown eyes that were so disturbingly familiar. The seconds seemed to stretch to minutes as they stared at one another, the champagne seemingly forgotten. But then his eyes darkened and he accepted the glass from her hand.

'I should…' She glanced round for another gentleman to whom she might pass the second glass but all of the men were already drinking and their attentions most definitely engaged in so obvious a manner that made Arabella feel as embarrassed as if she had been an innocent.

'It is for you, I believe,' Dominic said. He paused and

the dark gaze held hers once more before adding, 'Perhaps we can drink our champagne together...upstairs?'

Arabella's heart stumbled and missed a beat before galloping off at full tilt. The breath caught in her throat. The whole world seemed to turn upside down.

She knew what his suggestion meant.

Dominic had chosen her.

Her whole body trembled at the knowledge and she did not know whether it was the worst thing that could have happened or the best. Nearly six years, and yet it was as if her lips still burned from his kisses, her body still tingled from his love-making. To give herself to him again, and for money, flayed her pride more than anything.

Her hand itched to dash the contents of her glass in his face, to shout at him, to refuse him in the cruellest of terms. A vision of him standing there, his face and hair soaked from her champagne, his pride slurred before his friends swam in her mind, and that imagining was the one glimmer of light in the grim darkness of what was happening. But Arabella did not indulge her fantasy; she could not afford to. Even through the force of all that raged within her, she did not forget the stark truth of why she was here at Mrs Silver's House of Rainbow Pleasures. She had her responsibilities.

And she was honest and practical enough to admit to herself that, if she must couple with a gentleman this night it was better that it was Dominic rather than some stranger.

She glanced again at the other men in the room, at their faces glistening with sweat and flushed from drink and the greedy lust and excitement in their eyes. No matter how much she was loathe to admit it, the knowledge that it would be Dominic, and not one of them, was something of a relief, albeit a bitter one.

And if she kept the mask in place he would never know the identity of the woman for whom he was paying. And that at least would make it tolerable.

Arabella swallowed her pride. Her eyes met his. She nodded and turned to lead the way to the room Mrs Silver had shown her.

Within the black-clad bedchamber Dominic could not take his gaze from Miss Noir. He knew that he was staring and still he could not stop. His intention of watching over Northcote had been forgotten the moment he had set eyes on her downstairs in Mrs Silver's drawing room. God help him, but he could no more have turned away from her than stop breathing. It was as if the years had not passed and it was another woman standing before him.

'Is something wrong?' she asked.

Hell's teeth, he thought, but she even sounded like her.

Miss Noir's fingers fluttered nervously around the edges of her mask.

'Forgive my manners, but your appearance stirs memories from my past. You have the very likeness of someone I once knew.' It was the reason he was standing here with her now in the bordello's bedchamber and the very same reason why he should have turned his back and walked away. The pain had returned, and the bitterness, but when he looked at this woman he wanted her with what could only be described as desperation.

He wanted her because she looked like Arabella Tatton.

She did not smile or simper or offer playful seductive words. She did not unlace her bodice or stand before the fire to reveal the outline of her legs or lie upon the daybed with her skirts arranged to show her stockings. Rather her expression was serious, and her manner, for all she tried to hide it, was one of unease. She just stood there and watched him, all calm stillness, yet the white-knuckled clasp of her hands gripping together betrayed that she was not as calm as she was pretending. And beside her on the small occasional table, amidst the coil of dark silken ropes and the feathers and fans, the bubbles sparkled and fizzed within her untouched glass of champagne.

He drained the contents of his own glass in an effort to dampen the strength of emotion the woman's startling resemblance stirred.

'You seem a little nervous this evening, Miss Noir.'

'It is my first night here. Forgive me if I am unfamiliar with the usual etiquette. I...' She hesitated and seemed to have to force the remainder of the sentence, 'I wish only to please you.' Her head was held high and the glint in her eyes belied the subservience of the words. She raised her chin a notch and everything of her stance was as defiant and tense as if she were facing a combatant rather than a man whom she was trying to seduce. 'Do you wish me to undress now?'

He rose, setting his empty glass down next to her full one.

She looked so like Arabella that he felt like he had been kicked in the gut. His blood was rushing too hot, too fiercely. And no matter how hard he tried to suppress them, the memories were as strong and vivid as if all that had happened between them had been only yesterday.

The depth of his desire shocked him for he would have thought his anger at her to have long since tempered that. Yet his body was already hard and throbbing with impatience…as if it really were Arabella standing there. And because she looked so like Arabella, Dominic knew that he would not reject what she offered. He gave not another thought to Northcote and stripped off his tailcoat.

'There is more pleasure for us both if I undress you,' he said, never taking his eyes from hers. Her lashes swept low, not in a teasing manner, but as if she sought to hide something of herself from his scrutiny. He resolved to stop staring. But he could not.

'As you wish.' She walked to stand before him, and the dress she was wearing seemed to accentuate rather than hide the curves of her figure. In this, at least, she differed from Arabella, for although Arabella had been quite as tall as this woman, she had been more slimly built.

Arabella. Her very name seemed to whisper through the silence of the room. And the images were flashing through his mind, of Arabella lying beneath him, of her laughter and her smile; of him burying his face in the golden silk of her hair spread across his pillow, and his mouth whispering words of love upon hers while his hands stroked a caress over the naked satin of her skin.

And for all the anger in his heart, Dominic's body grew harder. With an effort he reined himself back under some measure of control. Arabella Tatton. He despised her. He should walk away from this woman, she, whose resemblance to Arabella had unleashed all that he had hidden away in the dark recesses of his mind. The logical part of his mind knew that with absolute certainty. Yet Dominic did not leave.

Instead, he reached over and untied the laces of her dress, loosening them until the bodice gaped wide to reveal the lush perfect breasts beneath. They nosed at the fabric, the nipples a rosy pink beside the pale perfection of her skin. And when his fingers brushed against them he felt the nipples harden and peak.

He leaned down and touched his lips against the soft skin of first one cheek and then the other, and when he looked through the holes cut within the feathered mask he saw her pupils widen, black as ebony, within eyes that were the same colour as Arabella's, the true clear blue of a sunlit summer sky.

Arabella. The pain was in equal measure to the depth of his desire.

His mouth traced down the slender column of her throat, to kiss each hollow of her collarbone as he eased the dress halfway down her arms. The laces were undone enough to expose her breasts in full and he moved his mouth over them so close yet without touching. Her nipples beaded harder as he caressed them with his breath. Slowly, teasingly he touched his tongue to her.

She closed her eyes and tried unsuccessfully to catch back the rush of breath that escaped her. Beneath his lips he felt the shiver pass right through her.

Very gently, very slowly he laved her, sucked her, measured the weight of each delicious breast within his hands. He could feel the fast hard beat of her heart and, more surprisingly, the slight tremor within her body.

And when he drew back her cheeks were faintly

flushed and behind the mask her eyes were open again, and just for a moment he saw that they glittered with desire before she hid them once more from his view. She slid the rest of her dress from her arms and unfastened the buttons by her waist so that the skirts slithered down her legs to pool upon the floor. She stepped out of the pile of silk, naked save for her high-heeled shoes and stockings, and the mask upon her face.

Miss Noir did not posture to encourage him, not that she needed to. She just stood there, proud and watchful.

Arabella, he wanted to whisper, and even though the name had never left his memory for all of these years past, having this woman who bore so much of her resemblance had slashed the bindings on all of those old wounds. And yet he wanted her more than ever. He wanted her as if she were Arabella herself.

Dominic shrugged off his waistcoat, unfastened his cravat and peeled off his shirt. He saw Miss Noir's gaze move over his chest and down to take in the bulge of his manhood straining in his pantaloons. And when her eyes met his again there was the strangest expression in them, one that he could not quite fathom.

He closed the distance between them and, pulling her into his arms, kissed her as thoroughly as he had wanted to from the moment he had laid eyes on her. She was rigid at first, but then she succumbed to his kisses and melted against him, and it was just like having the real Arabella in his arms. He did not even have to close his eyes to pretend it was her.

He kissed her as if she were the woman that he had loved. He kissed her with all the anguish that was in his soul…and in the answer of her lips he was shocked to feel an echo of how it had been between Arabella and himself. He stilled and eased back that he might look into her eyes but, just as quickly, Miss Noir turned away and bent to unfasten the garters of her stockings.

Dominic stayed her. 'Leave them,' he murmured. 'I want to look at you.'

She misunderstood and took a few steps away, opening up a small distance between them so that he might view her. He could not ignore the invitation, swallowing hard as his gaze swept over the long white legs that rose out of her dark stockings, over the smooth curve of her hips and the small triangle of fair hair that sat between her legs, and the soft feminine belly.

She blushed beneath his scrutiny, as if she were not a well-practised courtesan that rode different men every night of the week, as if she really were his Arabella. His manhood strained all the harder against the fine wool of his pantaloons.

She made no move to unfasten the mask from her face, nor did he ask her to do so, for he had no wish to shatter the illusion that had him standing here in the first place.

He stripped off his clothing and then took her in his arms once more.

Arabella, he mouthed silently against her throat as she wound her arms around his neck.

Arabella, as he carried her to the bed and laid her down. The contrast of her pale naked skin against the black silken sheets seemed to emphasise her similarity to Arabella all the more. He wanted her so much he was aching for her, so much that he could think of nothing else. His body covered hers, one hand thrumming at her nipple as he positioned himself between her legs.

She was open to him, moist and ready, and he was

rock hard as he stroked against her. Everything of her—
the scent, the taste, the feel—was so like Arabella that
as he slid into her silken heat in his mind it was Arabella
he was entering. And when he rode her it was Arabella
he was riding until both their breaths were ragged and
their bodies were slick with sweat. He rode her until
he found the relief of his climax, pulling out of her just
before he spilled his seed.

Such exquisite torture.

But the minute that his body was spent he rolled off
her, already regretting his decision to come upstairs
with her.

She was not Arabella, and all that he had done was
tear asunder ill-healed wounds of the past. He felt as
empty and alone and unhappy as ever he had been and
longed to be gone from this place. Throwing the covers
back, he climbed from the bed.

'Thank you,' he said awkwardly, but could not bring
himself to use the woman's name. He walked away,
found his shirt and pantaloons and pulled them on.

A faint breathy noise sounded from the bed, a noise
that sounded suspiciously like a silenced sob.

Dominic looked back at the bed and the woman who
lay there so still and unmoving. And as his gaze found
hers, she turned quickly away, rolling on to her side to
present him with her back, as if she sought to block him
out.

His eyes traced the golden tendrils that had escaped
from the pile of curls pinned upon her head, over her
pale shoulders and down the straight line of her back.
Her waist was narrow before the flair of her hips and
her perfect bottom.

His fingers froze in the act of fastening the buttons

of his pantaloons. His blood turned to ice. He could not move, could not so much as take a breath. He stared at the fullness of her rounded buttocks, stared at the soft white skin...and the distinctive dark mole upon her right cheek that he remembered so well.

The shock was as explosive as if someone had taken a pistol and shot him at point-blank range. Everything else in the world seemed to diminish. Dominic gaped with utter incredulity, staring at a truth so blatant that he marvelled he had not realised right from the very start.

'Arabella?' His whisper was barely more than a breath, yet it seemed to resonate within the room as loudly as if he had roared it at the top of his voice.

Every line of her body stiffened and tensed, the reaction confirming the suspicion his mind had been too slow to form. He saw the small shiver that rippled through her before she pulled the top cover free and then, holding it against her body to cover her nakedness, climbed from the bed. Only then did she turn to face him.

They stared at one another across the rumpled mess of sheets, and the very air seemed to vibrate with a barely contained tension.

Even now his mind could not accept the enormity of the discovery. Even now he thought she would deny it. But in her silence and stillness there was nothing of denial.

Dominic reached her in an instant. With one hand he pulled her to him, barely noticing that he had displaced the bedcover from her in the process. He was too busy untying the ribbons of her face mask, too busy tearing it from her. Even as she gasped, the black-feathered object

tumbled to lie at their feet. And he stared down with
horror into the shocked white face of Arabella Tatton,
or Arabella Marlbrook as she was now.

Chapter Two

Arabella's naked body was hard against the length of Dominic's, their hips so snug that she could feel the press of his manhood. For a moment the shock of him discovering her was so great that she could do nothing other than stare right back into the eyes of the man she had loved. But then she recovered something of her wits and struggled to free herself.

'Arabella!' He tried to still her.

She hit out at him and tried to escape. But Dominic caught her flailing arms and hauled her back to him, securing her wrists behind her in a grip that was gentle yet unbreakable.

'Arabella.' Quieter this time, but no less dangerous.

'No!' she cried, but Dominic was unyielding. He stared down at her with implacable demand.

'What the hell are you doing here?' His eyes had darkened to a black glower that smouldered within the pallor of his face. And there was about him a simmering, barely contained rage so unlike the man she remembered.

She strove to stay calm, but her breath was as ragged as if she had been running at full pelt and with every breath she took she could feel the swollen tips of her breasts brush against his unfastened shirt.

'At least grant me the honour of allowing me to clothe myself before we have this conversation,' she said with a calmness that belied everything she was feeling.

His gaze dropped to rove over her nakedness with deliberate and provocative measure so that she thought he meant to refuse her but, just as she thought it, she felt his grip loosen and drop away.

She gathered up the black dress from where it lay on the floor and, turning her back to him, quickly garbed herself. She stretched around and tightened the laces of the bodice that she could reach, but had no other option than to leave the remainder loose. The dress gaped from the untied laces, revealing far too much of the pale swell of her bosom. It was the antithesis of respectable clothing, but it was better than facing him naked. She hoisted the neckline of the dress and clutched it in place. Dominic had finished his own dressing and now watched her with eyes burning with a shock that mirrored her own and an unmistakable anger.

'I will ask you again, Arabella,' he said with a quietness that was deadly, 'what are you doing here?'

'The same as any woman does in a place such as this.' She faced him defiantly, and with a determination to hide the shame and wretchedness beneath that façade.

'Whoring.' His voice was harsh.

'Surviving,' she said with as much dignity as she could muster and stared down his contempt.

'And where in damnation is Henry Marlbrook while you are "surviving" in a brothel? What manner of husband is he that you have been reduced to this?' His voice changed, hardened, as he spoke Henry's name and the word 'husband.'

'Do not dare to mention Henry's name.' Arabella would not stand here and hear it.

'Why ever not?' he threw back at her. 'Frightened that I find him and run him through?'

'Damn you, Dominic! He is dead!'

'Then he has saved me the trouble,' he said coldly.

Arabella gasped at Dominic's cruelty and then, before she could think better of it, she slapped him hard across his face. The crack resounded in the room around them and was followed by silence. Even in the soft flickering candlelight she could see the mark her palm had left upon his cheek.

His eyes had been dark before, but now they appeared as black and deadly as the night that surrounded them. But Arabella would not back down.

'You deserved that.' For everything he had done. 'Henry was a good man, a better man by far than you, Dominic Furneaux!'

Henry had been kind.

And Arabella had been grateful.

She saw something flicker in the darkness of Dominic's eyes.

'Just as he was all those years ago,' he said in a chilled voice. 'I have not forgotten, Arabella, not for one single day.'

Neither had she. With those few words all the past

was back in an instant. Of the joy of losing her heart to Dominic, of her happiness and expectations for the future, of the lovemaking they had shared. Lies and illusions, all of it. It had meant nothing to him. *She* had meant nothing to him, other than another notch upon his bedpost. At nineteen she had not understood the base side of men and their desires. At four-and-twenty Arabella knew better.

'You wasted no time in wedding him. Less than four months from what I hear.'

She could hear the accusation in his voice, the jealousy, and it fanned the flames of her ire. 'What on earth did you expect?' she shouted.

'I expected you to wait, Arabella!'

'To wait?' She stared at him in disbelief. 'What manner of woman did you think me?' Did he honestly think that she would have welcomed him back with open arms? That she would have given herself to him again after he had discarded her in such a humiliating way? 'I could not wait, Dominic,' she said harshly. 'I was—' Her eyes sought his.

His gaze was dark and angry and arrogant, every inch the hard, ruthless nobleman she knew him to be.

'You were…?'

She hesitated and felt the pulse in her throat beat a warning tattoo.

'A fool,' she finished. A fool to have believed his lies. A fool to have trusted him. 'You have what you came here for, Dominic. Now be gone and leave me alone.'

'So that you might rush down to Mrs Silver's drawing room to offer a "glass of champagne" to the next gentleman who is doubtless already waiting there.' Contempt dripped from his every word. 'I do not think so.'

How dare he? she thought. *How damnably dare he stand there and judge me after what he has done?* And in that moment she hated him with a passion that was in danger of driving every last vestige of control from her head. She wanted to scream at him and hit him and unleash all of her anger, for all that he had done then, and for all that he had done now. But she hung on to her self-control by the finest of threads.

His eyes held hers for a moment longer and the very air seemed to hiss between them. Then he walked over to stand behind one of the two black armchairs by the fireplace.

'Sit down, Arabella. We need to talk.'

She gave a shake of her head. 'I think not, your Grace,' she said and she was proud that her voice came out as cold and unemotional as his, for beneath it she was shaking like a leaf.

'If it is the money you are concerned over, rest assured that I have paid for the whole night through.' He looked at her with flint in his eyes.

There was a lump the size of a boulder in her throat that no amount of swallowing would shift. She faced him squarely, pretending she was not ravaged with shame, pretending that she was standing there completely untouched by the fury of emotion that roared and clashed between them.

Pretending that she had no secrets to hide.

He gestured to the armchair before him. 'Come, Arabella, sit. After what has just passed between us there is no room for coyness.' His voice was harsh and his face was set harder, more handsome, more resolute than ever she had seen it. And she knew that he would not change his mind.

'Damn you,' she whispered and the scars throbbed as if they had never healed and his reappearance, after all these years when Arabella had thought never to see him again, sparked fears that she was only just beginning to grasp.

Only once Arabella was seated did Dominic take the chair opposite hers.

'Did you know it was me from the start?'

'Of course I did not!' The fury he felt for both her and himself made his voice harsh. It did not matter what she had done, he would never have taken her out of vengeance.

'Then how did you realise?'

'How did I not realise sooner?' he demanded, but the question was not really for her but, rather, for himself. 'Me, who has known every inch of your body, Arabella.' *One flimsy black-feathered mask alone had been enough to fool him,* he thought bitterly, and knew that was not quite true. It was the fact that this, a bordello, a bawdy house, a brothel, was the last place on earth he would have ever thought of finding her.

The thought of what she had become shocked him to the core. The thought that he had treated her as such shocked him even more. He had dreamt of finding her, both longed for it and dreaded it. But never in all of his imaginings had it been like this. He raked a hand through his hair, trying to control his feelings.

He glanced across at her. Her face was pale, her expression guarded.

Time had only served to ripen her beauty so that she was now a beautiful woman when once she had been a beautiful girl. There was about her a wariness that had not been there before. Then, she had been innocent and carefree and filled with an irrepressible joy. Now what he saw when he looked at Arabella was a cold, angry, determined stranger he did not recognise. And then he remembered the muffled sob he had heard and the sheen of tears in her eyes…and something of his own anger died away.

'You said Marlbrook died.'

She gave a cautious nod. 'Two years since.'

'And left you unprovided for?' He could not keep the accusation from his tone.

'No!' The denial shot from her lips in her desperation to defend the bastard she had married. 'No,' she said again, this time more calmly. 'There was money enough left for a careful existence.' She hesitated as if deliberating how much to tell him.

The questions were crowding upon his lips, angry and demanding, but he spoke none of them, choosing instead to wait with a patience that he did not feel for her explanation.

But Arabella's explanation was not forthcoming. Her expression closed. Her mouth pressed firm and she glanced away.

The seconds ticked by to become minutes.

'Then you are here by choice rather than necessity?' he said eventually and raised an eyebrow.

'Yes.' She tipped her chin up and met his gaze unflinchingly, almost taunting him. 'So now you see the woman I have become, have you not changed your mind about leaving?'

'I am staying, Arabella,' he said, his eyes still holding hers with every inch of the determination he felt.

She bowed her head and glanced away, sullen and angry.

'What does your father make of your chosen profession?' he demanded. 'What does your brother?'

'My father and Tom were taken by the same consumption that claimed Henry.'

'I am sorry for your loss,' he said. The news shocked him, for he had known the family well and liked them. 'And Mrs Tatton? What of her?'

'My mother was brought low by the disease, but she survived.'

'Does she know that you are here, Arabella?'

A whisper of guilt moved across her face. 'She does not.' She tilted her chin, defiant again. 'Not that it is any of your concern.'

In the ensuing silence they could hear the faint rhythmic banging of a bedstead against a wall. Neither of them paid it the slightest attention.

His eyes raked hers. There was another question he needed to ask, even though he already knew the answer by the very fact that she was here in Mrs Silver's House of Rainbow Pleasures.

'There is no other man since Marlbrook? No new husband or protector?'

'No,' she said in a tight voice and eyed him with unmistakable disdain. 'But if there were, it would be no business of yours.'

Their eyes held for a moment and a storm of anger seemed to fire and crackle between them before she rose and moved away to stand over by the long black curtains that covered the window.

Arabella could not just sit there and let the questions continue, not when she feared where they might lead.

Besides, Dominic had no right to question her. He had forfeited the right to know anything of her life when he had made his decision all those years ago. Let him think the worst of her if it prevented his questions and made him leave. Let him think she was the whore he had just made her. Better that than the alternative.

She could not bear for him to see how much she was hurting. And she could not bear for him to know the truth of her situation, of the desperation that had led her to this place. Better his contempt than his pity, and better still that he left knowing nothing at all.

The chink of night sky, between the edge of the curtain and the wall, was very dark. There were no stars, and the street lamps outside remained black and unlit and everything seemed to be waiting and edged with danger. And when she glanced round at Dominic he was sitting staring into the small flames that flickered amongst the glowing coals, the expression upon his face as dark and brooding as the night outside.

'I cannot believe that I have found you here...in a damnable brothel!' Dominic was still reeling from the shock of it. All these years he had imagined that one day he might find her. He had imagined a thousand different scenarios, but not one of them had come close to the reality. She was a lightskirt in an upmarket bordello. Miss Noir, in Mrs Silver's rainbow selection for those men who had enough blunt to pay. He felt sick at the thought.

'Then walk away and pretend that you have not,' she said in a low voice, but she did not look round.

In the silence there was only the crack from the remains of the fire upon the hearth.

'You know that I cannot do that, Arabella.' It did not

matter how aggrieved he was, she did not deserve life in such a place.

He glanced across at her standing there in the flimsy black silk that revealed more of her figure than it covered, and the nakedness of her back where the laces hung loose and, despite everything, he felt desire.

It disgusted him that he could still want her after her faithlessness with Marlbrook and after all he had already taken from her this night in such despicable circumstances. He was not proud of having treated her like a whore, even if that was what she was. And he swore to himself that, had he known that she was Arabella, he never would have touched her. But it was too late for that. He had done a great deal more than touch her.

'Why not? It is what I want. For you to leave…and not come back.'

Dominic felt the stab of her words, but he did not retaliate, nor did he take his eyes from the fire. A section of the molten embers cracked and collapsed and in the space where they had been one small flame remained, burning hotter and more brightly than all the other.

'For the sake of what was once between us, Arabella—'

'I do not want your pity, Dominic!' She swung round to face him, standing there with her hands on hips, her face proud and angry. 'And whatever was between us is long dead.'

'Oh, I am more than well aware of that, Arabella.' Her eyes flashed with a fierceness he had never seen there before. Her lips were flushed and swollen from his kisses, and the creamy swell of her breasts rose and fell with the raggedness of her breath. His gaze dropped to where her rosy nipples were beginning to peep over the black silk.

She saw his gaze and, with a fury, wrenched the bodice higher and held it in place.

'It is a bit late for that, Arabella.'

She might pretend otherwise but, unlike him, Arabella had known with whom she was coupling and Dominic had felt the spark in the response of her lips to his, an echo of what had once been. The love might be dead, but there was still a physical desire that burned strong between them.

His gaze dropped from her back to the fire.

He had not forgiven her, but he could not leave her here.

He could not forgive her, yet he wanted her still.

An idea started to form in his head, one that might finally allow Dominic to purge the demons that drove him.

She was watching him when he got to his feet and moved towards her. He saw the shiver that ran through her body and he found his coat and wrapped it around her shoulders.

Her eyes met his and he saw the surprise and wariness and unspoken question in them.

'You do not have to do this, Arabella.'

'I've already told you that what I do is none of your concern.' Her voice was curt and her eyes cold.

'I could help you.'

'I do not need your help, your Grace,' she countered.

'That may be, but you will hear me out just the same, Arabella.'

She stared at him, her expression closed, yet he could sense her caution and suspicion.

'It would mean that you would not have to sleep with one different man after another, at the mercy of whatever demands they might make of you. You would not fear to be cast out into the streets. Indeed, you would never want for anything again.'

She frowned slightly and shook her head as if she did not yet understand.

'I would give you a house, as much money as you need. You would be safe. Protected.'

'Protected?' She echoed the word and he saw her eyes widen.

'We would come to an arrangement that would be mutually beneficial to us both.'

'You are asking me to be your mistress?' She gaped at him.

'If that is what you wish to call it,' he said.

The silence was tense. From outside the room came the sound of a woman's giggle and a man's booted steps receding along the passageway.

He saw the shock so stark and clear upon her face and knew that whatever Arabella had been expecting it had been nothing of this. And just for a minute he thought he saw such a look of sadness in her eyes, of a pain that mirrored the one he had carried in his heart all of these years past, but it was gone so fast that he was not sure if he had imagined it.

'Arabella,' he said softly and could not help himself from touching a hand to her arm.

He felt the slight tremor that ran through her body before she snatched her arm away.

'You think it to be done so very easily?' she asked.

Her tone was cynical and when she raised her face to his again there was the glitter of some strong emotion in her eyes.

'It can be done easily enough,' he said carefully. 'I would pay off Mrs Silver; she would give us no trouble, I assure you.'

He saw her swallow, saw the way she gripped her hands together as if it was such a difficult decision to make.

'I have come into my father's title, Arabella. I am a very wealthy man. I would rent you a fine town house, furnish it as you wished. Your every want would be satisfied, your every whim met. I am offering you *carte blanche,* Arabella.'

'I understand what you are offering me,' she said and her voice was cool and her expression unmoving.

'Well?' he asked. 'Will you give me your answer?'

'I need time to think,' she said stiffly. 'Time to fully consider your offer.'

'What else can you have to consider?' He smiled a cynical smile. 'Have I not covered it all already?'

Her pause was so slight that he barely noticed. A heartbeat of time in which their eyes met across the divide. And there was something in her gaze that was contrary in every way to the strong cold woman standing before him. A flash of misery and hurt and…fear. But as quickly as it had arrived, the moment was gone.

'Nevertheless, your Grace, I will not give you an answer until I have had some time to think about it.'

Her sullen resolution irked him, as did her whole attitude of contempt. Any other woman in her position would have been eager for such an offer.

'You may play your games, Arabella, but we both

know that whores do as rich men bid, and I am now a very rich man. It is a new day. You have until my return tonight to make your decision. And in the meantime Mrs Silver will be paid so that you are not touched by another. What I have, I hold, Arabella. And what is mine, is mine alone. Be sure you understand that fully.'

Her lips pressed firmer as if she sought to suppress some sharp retort. She slipped his coat from her shoulders and handed it to him.

Dominic donned the rest of his clothing, gave a small bow and left.

And as dawn broke over the city he walked away from Mrs Silver's House of Rainbow Pleasures, leaving behind its black-clad bedchamber with its dark drawn curtains. But his mind was still on the woman that he had left standing there, with the black silk dress clutched to her breasts.

Chapter Three

It was only a few hours later that Arabella made her way up the stairwell of the shabby lodging house in Flower and Dean Street. The early morning spring sunlight was so bright that it filtered through the windows, that the months of winter rain and wind had rendered opaque, and glinted on the newly replaced lock of the door that led from the first landing into her rented room.

The damp chill of the room hit her as soon as she opened the door and stepped over the threshold.

'Mama!' The small dark-haired boy glanced up from where he was sitting next to an elderly woman on the solitary piece of furniture that remained within the room, a mattress in the middle of the floor. He wriggled free of the thin grey woollen blanket that was wrapped around his shoulders and ran to greet her.

'Archie.' She smiled and felt her heart shift at the sight of his face. 'Have you been a good boy for your grandmama?'

'Yes, Mama,' he answered dutifully. But Arabella

could see the toll that hunger and poverty had taken in her son's face. Already there were shadows beneath his eyes and a sharpness about his features that had not been there just a few days ago.

She hugged him to her, the weight of guilt heavy upon her.

'I have brought a little bread and cake.' She emptied the contents of her pocket on to the mattress. Everything was stale as she had pilfered it last night from the trays intended for Mrs Silver's drawing room. 'Wages are not paid until the end of the week.'

Arabella split the food into two piles. One pile she sat upon the window ledge to sate their hunger later, and the other she shared between her mother and son.

It broke her heart the way Archie looked at her for permission to eat those few stale slices, his brown eyes filled with a look which no mother should ever have to see in her child.

There was silence while they ate the first slice of bread as if it were a sumptuous feast.

Arabella slipped off her cloak and wrapped it around her mother's hunched shoulders before sitting down beside her on the edge of the mattress.

'You are not eating, Arabella.' Her mother noticed and paused, her hand frozen en route to her mouth, the small chunk of bread still gripped within her fingers.

Arabella shook her head and smiled. 'I have already breakfasted on the way home.' It was a lie. But there was little enough as it was and she could not bear to see them so hungry.

The sun would not reach to shine in here until later in the day and there was no money for coal or logs. The room was cold and bare save for the mattress upon which they were now sitting. Empty, just as they had arrived home to find it four days ago.

'How was the workshop?' Mrs Tatton carefully picked the crumbs from her lap and ate them. 'They were satisfied with your work?'

'I believe so,' Arabella answered and could not bring herself to meet her mother's eyes in case something of the shame showed in them.

'You look too pale, Arabella, and your eyes are as red as if you have been weeping.' She could feel her mother's gaze upon her.

'I am merely tired and my eyes a little strained from stitching by candlelight.' Arabella lied and wondered what her mother would say if she knew the truth of how her daughter had spent the night. 'A few hours rest and I shall be fine.' She glanced up at Mrs Tatton with a reassuring smile.

Mrs Tatton's expression was worried. 'I wish I could do more to help.' She shook her head, and glanced away in misery. 'I know that I am little more than a burden to you.'

'Such foolish talk, Mama. How on earth would I manage without you to care for Archie?'

Her mother nodded and forced a smile, but her eyes were dull and sad. Arabella's gaze did not miss the tremor in the swollen knuckled hands or the wheeze that rasped in the hollow chest as Mrs Tatton reached to stroke a lock of her grandson's hair away from his eye.

Archie, having finished his bread and cake, wandered over to the other side of the room where there was a small wooden pail borrowed from one of the neighbours. He scooped up some water from the pail using the small wooden cup that sat beside it and gulped it down.

Mrs Tatton lowered her voice so that Archie would not hear. 'He cried himself to sleep through hunger last night, Arabella. Poor little mite. It broke my heart to hear him.'

Arabella pressed a fist to her mouth and glanced away so her mother would not see her struggle against breaking down.

'But this new job you have found is a miracle indeed, the answer to all our prayers. Without it, it would be the workhouse for us all.'

Arabella closed her eyes against that thought. They would be better off dead.

Archie brought the cup of water over and offered it to her. Arabella took a few sips and then gave it to her mother.

And when the food was all eaten and the water drunk, Archie and Mrs Tatton lay down beneath the blanket.

'It was noisy last night,' Mrs Tatton said by way of explanation. And Arabella understood, the men's drunken shouts and women's bawdy laughter echoing up from the street outside would have allowed her son and mother little sleep.

Arabella spread her cloak with her mother's shawl on top of the lone blanket and then climbed beneath the covers. Archie's little body snuggled into hers and she kissed that dark tangled tousle of hair and told him that everything would be well.

Soon the only sounds were of sleep: the wheeze of her mother's lungs and Archie's soft shallow rhythmic breathing. Arabella had not slept for one minute last night, not after all that had happened. And she knew that she would not sleep now. Her mind was a whirl of thoughts, all of them centred round Dominic Furneaux.

When she thought of their coupling of last night she felt like weeping, both from anger and from shame, and from a heart that ached from remembering how, when she had given herself to him before, there had been such love between them. And the anger that she felt was not just for him, but for herself.

For even from the first moment that he had come close and she had smelled that familiar scent of him, bergamot and soap and Dominic Furneaux, she had been unable to quell the reaction of her body. And when he had taken her, not out of love, not even knowing who she was, her traitorous lips and body had, in defiance of everything she knew and everything she felt, welcomed him. They had known his mouth, recognised his kiss and the caress of his hand, and responded to him. And the shame of that burned deeper than the knowledge that she had sold herself to him.

She thought of the offer he had made her. To buy her. To be at his beck and call whenever he wished to satisfy himself upon her. Dominic Furneaux, the man who had broken her heart. Lied to her with such skill that she had believed every one of those honeyed untruths. Could she put herself under the power of such a man? To be completely at his mercy? Could she really surrender herself to him, night after night, and hide the shameful response of her body to him, a man who did not love her, a man who believed her a whore for his use?

She clutched her hands to her face as the sense of despair rolled right through her, for she knew the answer to each of those questions and she knew, too, the ugly truth of the alternative.

Arabella relived the moment that the group of gentlemen had entered Mrs Silver's drawing room, and it did not matter how hard she had tried to deaden her feelings, no matter how much she could rationalise the whole plan in her head, when it had come to the point of facing what must happen she had felt an overwhelming panic that she would not be able go through with it. She closed her eyes against the nightmare, knowing that there was only one decision she could make. Even if there were certain aspects of the negotiations that she would have to handle very carefully.

And as she lay there she could not help but think how differently things might have turned out if Dominic Furneux had been a different sort of man. If he had loved her, as he had sworn that he did, and married her, as he had promised that he would, how different all their lives would have been.

Dominic arrived at Mrs Silver's early and alone. The drawing room was filled with a woman of every colour of Mrs Silver's rainbow, every colour save for black. He knew with one sweep of the room that Arabella was not there and he felt a whisper of foreboding that perhaps everything was not going to go quite how he had planned.

'Variety is the spice of life, your Grace. Perhaps I could tempt you with another colour from my assortment?' Mrs Silver smiled at him and gestured towards the girls who had arrived looking a little breathless and rushed following his early arrival.

'I find I prefer black,' he said. 'Miss Noir...' He

stopped as the thought struck him that perhaps following his discovery of her Arabella had gone, fled elsewhere, to another part of London, another bordello…
somewhere he could not find her.

'Will be here presently, your Grace, I am sure,' the
woman said with supreme confidence but her eyes told
a different story.

He had not contemplated that Arabella would choose
this wretched life over the wealth and comfort he had
offered. That she would actually run away had not
even occurred to him. His mouth hardened at his own
naïvety. A man was supposed to learn from his mis-
takes.

'If you are content to wait for a little.' Mrs Silver
smiled again and gestured to one of the sofas.

Dominic gave a curt nod of his head, but he did not
sit down. He stood where he was and he waited, ignor-
ing the plate of delicacies and the glass of champagne
by his side.

Five minutes passed.

And another ten. The women ceased their attempts
to engage him in seductive conversation.

What would he do if she did not come?

By twenty minutes he was close to pacing.

By forty minutes there was only Miss Rouge and
himself left in the room and a very awkward silence.

At fifty minutes, Miss Rouge was gone and he felt
like he had done that day almost six years ago—angry
and disbelieving, a fool and his wounded pride.

He had requested his hat, cane and gloves and was
about to leave when Arabella finally arrived.

'Miss Noir, your Grace,' announced Mrs Silver, all

smiles and solicitude as she brought Arabella into the room and left.

The door closed behind Mrs Silver.

The clock on the mantel punctuated the silence.

Dominic's glass sat beside it, the champagne flat and untouched.

She was wearing the same scandalous dress, the same black feathered mask and beneath it her face was powder white. She came to stand before him and he found he was holding his breath and his body was strung tight with tension.

He swallowed and the sound of it seemed too loud in the silence between them.

He waited, not daring to frame the question, any certainty of what her answer would be long forgotten.

'I accept your offer, your Grace,' she said and her voice was low and dead of any emotion. She seemed so pale, so stiff and cold, that he had the absurd urge to pull her into his arms and warm her and tell her everything would be well. But then she moved away to stand behind the cream-coloured armchair and the moment was gone. 'Let us discuss the details.'

He nodded and, like two strangers arranging a business deal, they began to talk.

When Arabella returned to the little room in Flower and Dean Street later that same night it was to find Mrs Tatton and Archie curled again upon the mattress.

'It is only me,' Arabella whispered in the darkness, but Mrs Tatton was already struggling to her feet, armed with the chamber pot as a makeshift weapon.

'Oh, Arabella, you startled me.'

'Forgive me, Mama.' Arabella made her way across

the room by the light of a nearby street lamp that glowed through the little window.

'What are you doing home so early? I had not thought to see you until the morning.' Her mother's hair hung in a heavy long grey braid over one shoulder and she was wearing the same crumpled dress she had worn for the last five days. Then her eyes widened with fear. 'The workshop have turned you off!'

'There has been a change of plan, it is true,' Arabella said and quickly added, 'But you need have no worry. It is for the better.'

'What do you mean, Arabella? What change?'

'It is an arrangement that will ensure we do not end up in the workhouse.' She glanced towards the sleeping form of her son. 'We will live in a warm furnished house in a good respectable area, wear clean clothes and have three square meals a day. I will have enough money that Archie need not go without. And you, Mama, can have the best of medicines in London. We will not be cold. We will not be hungry. And…' She glanced towards the footsteps that passed on the landing outside. She lowered her voice, 'We will be safe from robberies and fear of assault.'

Her mother set the chamber pot down on the floor and came to stand before Arabella, staring into her face.

'What manner of arrangement?'

Arabella felt herself blush and had to force herself to meet her mother's gaze. She had known this moment would come and could not shrink from it. Better they spoke of it while Archie was not awake to hear. They would be moving out of here in a few days and there was no way that Arabella could continue her pretence. She had to tell her mother the truth…just not all of it.

'With a gentleman.'

'Oh, Arabella!' Her mother clasped a hand to her mouth. 'You cannot!'

'I know it is a very great shock to you,' she said in a calm reassuring voice that belied everything she was feeling. 'And I am not proud of it.' She was ashamed to the very core of her being, but she knew in order to make this bearable she must hide her true emotions from her mother. She must stand firm. Be strong. 'But believe me when I tell you it is the best of the choices available. Do not seek to dissuade me from this, Mama, for my mind is quite made up.'

'There was no workshop, was there?' her mother asked in a deadened voice.

'No.' She saw the tremble in the old swollen hand that Mrs Tatton still clutched to her mouth and felt as bad as if she had just reached across and dealt her mother a physical blow.

'And the gentleman?'

Arabella swallowed and averted her gaze. 'It is best that he remains nameless for now.' If her mother knew it was Dominic to whom she was selling herself there would be no force in heaven or on earth that could stop the awful cascade that would ensue.

'Really?' Mrs Tatton said in a hard voice that revealed to Arabella everything of her mother's disillusionment and hurt. 'And have you told him yet of Archie and of me?'

'No,' said Arabella quietly and her heart was racing and all of her fears rushed back as fast and frantic as a spring tide racing up a shore. 'He need know nothing of either of you.'

'It will be his house, Arabella. Do you not think

he will notice an old woman and a child cluttering his path to his fancy piece?' Mrs Tatton's nostrils flared, revealing the extent of her distress.

Oh, indeed, Dominic would more than notice Archie in his path, Arabella thought grimly.

'It will be a large house and he will not visit very often.' She had been very careful in her negotiations with Dominic, forcing herself to think only of Archie's safety and not the baseness of what she was doing, laying out her demands like the most callous of harlots. 'All we need do is keep you both hidden from his sight when he does come.' Words so simply spoken for her mother's sake, but Arabella knew that they would have to be very careful indeed to hide the truth.

'You think you are so clever, Arabella. You think you have it all planned out, do you not?' Mrs Tatton said. 'But what of the servants? It is the gentleman's money that will pay their wages. They will be loyal to him. At the first opportunity they will be running to him behind your back, eager to spill your secrets. And he shall send Archie and me away.'

'Do you think I would stay without you?' she demanded. 'It is true that it is his money that will pay the servants. But it is also true that if I dissolve our agreement, which I would most certainly do were they to tell him of your and Archie's presence, then they shall be out of a job as much as me. I shall put it to them that it is in their interest, as much as mine, that we keep your presence secret from the gentleman.'

'For men like him there are plenty more where you came from. Do not hold yourself so precious to him, Arabella,' her mother warned.

The smile that slipped across Arabella's face was

bitter. 'Oh, Mama, I know that I am not precious to him at all. Do not think that I would ever make that mistake.' The word *again* went unspoken. 'But he will take the house and the servants for me. And were I to leave, he would let them go again just as easily.'

'Then we best pray that you are right, Archie and I.' Mrs Tatton turned her face away but not before Arabella saw the shimmer of wetness upon her cheeks.

Mrs Tatton did not look round again, nor did she return to bed. She just stood there by the empty black fireplace, staring down on to the bare hearth. And when Arabella would have placed an arm of comfort around her mother's shoulders, Mrs Tatton pulled away as if she could not bear the touch of so fallen a woman.

Arabella's hand dropped back down to her side; inside of her the shame ate away a little more of her soul. She wondered what her mother's reaction would be if she knew what the alternative had been. And she wondered how much worse her mother's reaction would be if she ever learned that the man in question was Dominic Furneaux.

Chapter Four

Dominic was supposed to be paying attention as his secretary continued working his way through the great pile of correspondence balanced on the desk between them.

'The Philanthropic Society has invited you to a dinner in June.' Barclay glanced up from checking Dominic's appointments diary. 'You are free on the evening in question.'

'Then I will attend.' Dominic gave a nod and heard Barclay's pen nib scratch upon the paper. But Dominic's attention was barely fixed on the task in hand. He was thinking of Arabella and the discomposure he had felt since seeing her last.

'The Royal Humane Society has written of its need for more boats. As one of the society's patron you are in receipt of a full report of…'

Barclay's words faded into the background as Dominic's mind drifted back to Arabella. While making her his mistress had seemed the perfect solution at the time, in the cold light of day and after a night of fitful sleep, Dominic was not so sure. He had revisited their meeting during the long hours of the night, seeing it again in his mind, hearing every word of their exchange, and he could not remain unaware of a growing uneasiness.

Surviving. The word seemed to niggle in his brain. Her explanation of what she was doing there did not sit well with the later claim that she was in Mrs Silver's House out of choice. *Surviving.* The word pricked at him.

Barclay gave a cough in the silence and cleared his throat loudly.

'Most interesting,' Dominic said, having heard not a word of what the report had been about. 'Organise that they receive a hundred pounds.'

'Very good, your Grace.'

'Is that all for today?' He could barely conceal his impatience. He wanted to be alone. He wanted to think.

'Indeed, your Grace.' Barclay replied, checking the diary again. 'Except to remind you that you are due at Somerset House for a Royal Society lecture this afternoon at two o'clock and that you are sitting in the House of Lords tomorrow to debate Sir John Craddock's replacement in Portugal by Sir Arthur Wellesley.'

Dominic gave a nod. 'Thank you, Barclay. That will be all.'

And when his secretary left, taking with him the great pile of paper, Dominic leaned back in his chair and focused his thoughts fully on Arabella.

Arabella had to endure two days of pleadings. Mrs Tatton begged that Arabella would not cheapen herself and warned her that once it was done there would be no going back. She cried and shouted, persuaded and coerced, but once the shock had lessened and her mother saw that Arabella would not be moved, then Mrs Tatton's protestations fell by the wayside and, to Arabella's relief, no more was said about it. She seemed to have accepted the inevitability and necessity of what would happen and steeled herself to the task every bit as much as Arabella.

Which was well, for on the Friday morning of that week a fine carriage and four arrived outside their lodgings in Flower and Dean Street. Every face in the street stared at the carriage, for nothing so grand had ever been seen there before. Archie stared in excitement at the team of bays and kept asking if he might run down the stairs to see them more closely. It pained Arabella to deny him and to force him away from the window for fear that Dominic himself might be within the carriage.

'Soon,' she whispered, 'but not today.'

'Ohh, Mama!' Archie groaned.

'He must be wealthy indeed,' observed Mrs Tatton drily with a glance at her daughter that made Arabella curl up inside. And she was all the more glad that the carriage was a plain glossy black with no sign of the Arlesford coat of arms. She worried that her mother would recognise the smart green livery of the footman, groom and coach man, but Mrs Tatton showed no sign of realising the uniform's significance.

'I think he might be awaiting me in the house and I need time to speak to the servants. Either the carriage will come back for you, or I will return alone.'

Her mother nodded stoically and Arabella pushed away the little spasm of fear.

'Either way we should not be parted for too long.'

She hugged Archie. 'I have to go out for a little while, Archie.'

'In the big black carriage?' he asked.

'Yes.'

'Can I come with you?'

Arabella ignored the pain and the guilt and forced herself to smile. 'Not just now, my darling. Be a good boy for your grandmama and I will see you soon.'

'Yes, Mama.'

She kissed his head and took the time to blink away the tears before she rose to embrace her mother. 'Look after him, Mama.'

Mrs Tatton nodded, and her eyes glistened with tears that she was fighting to hold back. 'Have a care, Arabella, please. And…' She took Arabella's face between her worn hands and looked into her eyes. 'For all that I dislike this I know why you are doing it and I thank you. I pray that your plan is successful and that it is the carriage that returns for Archie and for me.'

Those few words from her mother's lips meant so much to Arabella. They strengthened her resolve that was fast crumbling at the prospect of facing Dominic once more.

'Thank you, Mama,' Arabella whispered and she kissed her mother's cheek and, before she could weaken to the tears, she pulled the hood of her cloak over her hair and walked away, closing the door behind her.

The carriage was empty. Of that Arabella could only be glad, for she had no wish for Dominic to see her cry at the sight of her son and her mother peeping from the edge of the dirt-encrusted windows.

Nor was Dominic waiting in the town house that he had rented for her.

It was a fine property in respectable Curzon Street, as different from the hovel in Flower and Dean Street as was possible. The servants were lined up in the hallway for her arrival just as if she were Dominic's duchess rather than his mistress. In some ways their respectful attitude made the whole thing easier, and in other ways, so much harder, for it reminded her of the hopes and expectations she had held for the future all those years ago when she had been a foolish naïve girl in love with a boy who would be duke.

The elderly butler bowed. 'I am Gemmell. Welcome to Curzon Street, Miss Tatton. We are very glad that you are here.'

It was so long since anyone had called her that name. She was Arabella Marlbrook now, even though Henry was dead these two years past. It angered her that Dominic wished to remove any reminder of the man who had saved her. She wanted to correct the butler, to tell him that her name was Marlbrook and not Tatton, but that would only be foolish. It was Dominic's house and Dominic's money; besides, she had no wish to make matters awkward between her and the servants, not when she would be counting on their good favour to keep her secret. So she smiled and walked down the line of servants, smiling and repeating each of their names and telling them how pleased she was to meet them and how she was sure that they would deal very well together.

Gemmell gave her a tour of the house during which she worked hard to breach his wall of formal and very proper servitude. By the time he had served her tea in the drawing room she had managed to coax from him all about his three little granddaughters and ten little grandsons; that his wife Mary, who had been the best housekeeper in all of England, had died three years past; and that he and Mary had previously been employed in the Duke of Hamilton's hunting lodge in Scotland for twenty years before moving south on account of their children and grandchildren because family was what was important.

Arabella knew then that the time was right to raise the subject of her own family, of her son and her mother. And after she had finished explaining, to a limited extent, the matter, Mr Gemmell was just as understanding as Arabella had hoped.

She knew that what she was asking the staff to do was not without risk and so did Gemmell. But she also knew she could do nothing other than ask. And the answer was yes. He promised to instruct the rest of the staff and then he brought her the note that Dominic had left for her.

She recognised the handwriting on the front of the note: determined lettering, bold and flowing from a nib that pressed firmly against the paper. She felt her heart begin to speed and her mouth dry as she broke the seal and unfolded the sheet.

The words were brief, just a couple of lines, saying that he hoped she approved of the house and its contents and that he would call upon her that evening.

Of course he would come in the evening; gentlemen did not visit their mistresses during the day. Not when everyone knew the purpose of their visit. She tried not to think ahead to the evening. She would deal with that when it came. For now she turned her mind to more comfortable thoughts.

She rang the bell for Gemmell, and sent the carriage back to Flower and Dean Street for Archie and her mother.

The sun came out that afternoon. It was a good omen, boding well for their future, Arabella told her mother as they wandered through the rooms of the town house in Curzon Street. Mrs Tatton kept stopping to examine and exclaim over the fineness of the furniture, the rich fabrics of the curtains and the sparkling crystal of the chandeliers.

'Arabella, these chairs are made by Mr Chippendale' and 'Arabella, this damask costs almost thirty shillings a yard,' and 'I have heard that the Prince of Wales himself has a wallpaper similar to this in Carlton House.'

Arabella did not tell her that the gentlemen's clothing hanging in one of the wardrobes within her bedchamber was made by the *ton*'s most expensive tailor, John Weston, nor that it bore the faint scent of Dominic and his cologne.

Having been cooped up for so long in the tiny room in Flower and Dean Street, Archie shouted and ran about in mad excitement at such space and freedom.

'It is all so very grand that he must be very wealthy indeed, this…gentleman,' said Mrs Tatton and she stopped and frowned before her face was filled with worry once more. 'I blame myself that it has come to this,' she said quietly so that her grandson would not hear. She dabbed a small white handkerchief to her eyes.

'Hush now, Mama, you will upset Archie.' Arabella glanced over towards her son and was relieved to see that he was too busy with his imaginary horse games to notice.

'I am sorry, Arabella, but to think that you have become some rich man's mistress.'

'It is not so bad a bargain, Mama. I assure you it is the best I could have made.' A vision of the crowd of drunken gentlemen in Mrs Silver's drawing room appeared in her head and she could not stop the accompanying shiver. She thrust the thought away and forced herself to smile a reassurance at her mother. 'And we will all do very well out of it.'

'You have spoken to the servants?'

Arabella nodded.

'And you are sure that they will keep Archie's and my existence a secret?'

'I do not believe that any of them will be in a hurry to whisper tales in his ear.'

'Then in that, at least, we have been fortunate.'

'Yes.'

Mrs Tatton's gaze met Arabella's. 'What manner of man is he, this protector of yours? Old, bluff, married? I cannot help but worry for you. Some men...' She could not go on.

'He is none of those, Mama,' said Arabella and rubbed her mother's arm. 'He is...' But what could she tell her mother of Dominic? A hundred words sprang to mind, none of which would relieve her mother's anxiety. 'Generous...and not...unkind,' she managed. But what he had done almost six years ago was very unkind. 'Which is what is of importance in arrangements of the purse.'

Mrs Tatton sighed and looked away.

'We will be careful with the money he gives me. We

will save every penny that we can, and soon, very soon, there will be enough for you, me and Archie to leave all this behind. We will go back to the country and rent a small cottage with a garden. And no one need be any the wiser to this whole affair.'

'We will be able to hold our heads up and be respectable once more.' As if Arabella could ever be respectable again. For all that illusions could be presented to the world, she would always know what she had done. Nothing could ever cleanse her of that shame. She linked her arm through her mother's and smiled as if none of this affected her in the slightest. 'It will work out all right, you will see.'

'I would like that, Arabella.' Mrs Tatton nodded and something of the anxiety eased from her face. 'Your papa and I were very happy in the country.' She smiled with the remembrance and the two strolled on together, pretending to each other that the situation was anything but that which it really was. And oblivious to the undercurrent of tension Archie played and ran about around their skirts.

Dominic pretended it was just a day like any other, but it was Friday and there was not a moment when he was not aware that Arabella would be waiting for him at Curzon Street that night.

He spent most of the day closeted with his steward who had come up from Amersham to discuss agricultural matters, namely moving to increased mechanisation with Andrew Meikle's threshing machine. After which Dominic went off to watch a four-in-hand race between young Northcote and Darlington, before going on to White's club for a drink with Hunter, Northcote and Bullford. But for all that day he was distracted and out of sorts. Indeed he had not been *in* sorts since the night of meeting Arabella. His usual easy temperament was gone and with each passing day the unsettled feeling seemed to grow stronger. It should have been desire that he was feeling, an impatience to satisfy his lust upon her, to have her naked, warm and willing beneath him.

But it was not.

Surviving. The word whispered again through his mind and he set the wine glass down hard upon the table before him.

'Arlesford?' Bullford said more loudly.

Dominic glanced round to find Hunter, Bullford and Northcote looking at him expectantly. 'Did not catch what you said.' Dominic's voice was lazy and his fingers moved to toy with the stem of his glass as he pretended a normality he did not feel.

'I was just saying that young Northcote's keen to try out some new gaming hell in the East End,' said Bullford. 'Apparently it is quite an experience and certainly not for the faint of heart. If anyone can wipe their tables it would be you and Hunter. Never known a couple of gamblers with as much luck. Hunter's up for it. Will you come and make a night of it?'

'Not tonight,' he said carefully, 'I have other plans.' The echo of her voice whispered again in his head. *It is my first night here. Forgive me if I am unfamiliar with the usual etiquette.* He tried to ignore it.

Bullford smiled in a leery knowing way. 'Ah, the mysterious Miss Noir. Heard you bought her from Mrs Silver. Got the luscious girl stowed away safe and good from the attentions of the rest of London's most eager males?'

Dominic felt his teeth clench and his body go rigid at the manner in which Bullford had just spoken of Arabella. His response shocked him, for Bullford did not know that Miss Noir was Arabella. And Arabella was indeed a lightskirt. But the rationalisations did little to appease his anger and he had to force himself to slow his breathing and uncurl his tightly balled fists.

But Bullford seemed oblivious to the danger and waded in further. 'Liked the look of her myself in Mrs Silver's. Unfortunate for me that you got to her before I did, or the little lady could have been warming my bed tonight.'

'Rather, I assure you that the turn of events was most fortunate for you.' Dominic's voice was cold and hard. He did not understand why he felt so livid. He only knew that if it had been Bullford that had gone upstairs with Arabella in the brothel... Dominic swallowed hard and felt the fragile thread of his self-control stretch thinner.

'Bullford.' Hunter attracted the viscount's attention and gave a warning shake of the head.

'Oh, I see,' said Bullford smugly. He tapped the side of his nose and winked at Dominic. 'Say no more, old man. Affairs of the breeches and all that. Strictly hush, hush. We will move the plans to another time and let you enjoy Miss Noir tonight.'

It was all that Dominic could do not to grab Bullford by the lapels of his tailcoat and smash a fist into his mouth, even though the man had only said aloud the very thing that Dominic planned to do. It was as if some madness had come upon him.

Hunter adroitly changed the subject.

But Dominic was already out of his seat and walking away, leaving all three men staring behind him.

Archie was fast asleep in bed in a snug little bed-chamber at the top of the house in Curzon Street with his grandmama by the time the carriage rolled to a stop outside.

Arabella had been pacing the drawing room nervously, unable to settle to anything through the evening. Dominic's imminent arrival was foremost in her mind. She knew that it was him as soon as she heard the horses. She did not need to wait to hear the footsteps upon the outside steps or the opening of the front door or the gentle murmur of voices to know that she was right. The tempo of her heart began to increase. Her hands grew clammy and she prayed that Gemmell's assertion of the servants' discretion could be trusted.

She grabbed a piece of needlework and sat swiftly down in a chair by the fireplace so it would look as if she was not bothered in the slightest over his visit. She heard the drawing-room door open and close again. And quite deliberately kept her attention focused on the sewing for a moment longer, even though she knew he was standing there.

She steeled her courage. Told herself that this… coupling need mean nothing to her. That she could give him her body while locking away all else. Don so much armour that he would not so much as glimpse her heart, her soul, her feelings, let alone get near enough to hurt them again.

She would not let herself think of him as Dominic. He was just a man. And Arabella was not naïve enough to think that a woman had to love a man before she could give herself to him. After all, she had slept with Henry when what she had felt for him was affection and gratitude, and nothing of love.

The moment could not be delayed for ever so she set the needlework down on the little sewing table with care and rose to her feet, skimming a hand down as if to brush out the wrinkles in her skirt.

Only then did she look at him.

Arabella was a tall woman, but Dominic stood a good head and shoulders above her. Tall with broad shoulders and a build that was well muscled. His tailoring was a deep midnight blue over the pristine white of his shirt, waistcoat and cravat. His tailcoat of superfine looked as if it had been fitted by a master tailor. Long legs clad in dark breeches showed too well the musculature of his thighs, leading down to matching top boots, the gloss of which could be seen even by the candlelight.

His face looked paler than the last time she had seen him, his features as breathtakingly handsome as the man from her nightmares. She knew every plane of that face, had kissed every inch of it. His expression was intense and unreadable. And when her eyes finally met his she knew in that instant that all of her resolve was in vain. For she could not even look at him and remain unaffected.

Her heart skipped a beat and then raced off at a canter.

'Dominic,' she heard herself whisper, and all of the old emotions were back, all of the love, all of the hurt, all of the hate. She felt her eyes begin to well and looked hastily away so that he would not see it, furious with herself for such weakness. She thought of Archie and that gave her the strength that she needed. She might not be able to do this for herself, but she could most definitely do it for her son.

'Arlesford,' she corrected herself and this time she was glad to hear that her voice was strong with just a hint of disdain.

'Arabella.' He made a small bow, but otherwise did not move.

He stood there so quiet and still and yet she could sense the tension that surrounded him. It emanated from every pore of his body. It was betrayed by the slight clenching in his jawline, in his lips, in the way he was looking at her. His eyes were darker than she had ever seen them, so dark as to appear almost black, and he was looking at her with such intensity as if to glean every last thought from her head.

She felt the nervousness ripple right through her body at the thought of all that she sought to hide.

'The house is to your liking?' he asked.

'It is very nice, thank you, your Grace. Beautifully furnished with impeccable taste.' She kept her face impassive and her voice cool.

They looked at each other across the small distance and the silence was awkward and tense. She glanced away, waiting for him to shrug out of his tailcoat and suggest that they go upstairs. But that was not what Dominic said.

'I wish to talk to you, Arabella.'

'Talk?' Her heart gave a stutter. A shiver of warning rippled down Arabella's spine. She did not want to talk. Instinctively Arabella glanced up as if she could see through the floors above to the small bedchamber at the top of the house.

She feared what talking might reveal.

She feared that Dominic would learn of Archie, his son.

Chapter Five

If Dominic knew the truth, then God only knew what would happen to Archie. Her son would be branded a bastard, his life ruined before it had barely begun whether Dominic acknowledged him or not. If he knew he had such a fine son, he might wish to raise Archie himself or send him away to be raised by someone of his own choosing. For what man, especially a duke, as rich and powerful and ruthless as Dominic, would leave his child with a woman he had found in a bordello, no matter the explanations she could offer? Archie would be taken away from her to be with people who did not love him, who did not understand a small boy's tender needs. Arabella trembled from the force of the fear.

She wetted her suddenly dry lips and gave a false laugh to hide the fear. 'But what more is there for us to talk about, your Grace? We have already settled upon all of the relevant details.'

She saw the flash of anger in those dark eyes. 'I would have you call me by my given name. And there is the whole of the last six years that we have barely begun to discuss, Arabella.'

'I thought you already knew.' *Attack is the best form of defence,* she thought and gathered her weapons as best she could. 'I married Henry Marlbrook. He died. I went to Mrs Silver's. That is all you need know, *Dominic.*' She turned away to gain some semblance of control over her emotions once more.

'On the contrary, Arabella. I think I need to know a great deal more than that.'

'What do you want me to tell you?' she demanded bitterly. 'How good a man Henry was?'

'Infinitely better than me. You made that very clear.' His eyes bored into hers.

'He was a thousand times the man you are,' she taunted.

'You forget your position, Arabella.'

'No,' she said and tried to control the raggedness of her voice. She forced a tight smile to her mouth. 'I understand my position exactly.' She glared at him. 'Do you want me in here? Perhaps on the sofa? Or on the rug before the fireplace? Shall I undress for you now?' she demanded.

'Arabella!' he said harshly, but there was a flash of pain in his eyes that matched the pain in her heart.

And she realised that she was doing this all wrong, risking everything.

She closed her eyes, rallied her senses. 'Forgive me,' she said in her normal voice and when she opened her eyes she did not look at him.

'Arabella,' he said more softly.

But his kindness was worse than his contempt. It reminded her too much of the man she had loved.

'What has happened to you?'

'You already know the answer to that question,' she said quietly.

'No, Arabella, I do not.' His eyes studied hers. 'I wish that you would tell me.'

Her heart was knocking so hard against her ribcage that she was surprised he could not hear it.

'All of it that happened across the years,' he said.

She shook her head and forced a smile, trying to fool him.

His gaze did not waver.

'In Mrs Silver's, when you were pretending to be Miss Noir, you said that it was your first night there.'

'A harlot's lie. It is what men want to hear, is it not?' She glanced away and pressed her fingers hard against her lips, hating the words she must say. But say them she would, for she did not want his pity. And she did could not risk his questions.

Dominic stood there still and silent.

'Shall we go upstairs?' She knew her part in all this, knew what he had come for. And once he had it, he would go and the ordeal would be over…at least for now.

He said not one word, but he followed her up the stairs to the large cream-coloured bedchamber on the first floor.

There could be no room for modesty, nor the last remaining shreds of her pride. She knew what was required, knew what she must do.

She turned away from him and forced herself to strip off her clothing, every last stitch. And when she was naked she sat down at the dressing table and took the pins from her hair, uncoiling its long length while her eyes watched his reflection in the looking glass. She watched while he slipped off his tailcoat and abandoned it over a chair. His waistcoat followed.

She sat there, waiting for the inevitable. Gathering her courage for what must come. But Dominic made no move towards her.

The nerves shivered right through her body. She swallowed. Did a mistress wait for her protector to come to her, or did he expect her to go to him? Arabella did not know the answer. But the quicker this was over, the better for herself. So she rose and walked to him. It took every ounce of Arabella's strength not to wrap her arms around herself to cover her nakedness, to make herself stand there before him and let him look at her.

His touch, when it came, was gentle, reverent almost, and she shivered at the sudden flash of unbidden memories from a lifetime ago—of the passion and the love that had been between them.

He ran a hand over her hair, his hand sliding round to the nape of her neck. His fingers rested there light as a butterfly and the tingle beneath them seemed to run through the whole of her body. Slowly, deliberately, he trailed the tips of his fingers down the column of her throat.

Arabella deliberately masked any sign of emotion from her face as she stood there and let him touch her, angling her head to allow him access. He was her protector. This was what he was paying for. It meant nothing. But already she could feel the hard thud of her heart and everywhere his fingers touched, her skin burned, and she felt like weeping.

His hand dipped lower, so that she felt his fingers trace all the way out to the end of her collarbone and all the way back again. She tried to control the unsteadiness of her breathing, the gathering sob, but that only seemed to make it worse.

Not one word did he say. Not once did he meet her eyes, just kept his gaze fixed on the magic that his fingers were working.

He paused.

Arabella held her breath.

And then inch by tiny inch his fingers followed the path down into the valley between her breasts.

Again he halted, but whether it was to torture her, or himself, she did not know. If he continued like this, Arabella did not know if she could bear it. He placed a palm upon her left breast and beneath it she felt her heart jump and race all the harder. Beneath the cover of his hand her nipple was already taut and tender.

Arabella willed herself not to respond. He did not love her. She thought of all he had done six years ago. But when his palm slid away and his fingers teased at her nipple, plucking it, there was nothing she could do to prevent it bead all the harder. Her wantonness appalled her.

She squeezed her eyes closed to prevent the tears, knowing what would follow.

But his hand halted and dropped away, so that he was no longer even touching her.

Each tight line of his body and the bulge in his breeches revealed that he was every bit as aware as she of the tension that hummed between them. Slowly, his gaze raised to meet her own and there was something in his eyes as he stared at her. The strangest expression. Not lust as she had expected. Not victory or even arrogance. Realisation, maybe. And something else that she could not quite define. Something that looked almost haunted.

'Dominic?' she whispered.

But Dominic gave no sign of having heard her. He stood there frozen, staring as if he could see into the very depths of her soul.

And then he backed away, raking a hand through his hair as he did so.

'I cannot...' he said and his face was white. He turned away, gathered up his waistcoat and tailcoat and made for the door.

'Dominic!'

He stopped where he was, hesitated with his hand stilled in its grip of the doorknob, but did not turn round.

And then he left, closing the door quietly behind him.

There was the tread of his boots upon the stairs, the murmur of voices in the hallway and, a short while after that, the sound of a carriage and horses outside.

Arabella watched the dark unmarked carriage drive away into the night. She shivered and pulled the shawl tight around her shoulders, not understanding what had just happened between them.

Dominic did not sleep for what remained of the night. He stood by the window of his library and looked out over the sleeping city and watched the dawn break over a charcoal sky.

He had been a fool to think that he could take Arabella as his mistress and use her as a whore, even if she was exactly that. The past was too strong between them. She might have slashed the ties that had bound them and walked away, but Dominic had only just come to see that what had bound them together could never be completely undone. She was his first and only love. And no matter what she had done, or what she had become, he could not forget that. Every time he looked at her it was flaunted before his eyes. Every time he touched her he felt it in his bones.

If he had thought it would be so easy to treat her just as he had treated all the other women who had come after her, without emotional attachment, he was wrong.

She was engrained upon his mind, engraved upon his heart. He had dreamt of nothing else for nigh on six years. He had longed for her and hated her and needed her all at once. It was Arabella whom he thought of constantly. It was Arabella he thought of even when he was bedding another woman.

He could taste her upon his tongue and smell her own scent, sweet and fresh like roses and summer rain. He could still feel the smooth softness of her pale skin, still feel the firm ripeness of her naked breasts. He wanted to possess every inch of her body with his mouth. He wanted to plunge his aching manhood into her silken flesh and take her in every way imaginable until this endless torment ceased.

But he could not.

The grey dress she wore in the bedchamber in Curzon Street was nothing of the courtesan's guise she had donned before. It was old and shabby and respectable, Arabella's own, rather than something of Mrs Silver's. And when she had stripped it off and stood before him, offering what he had thought he had the right to take, he had willed himself to accept it. He had touched her and tried to coax himself, for God only knew how much his body burned to possess her. But beneath his hand he had felt the flutter of her heart and he had known that he could not do it.

Arabella's words rang through his head. *He was a thousand times the man you are!... A harlot's lie. It is what men want to hear, is it not?* And he realised there had been a part of him that had thought that she would have welcomed him, wanted him. That she would have told him that what happened in the past was all a mistake, that she had loved him all along.

He shook his head with disgust at his own absurdity. Nothing had changed. It never would. She still had the power to hurt him…and was wielding it with deliberation.

He had made this arrangement; he would not break it and see her thrown back down into the gutter. But for Dominic there could be no more visits to Curzon Street.

The decision made, Dominic stood back to watch the new day dawn over London.

In the dining room that morning Arabella was watching Archie eating his breakfast. After seeing him brought almost to the point of starvation she could not help but worry whether that last week in Flower and Dean Street had left its mark upon him. But looking at him now, wolfing down his buttered eggs and sausages and excitedly telling his story, she felt a sense of relief at the resilience of children. She smoothed down his hair and concentrated on listening to how he was going to have a whole stable of horses when he was a grown-up man. But she knew Mrs Tatton's questions would not be deferred for long. Arabella could see from the corner of her eye the way her mother was watching her with concern written all over her face.

She tried to smile and act as if everything was just the same as it had been yesterday, but her heart was filled with humiliation and confusion and embarrassment over what had happened last night. She did not understand what she had done wrong. And she was relieved and angry and ashamed all at once.

Archie helped himself to another two sausages and then climbed down from the table and ran off to play a game of horses.

'Archie, come back. We do not leave the table until we have finished eating,' she called after him.

'Oh, leave him be, Arabella. He will do no harm and has been so well behaved of late despite all of our troubles,' said Mrs Tatton.

'You are right, of course,' Arabella said. 'It has not been easy for him.' The weight of guilt was heavy. She doubted that the memory of those awful last days when he had gone hungry would ever leave her.

'Nor for any of us,' answered her mother. 'Now I know it is not my place to ask and that events of the bedchamber between a man and a woman are best kept that way, but...' Mrs Tatton's brow furrowed with concern. 'I do not think that matters went so well for you last night.'

'Those matters were fine,' Arabella said quickly and felt her cheeks flush at the memory of Dominic's rejection. She was his mistress. She was supposed to bed him, to let him take his pleasure. And she had been prepared to do just that, however much she resented it. What she had not been prepared for was that he would tease a response from her body and then just walk away.

'Do not lie to me, girl. I have eyes to see and ears to hear. And I see your face is powder pale this morning and your eyes swollen and red as if you have spent the night weeping. And I heard him leaving the house before midnight.'

'My eyes are a little irritated this morning, nothing more. And D—' She stopped Dominic's name on her tongue before it could escape. 'And, yes, the gentleman had to leave early. There were others matters to which he had to attend.'

'At midnight?' her mother snorted. 'He was barely here.'

'If his visits are short, does it not suit us all the better?'

'Some men can be inconsiderate in their haste to… to satisfy their own…' Her mother's cheeks blushed scarlet and she could not finish her words.

'No,' Arabella said hastily. 'It was not like that.'

The sight of him. The scent of him. His fingers slowly tracing a line all the way along her collar bone, before meandering down to tease her nipples. The burn of her skin, the rush of her blood…

She winced with the shame of it.

'Tell me the truth, Arabella.' Mrs Tatton reached over and placed her hand on Arabella's.

Her cheeks warmed, and she felt the gall of bitterness in her throat. 'If you knew the truth, Mama, you would not believe it,' she murmured.

'Did he use you ill?' Her mother's face paled, the flash of fear in her eyes making Arabella feel a brute. She was supposed to be reassuring her mother, not worrying her all the more.

'He did nothing, Mama.' Even though she had offered

herself to him like the harlot she had become. She was so angry at herself…and at him.

She was relieved that he had not taken her, so why did she feel so humiliated? It was a confusing hurtful mess.

'Do not lie to me now, Arabella. If he has hurt you… Nothing is worth that. Better that we beg upon the streets than—'

She took her mother's hand in her own and stroked the fragile veined skin. 'Mama, he was gentle and demanded nothing of me. I wept only for what I am become.'

'Oh, Arabella, we should leave this house.' Arabella felt her mother's hands twist within her own.

'And return to Flower and Dean Street?' Arabella raised her brows.

'I could look for work. Between the two of us we could find a way.'

And the work would kill her mother. Arabella knew there was no other way. She shook her head. 'It is too late, Mama.'

What was done, was done. She was a fallen woman. Besides, the past had caught up with Arabella. *I cannot,* his words seemed to whisper through the room and she thought of the haunted expression in his eyes.

'Mama, we are staying here. I was foolish last night, that is all. Tonight will be different.' She hoped. 'You have nothing to worry over except to count the money and the days until we can return to the country.'

'If you are sure about this, Arabella?'

'I am quite certain.'

Her mother did not look happy, but she nodded and went back to eating her breakfast.

* * *

It was barely an hour later when the letter arrived.
Again, written in Dominic's familiar bold handwriting.
Arabella's heart began to trip as she broke the sealing
wax and read the bold penned words within.

'Well?' Her mother glanced up from the chair on
which she was sitting. The sunshine bathed the whole
of the drawing room in its warm pale golden light.

'He has arranged for a dressmaker to call tomorrow
afternoon.' Arabella folded the letter and slipped it into
the pocket of her dress so that her mother would not see
the crest embossed both upon the paper and impressed
within the seal.

'It is only to be expected,' Mrs Tatton said and went
back to pouring the tea.

'I suppose you are right,' Arabella murmured, and
a vision of the scandalous silk black dress swam in her
mind. She glanced down at her own grey gown and
knew she would rather wear this every single day, old
and shabby as it was, than anything Dominic would
buy for her.

'Archie and I will make ourselves scarce.'

Arabella nodded and glanced at her son, feeling a tug
of guilt and worry. Hiding them away at night was not
so very bad, for both her mother and son slept early. And
although the room was near to the attic it was warm and
cosy and nicely furnished, and better in every way than
the one they had left in Flower and Dean Street. But
to force them to stay quiet and hidden during the day
while Dominic sat downstairs and chose a wardrobe of
fast, provocative clothes in which to dress her sparked
an angry resentment in Arabella.

Something of her feelings must have shown in her

face for Mrs Tatton said, 'It is only for one day, Arabella, and it will do us no harm. And as for the rest... well, the clothes are the least of it.'

There was no sign of Dominic by two o'clock the next day when the dressmaker called. Arabella smoothed her skirts for the umpteenth time and forced herself to at least pretend to be attending to her needlework, although she had the sudden thought, just as she heard the knock at the door, that perhaps mistresses did not spend their time in needlework. It was the first time that anyone would be seeing her as Dominic's mistress and Arabella composed her face to conceal her humiliation.

When Gemmell showed the woman into the drawing room, Arabella's heart sank to meet her shoes. *Of all the dressmakers in London that Dominic could have chosen...*

And she remembered those final dark days that had led her to Mrs Silver's House of Rainbow Pleasures. It should not matter that it was Madame Boisseron waiting in the drawing room, for in her desperation Arabella had knocked on the door of every dressmaker, mantua maker and milliner, every corsetry house, tailor and seamstress, seeking work that was not to be found. Any one of London's dressmakers coming here today would have recognised her. But somehow, the fact that it was the woman in whose shop she had met Mrs Silver just seemed to add to the humiliation for Arabella.

But if Madame Boisseron recognised Arabella the dressmaker was wise enough to make no sign of it. Arabella took a deep breath, swallowed down her embarrassment and knew that she had no choice but to deal with the situation as best she could.

Dominic had still not arrived when the little dark-eyed woman, whose accent was soft and French, brought out a book of dress designs. Arabella glanced at the clock, knowing she ought to wait for his arrival before they proceeded, but the thought that Dominic could dictate the clothes she wore, even right down to her underwear, made her feel so angry that she took the book from the *modiste* and began to flip through it.

Some of the designs were positively indecent, barely covering breasts, revealing nipples and leaving little to the imagination when it came to a woman's figure. Not so very different from the black silk dress that she had been forced to wear within the brothel.

'This one but with a higher neckline,' she pointed to one of the sketches, 'and a thicker material.'

Madame Boisseron glanced up at her in surprise. 'You are sure, madam? Gentlemen, they usually prefer a little more...' she paused '...daring in their ladies' dress.'

'I have had quite enough of daring. So if you would be so kind.'

'Certainly, madam,' Madame Boisseron said. 'After all, the Duke, he said that the decision was with you.'

'He did?' Arabella heard the question in her own voice, and then tried to look as if she had known it all along.

'Indeed. There are not many men that would leave their ladies to order the entirety of their new wardrobes alone. I was most surprised when the Duke, he asked me to attend to you without his presence. He will pay only if you are happy—a most unusual nobleman, *non?*'

'Most unusual,' Arabella said and glanced away.

So Dominic would not be arriving this afternoon. She allowed herself to relax a little, and stopped looking at the clock.

By three o'clock, Arabella's measurements had been taken, they had been through the fabric sample book twice and Arabella had ordered a minimal and conservative wardrobe. Madame Boisseron must have been disappointed, given that she knew Arabella had *carte blanche* to order exactly as she wished and as much as she desired. But rather than be tight-mouthed, the dressmaker only smiled and looked at Arabella kindly and told her the clothes would be delivered as each dress became ready.

Immediately the door closed Arabella made her way upstairs to Archie and her mother's bedchamber and turned her mind away from Dominic Furneaux.

But she could not keep him from her thoughts for ever. Too soon the day faded into night and Arabella sat alone in the drawing room, waiting for him to arrive. She knew that he would expect her to thank him for the free rein with the dressmaker and for his generosity of purse, but the words stuck in Arabella's throat and she knew that she would be unable to bring herself to say them.

She waited; the clock ticked loudly and its hands crawled slowly, and the embroidery within her lap remained untouched. She worried over what he might say to her. And she worried over what she might say to him. But most of all she worried over the moment when he would take her to bed.

But Dominic did not come to the house in Curzon Street. Not that night, or the next, or the night after that.

Dominic was trying to check through the accounts for the land that encompassed his estate. It was a tedious task and one that required sustained concentration, which was the very reason he was sitting with the books spread before him this afternoon. Anything to keep his mind off Arabella Tatton.

The tactic was not proving successful and so Hunter's arrival in his study was something of a relief.

Hunter squinted at the pages lying open on the desk and then looked at Dominic with a knowing expression. 'There's enough crossed-out and overwritten ink on that paper to write a novel. Quite unlike your usual precision, Arlesford. Looks to me like you have got something—or some*one*—else on your mind.' Hunter smiled and arched an eyebrow.

Dominic ignored the bait and bent his head to the columns of numbers on the page before him. Hunter was right, he acknowledged dismally. The page had been clear and legible before Dominic had started his checking.

'Came by to drop you a warning.'

Dominic felt his stomach tighten. Hunter would not be here right now if it were not something concerning Dominic.

'You are not going to like it,' warned Hunter.

Dominic thought of Arabella.

Hunter helped himself to Dominic's decanter of brandy and filled two glasses. 'It's Misbourne. Trying a new approach.'

Dominic released the breath he had been holding as

he accepted the brandy from Hunter. He took a sip and watched his friend lounge in the chair on the other side of the desk.

'He is saying that there was some kind of old agreement made between your father and him years ago. An oath to bind the two families by marriage between you and his daughter.'

The news was not anything Dominic wanted to hear, but at least it did not regard Arabella.

'Aye, a pact sworn with the earl when the two of them were young, single and in their cups. My father never meant to hold me to a boy's drunken foolishness. And I'll be damned if I'm pushed to it by a louse like Misbourne.'

'Misbourne is risking much with his tactic; he must be very determined to make a match between you and Lady Marianne Winslow.'

Dominic's gaze met Hunter's and with the mention of marriage the awkwardness of the past—of what Arabella had done—was in the room between them.

Hunter gave a nod. 'Just have a care over him, Dominic. He is not a good man to have as an enemy.'

'I know and I thank you for the warning, my friend.'

There was a silence in which Hunter sipped at his brandy. Then he smiled. 'To change the subject to a lighter note…'

Dominic relaxed and raised the glass to his lips.

'You are creating quite a stir with Miss Noir.'

Dominic stilled, then set the glass down on the desk without having taken a mouthful.

'What do you mean?' He thought of the lengths he had gone to, to keep the transition of Arabella from Mrs

Silver's to his mistress a secret. 'You did not tell them anything of it?'

Hunter raised his brows and there was a genuine wounded look in his eyes. 'I hope you deem me better than that.'

Dominic gave a nod. 'Forgive me.'

'I do not know how, but the whisper is out about you and the mysterious Miss Noir. People are intrigued by the story. And they are asking questions.'

'Then let us hope that they find no answers.' It should not matter if all of London knew that it was Arabella he had taken as his mistress. After what she had done, it was the very least she deserved. But knowing that and doing it were two different things. He knew what the gossips would do to her if they discovered who she was. They would have a field day with the complete and utter destruction of every last aspect of her character.

'She must be something special that you are taking such a care to hide her,' mused Hunter. 'Who is she, Arlesford?'

'None of your damn business,' said Dominic and lifted his glass of brandy to his mouth. He wondered what Hunter would say if he knew the truth.

Hunter laughed. 'Now I really am intrigued, if you are keeping her secret even from me.'

'Especially from you, Hunter,' Dominic said as if in jest, but he had never been more serious.

'I am not such a bastard that I would steal my best friend's woman,' Hunter protested and finished his brandy in a gulp.

Dominic drew a wry smile. 'Knowing your reputation, I am not about to take any chances.' Better to blame it on that than let Hunter know it was Arabella.

Hunter laughed. 'She must be something special.'

All levity vanished from Dominic's face. He tapped the base of the glass against the wooden surface of his desk as he thought of Arabella.

'She is,' he said and glanced away.

'Dominic?' Hunter probed. But Dominic had no mind to discuss the matter even with Hunter, so he just shook his head.

'Do not go further, friend,' he said quietly.

Hunter gave a subtle nod, then smiled, refilled their glasses and raised his in a toast. 'Miss Noir, long may the *ton* fail to unmask her.'

Dominic chinked his glass against Hunter's, but he did not smile. And as he drank the brandy his mind was filled with Arabella Tatton and what it would mean to them both were she to be unmasked.

It was another reason he should not return to Curzon Street. And yet one more reason that did not relieve the compulsion that whispered to him night and day to retrace his steps straight back there.

Chapter Six

'He did not call upon you again last night?' Mrs Tatton enquired over the toast. 'That is the fourth night in a row.'

Four nights during which Arabella's initial relief at Dominic's absence was beginning to turn into something else. A niggle of worry that would not be stilled. She nodded, trying to let nothing of her true thoughts show upon her face, and spread some honey upon another slice of toast for Archie.

'Who did not call?' asked Archie.

Arabella's mother met her eyes over his head. The two women looked at one another.

'Your mama's friend,' said Mrs Tatton. 'Now eat up your toast, Birthday Boy, before it grows cold.'

Archie, mouth filled with toast, started to pretend two of the spoons were horses galloping across the tablecloth.

Arabella felt her cheeks heat from the deception she was weaving, but knew she had no choice. It would all be so much worse if the truth came out.

'Perhaps if his first visit was not entirely to his satisfaction he has changed his mind over the arrangement.' Embarrassment flushed Mrs Tatton's cheeks as she voiced the fear that had been gnawing at Arabella.

'Let us hope not, Mama.' God help them if he had, for Arabella did not think she could go back to Mrs Silver's. But the manner of their parting lent her little confidence.

A knock sounded at the door and Gemmell entered with a letter from Dominic upon a silver salver.

'Delivered first thing, ma'am,' he said and left again.

Arabella felt a stab of dread, wondering if it contained her *congé*.

Mrs Tatton looked on in anxious silence as Arabella opened the letter and scanned its contents.

'He enquires as to my happiness with the dressmaker,' Arabella said with relief.

'Then all is well?'

'It appears so, Mama.' As Arabella read the rest of the bold script she could not keep the surprise from her voice. 'He writes to say that he has given me the use of a carriage and a purse of money to spend so that I will not have to buy on credit using his name.' She glanced up to meet her mother's eyes. 'So no one need know of our…situation.'

Her mother's eyes widened. 'He is either a most thoughtful gentleman, or…' she raised a brow '…one who has much to lose if you are discovered.'

As far as Arabella could see Dominic had nothing to lose by her discovery. Indeed, she would have thought he would have been crowing it from the rooftops. *A most thoughtful gentleman.* Not a description that could ever be applied to Dominic Furneaux. Or so she had thought.

'Much as I detest that he must pay for us…' She glanced across at her mother's shabby dress. 'You and Archie are in dire need of some new clothes.'

'We should be saving the money so that we may leave this situation as quickly as possible. Archie and I can manage just fine as we are, Arabella.'

'Both of you have only the clothes upon your back, Mama, and nothing more. Your shoes have holes in the soles. And your hands have been paining you. His payment is generous.' She pushed away the thought of what it was he was paying for. 'I will ask Gemmell to organise new wardrobes for you. And I will visit the apothecary myself to fetch you something for your joints.'

Mrs Tatton worried at her lip. 'You are sure he will not notice? About the money?'

Arabella glanced again at the letter. 'He makes it clear he does not wish for an account of my spending.'

'Well, I suppose in that case…' Her mother nodded, but the furrow of worry between her brows lifted only a little.

Arabella pushed the thought of Dominic and her situation aside. There were other matters to be considered today, and she intended to apply herself fully to them. 'Let us talk of more pleasant matters. It is a certain boy's birthday.' She raised her voice so that Archie would hear and looked over at her son. 'And as a special treat I thought that we might take a trip to the park. Robert, the groom, has a little mare called Elsie. Would you like to sit up on Elsie's back while Robert walks her around the park?'

'Oh, yes, please!' Archie's eyes were wide with

delight and he slipped down from his chair and started to gallop around in excitement. 'Can we leave right now?'

'We had best get ourselves ready first!' Arabella laughed.

'Are you sure about this, Arabella?' Mrs Tatton asked.

'It is still early, Mama. There should be few enough people about to notice us; even if they do, there is nothing to associate us with this house or its master.'

Archie paused as he galloped past the mantel piece to stroke a hand against the ribbons that Arabella had festooned there. She smiled at the pleasure on his face and knew that the decorations had been worth it, even if she would have to take them down and hide them away just in case Dominic arrived.

'And remember that we are to have a special birthday lunch,' said Mrs Tatton. 'Cook is making a cherry cake and lemonade and some biscuits too.'

'Hurrah!' shouted Archie. 'I love birthdays.'

Gemmell came in to organise the clearing of the breakfast plates. 'And how old are you today, young master Archie?' he asked.

'I am a grown up boy of five years old,' said Archie with pride.

'That is very grown-up indeed,' agreed Gemmell with a smile and gave the little boy the small wooden figure of a horse that he had carved.

And the maid, Alice, chucked Archie under the chin and gave him a packet of barley-sugar twists that she had made herself and knew to be his favourites.

Arabella felt her heart swell at their kindness. 'Thank you,' she said with meaning. 'You are very kind to us.' And today all the shadows of the past and the present seemed very far away. Today they were a proper family—Archie, her mother, Arabella and all of the servants.

Dominic read the card in his hand and knew there was no way he could refuse Prinny's invitation without delivering the prince a monumental insult. How recently a night of drunken revelry and fireworks in Vauxhall Pleasure Gardens would have held appeal for Dominic. Now it did not. He wondered how little time he might need stay there before he could slip away.

He thought of Arabella sitting alone at her needlework in Curzon Street. And he felt that same surge of desire for her that he had always felt. He burned for her, just as he knew he could not take her. It was an absurd situation of his own creation. An insolvable paradox that tortured him more with each passing day. His brain told him that he should go round to Curzon Street right now and ease the ache in his loins upon her, to ride her as he had done in Mrs Silver's. But even the memory of what had happened in that place soured his stomach. And in his heart he knew that he could not do it. Even if she had been ridden by a thousand men before him.

He glanced again at the card, *Vauxhall and its masked carnival*, and an audacious idea popped into his head. An idea that was both daring and ridiculous. To be with her was a torture, but he craved it all the same. The carnival might be easier than being alone with her in a house he was paying for, with a bed too easily within reach. The thought of having Arabella by his side seemed to make the prospect of Vauxhall much more palatable. He slipped the card into his pocket. It would require another visit to Curzon Street.

Just to tell her of the carnival.

Nothing more.

Tonight.

He anticipated the visit with a combination of dread and impatience.

It was wonderful to escape the house in Curzon Street and it gladdened Arabella's heart to watch her son and her mother enjoy the morning in the fresh air of the park. The trip lifted all of their spirits and so too did the little party they had for themselves and the servants that afternoon.

Normally Gemmell served dinner at four o'clock, which was early for London's society, but it was an hour that gave Arabella and her family time enough to sit down and eat together before preparing for the evening. The preparation involved checking in each room that there was no evidence of either Archie or Mrs Tatton and ensuring that Archie was bathed, changed and tucked up in bed asleep before the master of the house's arrival, should he choose to call. But today, because of the park and the party, and the fact that come four o'clock they were still full of birthday cake and lemonade, everything was running late. And Arabella was loathe to bring a close to the day. Not once had she allowed herself to think of Dominic or her circumstances. She had been determined to make this day as enjoyable as possible for Archie's sake. And it had been. Arabella felt happy for the first time in weeks.

'Have we not had the very best of days?' she asked as they sat down to a light dinner within the dining room.

'Indeed we have, Mama!' His eyes were shining

and his cheeks had the healthy glow of the outdoors about them.

Arabella and her mother laughed.

'And Charlie thinks so, too.' He stroked the little wooden horse that Gemmell had made for him.

They were in the middle of eating when Arabella thought she heard a familiar-sounding carriage outside. *It cannot be,* she thought to herself. *It is barely quarter past six.* But then a very worried-looking Gemmell appeared in the doorway.

'Madam, it is the master!'

'Good Lord!' said Arabella beneath her breath.

'Oh, Arabella!' gasped her mother.

'Show him into the drawing room. I will come through and stall him there while Mama and Archie make their escape.'

Gemmell gave a nod and hurried away.

'What is wrong, Mama?' asked Archie.

'Nothing at all, little lamb. Grandmama wants to tell you a very exciting new story. So you must sneak upstairs to your bedchamber as quickly and quietly as you can. And once you are there you must climb straight into bed and be as quiet as a mouse and listen to Grandmama's new story before you go to sleep.'

'No bathing?' asked Archie, who was looking as if it was something too good to be true.

'Just for tonight,' said Arabella.

'Hurrah!' Archie began to shout.

Mrs Tatton put her fingers to her lips and hushed him. 'Shush now, Archie. Fasten that little button on your lips. Quiet as a mouse, remember?'

Archie nodded and made the button-fastening movement at his lips.

Arabella heard the front door open. She heard the murmur of Dominic's voice and the tread of his shoes on the polished wooden floorboards of the hallway.

Archie was grinning so much a tiny breathy snigger escaped him.

Arabella's and her mother's eyes shot to him, shaking their heads, touching their fingers to their lips in a silencing gesture.

Her heart was thudding as hard as a blacksmith's hammer striking against an anvil. She looked at the door, afraid that Dominic would come striding through it, demanding to know what was going on.

Please God, do not let him discover them.

But his footsteps walked straight on past the dining room door and on along the passageway to the drawing room.

A minute later, and without a single noise, Gemmell appeared at the door. There was a glimmer of sweat upon his brow. The poor man looked every bit as worried as Arabella felt.

She nodded to him. 'Help Mama and Archie. Wait until I am inside the drawing room speaking with him before you make a dash for it.' She thought of the infirmities of both Gemmell and her mother—'dash' was perhaps the wrong word to use.

'Be a good boy for Grandmama.' She kissed Archie on the forehead. And to her mother, 'Take off his shoes that they make no noise upon the floor.'

'I will carry him, ma'am,' said Gemmell.

Archie was quite heavy and she worried that Gemmell could not manage him, but she did not want to insult the old butler by suggesting any such thing. So she gave him a grateful, if nervous, smile. 'Thank you.'

And then, smoothing down her skirts, she made her way through to the drawing room and Dominic.

Arabella was looking a little flustered when she appeared in the drawing room.

'Forgive me,' he said, 'did I interrupt you?'

'Not at all.' She sounded slightly breathless. 'I had almost finished eating when I heard your arrival.'

'I did not mean to interrupt your dinner. It is nothing of importance. I merely wanted to speak with you. Let us go back to the dining room. We can speak just as well there.'

'No. Really.' She thought of the ribbons that still festooned the mantel, and the three settings at the table and their half-eaten meals…and her mother and son still within. 'Besides, I find my appetite has quite deserted me.'

He stiffened at her words, but when his eyes scanned her face there was nothing of disdain or sharpness there.

She caught his expression and only then seemed to realise what she had said. 'I did not mean…that is to say…'

Dominic looked at her in surprise. There was not one sign of her normal cool reserve, nothing of artifice. She was every inch the Arabella he had known and loved. Keeping her here as his mistress had never seemed so wrong, yet he was having trouble tearing his eyes away from her.

'I came to ask if you would accompany me on an evening at Vauxhall Gardens. The Prince of Wales is organising a masquerade and I am obliged to attend. I thought as it was a masked affair…your identity would

be quite hidden. And perhaps you would find it prefer-
able to an evening spent with your needlework.'

She opened her mouth to say something, then closed
it again. And something of the mask was back upon her
face.

They looked at one another across the distance.

'You may think about it, Arabella, and let me know
your decision.' He placed the card down upon a nearby
table and made to leave.

'Wait.' She stepped towards him, her hand held out
in entreaty. 'Please.'

Dominic stopped and looked round at her.

'I would like very much to go to Vauxhall with you.'

Some of the tension he had been feeling eased. He
gave a nod of his head. 'Thank you.' His eyes met hers.
'I will leave you to your dinner.' He bowed and turned
away.

'Dominic!' There was an urgency in her voice he had
not heard before. 'Will you not stay for a little while?'

He peered round at her, hardly believing this sudden
change in her.

She gestured to the sofa. 'Let us sit down and…talk.'

There was such earnestness in her face he could not
refuse. Besides, if she wanted to talk then he wanted
to listen. Maybe she would tell him the answer to the
question that had weighed heavy in his mind for every
single day of the last six years.

'Tell me about your day.' He could sense the nervousness running through her, see it in the way she wetted
her lips and clutched her hands together that bit too
tightly.

'You wish to know about my day?'

'Yes. I am interested to hear it. You have not told me

anything of your life.' She perched herself on the edge of the striped green sofa.

'You have not asked,' he said and sat down beside her.

'Then I have been remiss in my duty.' She smiled, but Dominic could not help but notice that the smile did not touch her eyes.

Her fingers were gripping the edge of the sofa. He laid his hand gently over them.

'I do not want you to ask out of duty, Arabella,' he said quietly.

Her gaze met his and the smile dropped away from her face.

A loud clatter sounded from the hallway and Arabella jumped.

'What on earth...?' He got to his feet to go out and see what was going on.

But Arabella was already on hers and standing before him. 'Gemmell is a little clumsy. Do not be harsh with him, Dominic, I beg of you.' Her face had paled and she looked almost frightened.

'I have no intention of chastising anyone, Arabella. I mean only to check that there has been no mishap.'

'Dominic...' She stepped towards him. He saw the intensity of her expression, the uncertainty in her eyes. Slowly she reached her hand out and brushed the tips of her fingers against his face.

And everything in Dominic's world seemed to stop.

She touched her fingers over his cheek as if she were reassuring herself that it really was him.

Dominic held his breath and did not move.

She traced down the line of his nose, omitting his mouth to move over the angles of his chin, first one way and then the other, before coming back to linger within its cleft. Her fingers were chilled as ice against his skin.

Not once did he move his gaze from her, just watched her following the path her finger was drawing.

And then slowly she inched her fingers higher...

Dominic's body tightened.

And higher...

His breath shook.

Until at last, her fingertips touched against his lips and stilled. They were light as a feather and trembling.

Dominic ceased to think. He responded in the only way he knew how with Arabella. He kissed those sweet delicate fingers, kissed each one in turn. And when she came into his arms and her body cleaved to his it seemed the most natural thing in the world to kiss her mouth.

Arabella kissed him and forgot that she was only doing this to prevent the discovery of Archie and her mother. She kissed him and everything else ceased to be. He held her as if he cared for her, kissed her as if he loved her. He was the same man she had known, the same man she had loved. And in this moment as she felt the fast beat of his heart beneath her hand and the warmth and the strength of his body, she felt everything that she had done as a girl of nineteen. He worshipped her with his lips and she believed the illusion his tenderness wove—of love and of protection. She slid her hand up around his neck and gave herself up to the kiss, revelling in it, wanting it all the more. All of these years without him. Her heart clung to his and refused to let go.

Lies, all lies, the little voice in her head whispered.

And she remembered all that he had done. And her son who had no father. And the memories cooled her ardour like a bucket of iced water.

She stumbled back, clutching a hand to her mouth, appalled at what she had just done.

'Arabella?' Dominic's eyes were dark and dazed. His voice sounded low and confused.

'I…' She backed away and shook her head, knowing that there were no words to explain how she was feeling. She did not know what to say to him. She could not even begin to pretend that she was unaffected by what had just happened between them or by anything of this situation.

'I…' she tried again and as her gaze lowered she saw the evidence of his arousal within his close-fitting pantaloons and realised that she had seduced him just like the courtesan she was. What she had done meant he would take her now. And she trembled at the thought of it.

Dominic looked right into her eyes, as if he could see every thought in her head, then walked away without saying a single word.

There was the thud of the front door shutting, and Arabella's eyes closed in anguish.

Chapter Seven

The night of the Vauxhall masquerade came around too quickly.

Arabella slipped the silver-beaded and feathered mask into place and turned to face Dominic. He had barely said a word since entering the drawing room of the Curzon Street town house and there was an atmosphere in the room thick enough to be cut with a knife.

Dominic's gaze perused her face, lingering for seconds that seemed too long, so that it was almost as if she had only just touched her fingers to his lips, only just kissed him with such wanton abandon. The sweat prickled upon her palms and the butterflies were flocking in her stomach.

It was not only the mask she was worrying over. 'My dress...' She had been so very determined to thumb her nose at him during its ordering; now she was aware that its very respectability might reveal more of her identity when she was by Dominic's side. 'It will not attract...'

Suspicion. Speculation '...attention,' she finished, 'will it?'

She watched his gaze drop to the bodice, then sweep down to the skirt and she bit her lip in worry.

It was a dress like none that Arabella had ever owned. Plain yet elegant. Pale silver silk cut to fit her body perfectly. With its small capped sleeves, bodice scattered with small crystal beads that sparkled in the light and décolletage that teased rather than revealed, the dress was beautiful but pure in a way that made it unsuitable for any courtesan. The irony of its styling was not lost on Arabella.

'How could you think it would fail to attract attention, Arabella?' he said in a quiet voice.

Her stomach gave a churn and her gaze shot to his, waiting for his anger.

'It is beautiful. *You* are beautiful.'

She gaped in surprise, and blushed and could think of not one thing to say.

Dominic swept the long black velvet domino around her shoulders. She jumped at the brush of his fingers against her collar bone as he fastened it in place, feeling nervous both at Dominic's proximity and the prospect of the night ahead.

Out there before all those people. At his side. As his mistress.

A wave of uncertainty swept through her. She bit again at her lip.

'No one will know your true identity, Arabella,' he said gently, and carefully pulled up the domino's hood to cover the curls piled high upon her head.

And then he took her hand in his and led her out to where the carriage waited.

* * *

The night was cool, but clear and dry. Tiny stars studded the blackness of the sky as they walked down the grassy bank towards the boats and barges that would carry them across the Thames to the carnival. They crossed the river in silence. Nor did they speak when they arrived at the other bank and the pleasure gardens that were Vauxhall. Dominic was too aware of Arabella by his side, and of the tension that flowed between them.

The gardens were more crowded than usual, with guests who had come to witness the Prince of Wales at the masquerade. Dominic made his meeting with the prince and, when he saw how Prinny was looking at Arabella, steered her away again just as quickly.

She had taken hold of the arm that he offered and they strolled together through the night, in a parody of all the other couples around them. But even in the lightness of her touch he could feel the tension that hummed through her body. He took her to the section of the gardens where there were shows and jugglers and acrobats. And something of the strain between them seemed to lessen as they stood there together and watched. Her grip even tightened a little as she watched with fascination a man who could swallow the blade of a sword. And when that display was done, he moved on, wanting to show her all there was to see.

There were jesters and gypsy women selling lucky white heather and offering to read their fortunes.

Near to the supper booths a group of musicians were playing, filling the surrounding gardens with the sweetness of their music. An area close by was ringed with tables and chairs in the middle of which a wooden dance floor had been laid down upon the grassy surface.

'Shall we dance?' He realised that he wanted to dance with her, to hold her close in his arms, very much.

She touched a hand against her mask, in the same gesture she had used that very first night in Mrs Silver's drawing room.

'No one will recognise you,' he reassured her and slid the dark voluminous hood down to reveal the glory of her hair. 'Even like this. Trust me.'

She looked up at him and nodded, and again Dominic felt something he thought to have long been destroyed stir in his heart.

'It is so long since I danced,' she said and there was uncertainty in her eyes as she glanced at the dance floor where other couples were moving together in each other's arms. 'And I have never waltzed.'

'Just relax and follow my lead.' He offered his hand for hers.

She looked at him and it seemed to Dominic as if she were making some pivotal decision in that moment, not merely deciding whether she would dance with him. Then, without saying a word, she placed her hand in his and let him lead her out on to the dance floor.

Arabella gave herself into Dominic's arms and waltzed with him. There was something soothing about the moonlight and the lilt of the music and the sway of their bodies in the dance. He was holding her scandalously close, so close that the fall of his breeches brushed against her skirts, so close that his heart beat against her breast. But this was Vauxhall and every other couple was dancing just as intimately.

He was looking at her with those dark soulful eyes

just as he had looked at her all those years ago. Whether it was the music or the moonlight or just plain madness, in that moment she let herself forget, and just felt—the music, her heartbeat…and him.

When the music stopped, he led her from the floor towards the buffet of food laid out upon the tables. There were fresh bread rolls and ham sliced fine and thin, and a selection of fruit perfect for the eating.

He fetched them two glasses of punch and filled two plates with a selection of food to tempt her and found them a small table in a spot that was not so crowded. He made a little conversation, polite pleasant words, nothing that touched near anything that was sensitive for them both. Something of her fears for the evening faded.

Afterwards they watched some boats, miniature replicas of the great Lord Nelson's, being sailed down the river, and then there were the fireworks, a burst of rainbow lights that exploded to shower the dark canvas of the sky. And she wished that Archie and her mother could see the spectacle.

Dominic was standing behind her, both of their necks craned back as they stared up at the sky. He bent his head forwards and said something to her, but the explosions all around were so loud that she could not hear. He stepped closer, easing her back against him so that he could whisper in her ear.

But she still could not make out his words, so she turned in his arms and all of a sudden she was looking into his face and he was looking into hers. And she could see the flash of the firework bursts reflected in the darkness of his eyes. But she was no longer thinking of the fireworks, and neither was he. They stared at one another. Alone in the crowd. Silent and serious in the midst of the riotous carnival.

'Arlesford?' The voice smashed the moment apart like a cannon. 'Your Grace, I thought it was you.'

Dominic turned, shifting his stance to manoeuvre Arabella slightly behind him so that he was partly shielding her with his body. 'Misbourne,' he said in his usual emotionless voice and faced the man.

Lord Misbourne was dressed in a domino the like of Arabella's and even wore a mask across his eyes. But there could be no doubt over the owner of the face that was beneath it, with its curled grey moustache and neatly trimmed beard. Misbourne's arm was curled around the waist of a woman young enough to be his daughter and whose large breasts were in danger of imminent escape from her bodice. The girl cast Dominic a libidinous glance and licked her tongue suggestively around her lips before taking a sip of punch from the glass she was carrying.

Misbourne did not notice; he was too busy staring at Arabella. 'Gentlemen must have their little distractions, Arlesford,' he said. 'Nothing wrong with that—as long as they are discreet, of course.' And Dominic understood the message that Misbourne was trying to send him—that his having a mistress would be no barrier to courting Misbourne's daughter.

The earl leered at Arabella and Dominic felt his fists bunch in response. He forced himself to stay calm. Brawling with Misbourne would only draw the wrong kind of attention to her.

'If you will excuse us, sir. We were just leaving.'

'But not before you have introduced me to your lady friend. Could this be the delectable Miss Noir about whom I have heard so many whispers?' He peered around Dominic at Arabella.

Dominic felt the rage flow through his blood. He could smell it in his nose and taste it upon his tongue. Every muscle was primed and ready. Every nerve stretched taut. His loathing of Misbourne flooded him so that he would have knocked the man down had he not felt Arabella's fingers touch his arm in the gentlest of restraints. Only then did he recollect his senses.

'Goodnight, Misbourne,' he said in a tone that brooked no refusal, and when he looked at the man's beady, glittering dark eyes behind his mask he saw that Misbourne understood. The older man took an involuntary step back from the threat.

Dominic took Arabella's arm in his and he was so grateful that she had stopped him.

She did not utter one question, nor throw so much as a glance in Misbourne's direction. She just held her head up and waited.

They walked away together, away from Misbourne and the fireworks. Away from Vauxhall and the wonderful night.

The carriage wheels were rumbling along the road carrying them back to Curzon Street and still Dominic had not spoken.

Arabella could sense the tension emanating from him, the echo of the anger she had seen directed against the man, Misbourne, in Vauxhall. All illusions had vanished the moment Misbourne and the woman had appeared.

'Does everyone know that you bought me from Mrs

Silver?' The words would not be contained for a minute longer.

The carriage rolled past a street lamp and in the brief flicker of light she saw his face through the darkness—handsome, hard edged, dangerous—before the night's darkness hid him again.

'How naïve of me not to have realised.' She shook her head and looked away, feeling sick at the thought. 'What else do they know, Dominic?' *What else have you told them?* she wanted to ask.

'Nothing, I hope. I paid Mrs Silver very well for her silence. And I trust my friends, who were with me that night, enough to make no mention of Miss Noir.'

'You did not tell them?'

'Of course I did not tell them, Arabella! My affairs are my own, not tittle-tattle for the amusement of others.' His voice was hard and angry. 'Do you think I would have gone to such lengths to hide you were it otherwise?'

'You guard your own reputation well.' This was all about protecting himself. How foolish to think it could ever have been about her.

'I am guarding what is left of yours,' he said grimly. Then his tone softened slightly. 'I am not unaware of the…sensitivity of this issue.'

She looked across at the shadowed man through the darkness and was not sure she believed him.

'Of what it would mean to your mother were she to learn the truth.'

'God forbid…' Arabella pressed a hand to her forehead, horrified at the prospect of that revelation, even if it were something rather different to that which Dominic envisaged. But even as she thought it she was wondering why Dominic should have the slightest care over her mother.

'They may know of Miss Noir, but they do not know the identity of the woman behind her mask.'

Yet.

The word hung unspoken between them.

'You may rest assured that I will do all in my power to keep it that way.'

She stared at him, not knowing what to make of his attitude.

'I will make discreet enquiries over—'

'No,' she said too quickly. If he started asking questions, who knew what he would discover. Everything that Arabella had striven so hard to hide. 'No,' she said more gently. 'Words already spoken cannot be unsaid. Asking questions will only make it worse. Besides—' she glanced away '—you are a duke; there will always be an interest in your dealings. And the lure of a coin will mean there are always tongues to be loosened.'

And she could not blame them. She of all people knew what it was like to be poor and in desperate need of money.

'Perhaps, but speed and generosity has always worked in the past to silence them,' he said.

'But not this time.'

'Seemingly not.'

There was a small silence.

'Thank you for trying.' Her words were stilted. Gratitude sat ill with her when it came to Dominic, but for all that she felt she knew how much worse it could be, had he taken her as his mistress as carelessly as he had abandoned her as his betrothed.

The carriage wheels rolled on.

She steered the conversation to safer ground. 'Who was he, the man in Vauxhall? Misbourne.' The man who had stirred in Dominic such barely leashed fury.

There was a small pause before Dominic answered, 'A delusional old fool, Arabella, but not one you need have a worry over.'

Another pause.

'I thank you that you stayed my arm,' he said. 'Brawling with an earl at Vauxhall would not have been conducive to our maintaining a low profile.'

She gave a nod of acknowledgement. And she wondered as to this man who she knew to be a rake and a scoundrel. A man who had made her his whore, yet did not flaunt or humiliate her publically. A man who went to such pains to preserve her privacy and who, it seemed, had a care for her mother's sensibilities.

The carriage came to a stop outside Curzon Street.

The hour was late. She did not know whether he would come in. Whether he would kiss her. Bed her. And she was not sure if she dreaded it or wanted it. Nervous anticipation tingled right through her.

He helped her from the carriage and into the hallway, dismissing James the young footman who was acting as the night porter.

Only two wall sconces were lit and the soft shadowed lighting lent the hallway an unusual intimacy. Or maybe it was the fact that they were standing there alone in the middle of the night facing one another.

Arabella did not know what she should say. She could feel the tension between them, feel the speed of her heart. Her mouth was dry from dread, her thighs hot from desire. She swallowed and it sounded loud in the silence.

'You need not worry, Arabella, I am not staying,' he said in a voice as dark and rich as chocolate. 'I came only to see you safely inside.' As if to reinforce his words she could hear the sound of the waiting carriage from the street outside.

In the flickering of the candlelight she thought he had never looked so dangerous or so handsome. There was a hardness to his face that had not been there all those years ago, but when she looked into his eyes, those dark velvet brown eyes, Arabella saw something of tenderness. And for all that she should have known better, for all of her common sense, she felt the stirrings of old feelings that she had thought never to feel again. There was such an allure of forbidden attraction that the atmosphere sparked with it.

Her breath was shallow and fast, her stomach a mass of fluttering butterflies. 'This arrangement between us. I thought that you would… That it would be different between us…' She met his gaze. 'I do not understand.'

'Neither do I, Arabella,' he said.

Her heart was thudding so hard she thought she could hear it in the silence.

He peeled off his gloves and came to stand before her.

They stared at one another for one beat of her heart and then another. And then he reached out his hand and touched his fingers to her cheek, caressing her face in a mirror of her own actions from an evening not so long ago. His touch was more gentle than she remembered, soft as the stirring of warm breath upon her skin. His movement was unhurried and sensual as he traced the outline of her cheek and up across her eyebrow.

He touched only her face yet every inch of her body

tingled in response. He trailed his forefinger down the slope of her nose, and her breasts felt heavy and sensitive. His thumb brushed against her lower lip and the sensation was as if he had stroked between her legs. She gasped and opened to him so that his thumb probed within the moisture of her mouth. Her lips touched to him, not because she was his mistress but because it felt instinctive and right.

'Arabella,' he whispered and there was something agonised and urgent in his whisper. And then he pulled her into his arms and kissed her.

Arabella kissed him back, their mouths moving in hungry reunion. She felt his hands upon her breasts, upon her hips. Their bodies clinging together, as if nothing of the pain had ever been.

She felt the press of his manhood against her, felt the heat of him, the need in him, and, God help her, but she wanted him too. Her thighs burned. She was moist for him. Her body recognised his and opened as if in invitation. And her heart began to open to him too, just as it had done all those years ago. And suddenly she was afraid, afraid of where this was leading, afraid of what she was feeling.

Dominic seemed to sense the sudden swirl in her emotions. He stopped, raised his head and looked into her eyes and she saw in them a desire and confusion that matched her own.

'No,' he whispered, but did not release her. 'No,' he said again and she knew that it was himself he was denying more than her. His breathing was ragged and she could feel the taut strain in every hard muscle of his body. She could sense his hunger, and yet there was a sudden wariness in his eyes, a restraint almost. She felt his grip loosen. He released her and left; there was only the sound of the front door clicking shut behind him.

Arabella stood there until the sound of his carriage faded into the distance and she touched trembling fingers to her swollen lips, not understanding how she could feel such attraction for a man whom she disliked and did not trust. He had hurt her in the past. He was humiliating her in the present. She knew all of that, yet tonight he had made her forget. He seemed too like the man she had fallen in love with. When she was with him, when he touched her, when he kissed her…

She clutched her hand harder to her mouth and closed her eyes against the memory, feeling confused and ashamed that he could still affect her so and not knowing what was wrong with her. How could she, who was so strong when it came to everything else, be so weak when it came to Dominic Furneaux?

But Arabella knew that she must not give in. Once it had only been her heart and her pride that he had taken. Now there was so much more at stake than that. She glanced upstairs towards the chamber where her mother and son slept and knew she must stay strong.

Chapter Eight

The night was not going well for Dominic in the gaming den.

He looked at the cards in his hands and, despite all his resolutions, thought again of Arabella. Two nights had passed since the night of the masquerade. Only two nights and in that time he had thought of little else.

'Arlesford,' Hunter prompted by his side, and he realised that everyone at the table was waiting for him. He shoved some more guineas into the pile at the centre of the table.

And, contrary to his usual play, promptly lost them. Indeed, he had not won a game since entering the seedy surroundings, much to the delight of the rather rough-and-ready patrons of the establishment. But then Dominic knew he was more than a little distracted.

It was a small tavern in the East End, most of the patrons of which looked like men you would not wish to meet on a dark night. Their clothing was coarse, their language too. The gin and beer flowed freely, in the hope of addling the wits of those that were fool enough to come here.

It was, surprisingly enough, the very latest place to be seen for Gentlemen of the *ton*. Although, Dominic thought wryly, those young fops that ventured in here would soon realise they had bitten off more than they could chew. Young Northcote had ignored all of Dominic's warnings and was now grinning to hide his nervousness and both drinking and betting more deeply than was wise. The boy was ill at ease in the surroundings, even if he did not want to admit any such thing; it had, after all, been his idea to come here.

Did she wonder as to his absence? Did he gnaw in her thoughts as she gnawed in his? Did she feel this same craving that plagued him night and day? He doubted it. To women like Arabella, their arrangement was nothing more than business. To women like Arabella… He caught the phrase back, and thought bitterly that there were no other women like Arabella.

He stared across the room, seeing not the overly warm, smoky den with its scored tables and rickety chairs and the men with their blackened teeth and their stubble-roughened faces, but the woman whose image had haunted him through the years.

The cards had been dealt. Again.

He lost. Again. And saw the way young Northcote's eyes widened with fear as the youngster realised the extent of his own loses even at this early hour.

Dominic ached for Arabella, wanted her with a compulsion that bordered on obsession, but each time he touched her it was both ecstasy and torture. When he took her in his arms he felt the wound inside him tear afresh.

She was Arabella Tatton, the woman he had loved, the woman who had so callously trampled the youthful tenderness from his heart. And he could not separate that knowledge from his body's craving for her. There would never be anything of relief. Yet he needed to be with her more with every passing minute. Even knowing that he could not touch her, even knowing the torture would be greater with her than without, he could not fight this growing addiction.

Dominic pushed his chair back, its battered legs scraping tracks through the sawdust that covered the floor.

'I think I will call it a night,' he said to the others and gestured for his hat and gloves to be brought.

Several faces looked up, surprise soon turning to menace.

Even Bullford seemed caught unawares. 'A tad early for you, Arlesford.'

'Certainly is, your Grace,' said a large ruffian employed by the establishment. 'Stay, see if you can win back them golden guineas that you've lost.'

'Perhaps another night, gentlemen,' he said.

The men did not look pleased, but Dominic met their gaze directly, knowing that he could handle himself against them. They looked back but only for a moment, then deliberately moved their attention elsewhere.

Hunter stood by his side.

'Best not leave Northcote here. They will only chew him up all the more and spit him out afterwards,' he said quietly to Hunter.

So the two of them guided Northcote out into the street.

After the haze of cigar and pipe smoke within the

den the clear chilled night air seemed to hit Northcote so hard that the boy staggered.

Dominic hailed a hackney carriage and helped Hunter manoeuvre Northcote into it.

'You are not coming with us?' Hunter asked.

Dominic met his friend's eyes. An unspoken understanding passed between them.

'You do not have your cane with you tonight,' said Hunter.

Dominic said nothing, just looked at his friend resolutely.

Hunter gave a sigh. 'Very well. Just have a care if you are so intent on walking to her,' said Hunter. 'The coves back there were not too keen to let you go. It is only a little after midnight and they had hoped to fleece you for hours yet. Watch your back, Dominic.'

'I will.' Dominic clapped Hunter on the shoulder and watched the carriage depart before he turned and began to walk in the opposite direction.

He had not gone far when he became aware that he was being followed. He scanned the street, seeing that one of the lamp-posts was out a little further along, just at an opening between the buildings. A nice dark spot and a conveniently positioned alleyway. He knew that was where they would attack him.

They struck just where he had expected. Two attackers, one large and burly, the other smaller with no teeth in his head. He recognised them both from the gaming den.

He dodged back into the alley to avoid the first punch.

'Not so fast, your Grace,' a coarse voice said so close to his ear that he could smell the foulness and feel the heat of the fetid breath. A fist swiped close to his face. Dominic ducked and retaliated with a blow hard and low in the belly and had the satisfaction of hearing the man grunt and stumble away clutching at his guts as he bent double and retched against the alley wall. As he turned the second assailant was almost upon him. Dominic twisted to avoid the blow arcing towards him, and managed to avoid the blade—almost. The sting of it sliced across his ribs.

Dominic grabbed the man's wrist and twisted. He heard the soft crack of bone and the yelp of pain as the man fell to his knees cradling his wrist. The knife clattered to land in the wet and filth of the cobblestones below. Dominic picked it up, and then grabbed the kneeling man's hair, jerking his head back and touching the edge of the blade against the exposed throat.

'See that the same does not happen to my friends. Do you understand?'

The man croaked a desperate acquiescence.

Dominic pushed the man away, then walked to face the man cringing against the wall, touching the knife's tip ever so lightly against the fat of the villain's belly.

'You too.'

'They won't be harmed, I'll see to it personally, your Grace,' the rogue promised.

Dominic stared at him for just a moment longer and then he slipped the knife into his pocket and walked away.

The ruffians were kicking at the door, laying siege to it with a hammer. The thuds of the splintering wood reverberated right through Arabella's body. She protected Archie with her body, but the men pulled her aside and wrenched the golden locket from around her neck. And when she looked across the road to the other side of the street where the narrow houses with their boarded windows should have stood, she saw the park and her mother standing waiting there. It was all mixed up and wrong, of course, but Arabella did not notice that in her nightmare.

She woke suddenly, with that same panicked feeling of fear in the pit of her stomach. But the sky was still dark with night, and she remembered that this was Curzon Street and there were no robbers and thieves here. She breathed her relief and relaxed her head back down on to the luxury of a soft feather pillow, and as she did she heard a voice cry out in shock. The cry was cut off as if abruptly hushed. She heard the low murmur of voices in the hallway below, the quiet opening and closing of a door. Hurried footsteps across the marbled floor tiles of the hallway.

Archie!

Arabella scrambled from the bed and, using only the glowing remains of the fire to guide her, was out of the bedchamber door and running down the stairs.

All of the wall sconces in the hallway had been lit. A maid, clad in her nightdress and robe, was coming out of the library with a bottle of brandy in her hand.

'Anne?'

'Oh, ma'am!' The girl jumped and spun round and Arabella could see that her face was wet with tears.

'What is wrong? What are you doing?' The fear was squirming in Arabella's stomach.

'I got such a fright when I saw him.' The maid's face crumpled and she began to sob again.

'What has happened, Anne?'

The drawing door opened and James the footman appeared. 'What on earth is taking you, girl? I would have been quicker fetching it myself.' And then he saw Arabella, and gave a quick bow. 'Begging your pardon, ma'am. I did not see you there.'

'What on earth is going on here?' Arabella demanded.

'It's the master, ma'am.'

'Dominic is here?' The thought had not even entered her head. Even though it was his house. And she was his mistress.

'His Grace has had a bit of an…accident.'

'An accident?' Arabella's stomach dropped to the soles of her feet. Her heart was thumping a fast frenzied tattoo of dread.

The footman lowered his voice even more. 'Not the best of sights for a lady to see, but he won't let me fetch a doctor, ma'am.'

A chill of foreboding shivered right through her. She pushed past James into the drawing room.

Three branches of candles had been lit, yet still their warm flickering glow did not reach to the shadows of the room, nor barely touched the tall dark figure that stood near to the cold fireplace. He had his back to her, but he appeared to be as he ever was, smartly dressed in dark tailcoat and pantaloons, with the air of authority and arrogance that he carried with him. He seemed well enough. She could smell the damp night air that emanated from his still figure. One hand hung loose by his side, the other looked to be tucked into the inner breast pocket of his tailcoat.

'I should not have come,' he said without looking round. 'I had not realised that the hour was so late.'

'James said you met with an accident.'

'James exaggerates. I did not mean to wake you. You should go back to bed.' Still he did not move. And the apprehension that had faded on her first sight of him was back as if it had never left.

'What has happened, Dominic?' she asked carefully.

He turned then, and still nothing appeared out of place, except that his right hand remained tucked beneath the left breast of his tailcoat.

'A minor altercation. Nothing of concern. As I said, go back to bed.'

And then she caught sight of the dark ominous stains upon the white cuff that protruded beneath the dark woollen sleeve of his coat and, lifting the closest candelabrum, she walked towards him.

'Arabella,' he said, holding out his exposed hand as if to stay her. But she kept on closing the distance between them, for she had a horrible fear of just what those stains were.

'This is not for your eyes.'

She felt sick to the pit of her stomach. Her body felt stiff and heavy with dread. 'Take off your coat.'

'Arabella…' One last warning.

She ignored him and took hold of his lapel, pulling back the left breast of his tailcoat.

She gasped at the sight that met her eyes. His white shirt and waistcoat were sodden with blood. She froze, and in that single moment everything changed in her world.

'Dominic!' she whispered.

His hand took hers, his grip strong and reassuring. But she felt that it was wet and when she looked she could see the blood that stained it glisten in the candle-light.

'Oh, my God!'

'It is but a scratch that bleeds too much.'

But there was blood everywhere, and all of it was his.

'Go. James will help me.'

She took a deep breath and raised her gaze to his. Their eyes held for a fraction of a second, a heartbeat in which everything she had told herself she felt about him these years past was revealed as a lie.

'No,' she said. '*I* will help you.' And then she glanced round at the footman and prepared to do what she knew must be done.

Dominic watched as Arabella shifted from shock to take charge of the situation. She sent the maid for clean linen and a glass, and instructed the footman with equal calm proficiency, directing James to help divest him of his upper clothing while she half-filled the glass with brandy.

Only once he sat on the sofa wearing only his panta-loons did she pass him the glass. 'Drink it.' Her voice was calm, but brooked no refusal.

He did not argue, just did as she directed, downing the contents in one go.

As he drank she rolled up the sleeves of her night-gown, tore a strip off the linen and dowsed both it and her hands in brandy.

Then she sat down by his side, eased him back a little against the sofa.

Her gaze met his. 'This is going to sting,' she warned. And her eyes held a concern that Dominic had never thought to see there again. It touched his heart much more than he could ever have imagined.

'Do your worst,' he murmured.

He could not prevent himself flinching from the initial touch of the brandy to the wound and saw the pain mirrored in Arabella's eyes. Yet she did not hesitate, or weaken from her purpose.

Her touch was gentle, her movements reassuring. She worked methodically and with a calmness that seemed to stroke away his tension despite the pain. With strip by patient strip of brandy-soaked linen she cleansed the blood away until all that remained was a thin red line against the paleness of his skin.

'We should send for the doctor. He may wish to stitch the wound.' She had not looked at him, not once, since she had taken control of the situation.

'No doctor,' he said. 'The cut is shallow. A week of binding and the skin will knit together well enough.'

'Dominic—'

'No doctor,' he said again.

'Very well.' She laid a pad of linen against the wound, then bound it in place. And then she got to her feet, passed the tray of bloodied rags to James.

'Thank you, James, Anne. You may leave us now.'

She waited until the door closed behind the servants before she sat back down. Side by side they sat on the sofa. Not looking at one another. Not speaking a word. The tension was still between them. But it was different somehow, as if some barrier that had been there before had given way.

The silence seemed to stretch between them.

He slipped his hand to cover hers.

'Are you going to tell me what happened tonight?' she asked.

'A small disagreement with two gentlemen from a gaming den.'

'I did not know you frequented such places.'

'There is a lot you do not know about me, Arabella.'

'And too much that I do know,' she said quietly. 'I cannot forget…'

'Nor can I.'

The clock's ticking seemed too loud. It seemed to match the beat of his heart.

'It was not supposed to be like this, Arabella.'

'None of it was supposed to be like this,' she said and he heard the huskiness in her voice.

'Arabella.' He looked at her, willing her to look round at him.

She shook her head at first, but he could hear the slight sob in her breath. He stroked his thumb against her fingers where his hand covered hers.

She turned her face to his, then met his gaze, and the emotions he saw there were as raw and aching as those that beat in his own heart.

'Dominic,' she whispered and the tears spilled from her eyes. He took her in his arms and he kissed each one away and then he held her.

He held her and the minutes passed.

He held her. And then as if by some silent communion they both rose. He blew out all save one branch of candles, then he took her hand in his and together they walked out of the drawing room.

Chapter Nine

Within her bedchamber they spoke not one word. Dominic stripped off his pantaloons, while Arabella unfastened the ties of her nightdress and loosened it so that it slid down her body to lie in a white pool around her feet.

The candles flickered upon the nightstand, so that she could see him standing there naked. His body as tall and strong and well muscled as she remembered. A sprinkling of dark hair covered his chest and narrowed to a line that led down to his manhood. His skin glowed a honey gold in the candles' light, the whiteness of the linen bandage stark against the rest of him.

There was no need for words. She sensed his feelings as keenly as her own. She wanted him. And needed him. Not out of lust. Not even out of desire. The need ran at a much deeper level than that, in a place that touched both her heart and her soul. She did not analyse the feeling. Nor did she think about the past.

Arabella knew only this moment. Dominic was alive.

And that, had a blade pressed a little harder this night, he would not be.

She placed her palm upon his chest over his heart and felt its strong steady beat. Beneath her fingers she could feel the roughness of his chest hair and in her nose was the scent of brandy and cigar smoke mingled with Dominic's cologne.

He threaded a hand through her hair at the scalp, angling her head so that he could look into her eyes.

She did not look away. She did not try to hide anything. They looked at each other with an honesty that belonged only to that moment. His eyes were deep and dark and sensuous and in them was a vulnerability that she had never ever thought to see.

Slowly he lowered his mouth to hers. Their lips touched, the kiss small and gentle. And touched again, before stilling so that their lips rested together, not kissing, but sharing their breath. She slid her hands up from his chest, to dip her fingers into the hollow between his collar bones, before spreading out to slide across the tense hard muscle of his shoulders. Their faces were so close she could feel the brush of his eyelashes every time he blinked.

His free hand followed down the line of her arm to capture her hand in his, hooking both their hands against the small of her back to arch her body all the closer into his. His chest was hard as a rock, the hair that covered it rough against her nipples. Her breasts felt heavy and sensitive, and deep in her belly was a heat that had never expired. She could feel the call of his body and the answer of her own. Just as it ever was, except this time it was different. She could feel the difference. And she knew that he could feel it too.

He bit gently at her lower lip, then salved the nip with his tongue. She tasted him, opened to him, felt his tongue accept the invitation as his lips slid against her own. They kissed. A deep sensual coupling of their mouths. A sharing of such intimacy and tenderness. They kissed and his every breath, every stroke of his tongue, every touch of his lips was a caress of her soul.

He sat down on the edge of the bed, drawing her in so that she was standing straddling his thigh. He kissed her again, then trailed his mouth down over her neck, his breath hot, his tongue tasting her. His hands caressed her breasts, weighing them, stroking skin that was sensitive to his touch, teasing at peaks that were already beaded hard. His hands stilled, his thumbs resting lightly on her nipples, as his gaze slid up to hers. And then, keeping his eyes locked on hers, he shifted one thumb aside and leaned his mouth down to take her nipple into his mouth.

He did not suckle. He did not even move his lips, but his breath was hot and moist against her. He was still watching her when his tongue began to flick against the tender swollen bud. A low soft moan escaped Arabella. She arched her back, driving her breast harder against his mouth. He began to kiss her nipple, to suck it, while his thumb and fingers worked upon the other. When she felt the gentle scrape of his teeth, she clutched that dark head to her, watching his mouth work thoroughly against first one breast and then the other.

His hands found her hips and drew them lower so that she felt the tease of the hairs on his broad muscular thigh against the hot wet centre of her womanhood. Her grip shifted to his shoulders and tightened as he rubbed his thigh gently against her. Arabella moaned again and slid higher up his thigh, until she could feel the probe of his manhood against her hip.

They stilled, his mouth coming back to find hers. And when he rolled her on to the bed their bodies clung together. He lay on his uninjured side, clutching her to him. And she could feel the raggedness of his breathing and the race of his heart as they positioned their legs to minimise the strain on his wound. And when at last she welcomed him into her body it had never felt so right. There was no dominant, no submissive. Nothing of taking, only of sharing. They moved together in a partnership, both rejoicing in their union and striving to the same end.

They loved, for there could be no other word for it. And Arabella was only aware of the moment and the man. Dominic filled her senses. Dominic filled her body.

'Dominic,' she gasped as she exploded into a thousand shards of shimmering pleasure.

'Arabella,' he groaned and she felt the warmth of his seed spill within her.

They lay in each other's arms, feeling the pulse of their bodies and the beat of their hearts.

And eventually they slept.

Dominic came every night to Curzon Street after that. And every night they made love. Arabella was no longer fool enough to believe that she could fight against the mire of complex emotions that she felt for Dominic. Since the night he had come to the house covered in blood she had known that much as she hated what he had done to her, she did not hate *him*. Indeed, there was a part of her that knew they would always be bound together, and not just through Archie. If Arabella had allowed herself to think too much of her situation it would have been unbearable.

She knew what she was—his mistress, a woman he had bought from a brothel.

And she knew what he was—a man who had betrayed her and ruined her life.

And she knew, too, that contrary to everything that she should feel she still cared for him.

Arabella did not want to think what that said about her. Or what it implied about Dominic.

Dominic watched Hunter as the other man pulled up the tails of his coat and stood with his back before the warm flame of the fire. There was only the slow steady tick of the clock on the mantelpiece and the soft sounds of the flames upon the coals.

'I am sure I saw Arabella Tatton coming out of an apothecary shop in Bond Street the other day.' Hunter's voice was steady and he was watching Dominic.

'Did you?' Dominic's heart picked up some speed but he feigned indifference.

'She was carrying her gloves…and she was not wearing a wedding ring.'

'Really?' Dominic pretended to examine his nails.

'And she asked her coachman to take her home to Curzon Street.' Hunter shifted his stance and Dominic could smell hot wool.

Silence.

'It all begins to make sense. Why you are so very protective of Miss Noir's identity. Why you have been so intent on keeping her hidden from view. Not one party. Not one ball, save Prinny's *masked* carnival at

Vauxhall, so I hear. Hardly your normal treatment of a woman…unless there is something of her identity that you wish to conceal.'

Still Dominic said nothing, but he felt his body tense as if in preparation for a fight. He thought of the tenderness of their lovemaking. And he wanted to protect her, even from Hunter.

'It is her, is it not?'

'You are mistaken, Hunter,' he said and the look in his eyes bellowed the warning that his words only whispered at.

'Hell's teeth, Dominic! I am not a fool. I know that Arabella is Miss Noir.'

Dominic did not remember moving, but the next he knew he was two inches in front of Hunter's face, staring down at him as if he would like to rip him limb from limb.

Hunter shook his head and met his gaze. 'Do you honestly think I would breathe one word of this outside of this room? Your secret is safe with me.'

Dominic knew that it was, but it did not make him feel any better.

'I think I am in need of a drink,' said Hunter weakly and ducked under Dominic's arm to stroll across the library and pour them both a large brandy. He passed one glass to Dominic and took several swigs from the other himself. 'I hope you know what you are doing.'

Dominic took a sip of brandy. 'Everything is under control.'

'Is it?' asked Hunter and the look on his face said that he did not believe it. 'Have you forgotten what she did to you?'

'I have not forgotten.' Nothing of the pain.

'Then this is some kind of revenge?'

Dominic set his glass down upon the mantelpiece with a thud that threatened to fracture the crystal stem. 'Hell, Sebastian, what kind of man do you take me for? I found her in Mrs Silver's that night! What did you expect me to do? Walk away and leave her there?' he shouted.

'After breaking your betrothal to run off and marry some other man? Yes. That is exactly what I would have done.' Hunter shook his head again. 'I thought you were over her. I thought you had learned your lesson from her. Lord, but she made a damn fool of you!' Hunter peered closer at Dominic's face. 'But you still want her,' he said slowly as if the pieces of the puzzle were falling into place to reveal the answer.

'Yes, I want her,' admitted Dominic. 'I have never stopped wanting her. Any sane man would. I do not have to like her to bed her.'

Hunter was still looking at him. 'Were that true you would not give a damn who knew she is your mistress. The shame would be on her, Dominic, not on you. No, there is more to it than that.' His eyes narrowed with speculation.

'Leave it alone, Sebastian,' Dominic warned.

But Hunter never could take a warning. 'You still care for her,' he said quietly.

The glass within Dominic's hand shattered, sending the splinters of glass flying across the mantelpiece and spilling the brandy to pool with the blood, but Dominic felt nothing of the pain.

Hunter pulled a clean white handkerchief from his pocket and appeared by his side. First he checked there were no glass fragments in Dominic's hand, then used the handkerchief as a bandage to staunch the bleeding. He eyed Dominic with concern. 'This is worse than I thought,' he said, and Dominic knew Hunter was not referring to the cut upon his hand. 'You do not want me to, but I will say it anyway. You are making a mistake with her, Dominic.'

'Be that as it may, I will not give her up,' said Dominic; he knew he sounded stubborn and bad tempered and that he should relax and pretend that she did not matter to him in the slightest.

'I did not think that you would,' replied Hunter quietly. 'You do care for her, Dominic.'

'I care only that she warms my bed,' said Dominic and knew that he was not fooling Hunter for a minute, yet his pride would not let him admit the truth. He did not think he even understood himself what the truth was any more.

He tensed against any more of Hunter's questions, but his friend let the matter drop, clapping a hand of support against Dominic's shoulder. 'I think you are in need of another brandy.'

'It is just an arrangement for sex,' he insisted. Except Dominic knew that he was lying. Even Hunter knew he was lying. There were other aspects to what was between Arabella and him that he did not wish to think about. Depths he had not yet come to terms with. 'I know what I am doing, Sebastian.'

'I hope so, Dominic.' But Hunter did not look convinced.

A fortnight had passed when Arabella awoke with the sunlight streaming in through a crack in the curtains. The bed was still warm from Dominic's presence although he had left before dawn, as he did every morning. Whatever else Dominic was, at least he was discreet.

From the chamber above she heard the scurry of little footsteps. Archie. She smiled as she pulled on her dressing gown and went to find her son and her mother.

'You two slugabeds had best get yourselves up and readied, for today we are going out.'

'Is that such a good idea?' Mrs Tatton glanced round at her in surprise.

'I have heard tell of a wonderful new apothecary in Oxford Street who can mix the best of liniments for the joints. Besides, we have not been out of the house since our outing to the park and such confinement is not good for Archie, or for you. The weather is fine and an outing will do us all good.'

'What if we are seen by your gentleman while we are out?' said Mrs Tatton.

'We will be very careful. And he hates shopping.' She doubted Dominic had changed in that respect. 'I cannot think that we would meet him in the apothecary.'

'But after that last time, when he almost caught us... My stomach has been sick with nerves.'

'We will make sure we return here in plenty of time.' Arabella placed a reassuring hand on her mother's shoulder. 'Please come, Mama. I think it would do you good. And I promise you, nothing will go wrong.' Arabella felt a shiver of foreboding as soon as the words had left her mouth. She turned to her son, and lifted him on to her knee. 'What say you, Archie? I thought we might visit Gunter's for some ices before the apothecary.'

'Oh, can we, Mama?' His eyes shone with excitement.

She kissed Archie's cheek and then her mother's. 'Chop chop, then,' she said with a smile.

There really was very little chance of something going wrong, she told herself again and again, but that stubborn feeling of unease sat right there in her stomach and refused to shift.

She would only later learn that the feeling was called instinct and that she should have listened to it.

Chapter Ten

'I am so glad that you persuaded me to come. It is a lovely day and Archie is having such a fine time.' Her mother smiled as she and Arabella strolled along arm in arm, with Archie running before them breathless with excitement.

'Ooh, do look at that display, Arabella!' Mrs Tatton pulled Arabella over to admire the array of perfume bottles in the shop window. 'All the way from Paris and with matching scented soaps. How lovely.'

'This is the place of which I was speaking to you of—the apothecary who is highly recommended. Gemmell was telling me that he bought some liniment for the stiffness in his joints and it has worked wonders for him. And Cook swore that a tonic brought her sister back to health when she was dreadfully weakened following a fever. I was thinking we could buy some remedy for you, Mama.'

'If you think it would help.'

'There will be no hurt in trying.' Arabella raised

her eyebrows. 'And perhaps we might treat ourselves to some of that fine French soap while we are on the premises.'

Mrs Tatton laughed. And when Archie copied her, even though he did not understand what his grandmother was laughing about, Arabella could not help but join in.

The bell rang as they entered through the door, making the women who were standing in the middle of the shop floor beside a display of glass bottles glance round and notice Arabella and her family. The bottles which the women were inspecting were the same expensive Parisian perfumes as displayed in the shop's window. On seeing that Arabella was no one that they knew, the ladies ignored her and went back to choosing their perfume. Arabella watched them taking great pains over sniffing the scents that the shop assistant had touched to their hands using a variety of thin glass wands.

Two of the women were older; Arabella would guess of an age similar to her own mother's. But they were as haughty as Mrs Tatton was not. One look at their faces and Arabella could not help but draw a less-than-flattering conclusion as to their characters. The third woman was much younger, barely more than a girl. In contrast to the older women, one of whom Arabella was sure was the girl's mother due to a faint family resemblance, the girl seemed very quiet and eager to please.

'What do you mean, you like the sandalwood, Marianne?' demanded one of the formidable matrons. 'It is quite unsuitable for a young lady. Whatever would Sarah say were she to receive that as her birthday gift?'

The matron looked quickly to her companion. 'Forgive Marianne, Lady Fothergill, she can be such a silly goose at times. I am quite certain that she will admit that the rose fragrance is quite the most appropriate scent for her friend, albeit one of the most expensive choices.'

Arabella felt a pang of compassion for the girl. *Life with a mother like that could not be easy,* she thought as she turned her attention back to the apothecary who had arrived at the counter to serve them.

In the background she could hear the drone of the women's conversation, but Arabella was not listening. Rather she was concentrating on showing the apothecary her mother's hands and explaining about her mother's lungs. He suggested a warming liniment for Mrs Tatton's joints and a restorative tonic for her lungs, and disappeared off into the back of the shop to prepare them.

Mrs Tatton fitted her gloves back on while they waited and Arabella looked down at Archie. He was crouched by her side making his little wooden horse, Charlie, gallop around his feet and clicking quiet horsy noises to himself. Arabella smiled at the look of absorption upon his face. It was then that she heard the name 'Arlesford' spoken as clear as a bell. She tensed and could not help but listen in to the women's conversation.

'Close your ears, Lady Marianne, this is not talk for you,' one of the women was saying.

'Yes, Lady Fothergill,' said the girl, and Arabella resisted the urge to turn around and see if Lady Marianne had actually put her hands over her own ears. Then in lower quieter tones as if it were the greatest secret, Lady Fothergill continued, 'I am afraid I have to tell you the latest word, my poor dear, but they say that he has a mistress, and not just any mistress, one he bought from a bordello. Can you imagine?'

Arabella felt her blood run cold. She tried to keep her face clear and unaffected. The apothecary returned carrying a dark blue bottle and a small brown jar and placed them both down upon the counter.

'Might we also view your perfumed soaps, the ones that you have displayed in the front window?' she managed, and the smile fixed upon her face was broad and false.

'This is such a treat, Arabella,' said her mother.

'Yes.' Arabella nodded, still smiling, but almost the whole of her attention was focused on the conversation taking place behind her.

The other woman's voice stiffened with a defensive tone. 'Lady Fothergill, gentlemen will have their little foibles, but Arlesford is a duke and he knows his duty. I am sure that he will make a good husband.'

Arabella saw her mother's ears prick up at the mention again of Dominic's name and her stomach clenched all the tighter. She felt Mrs Tatton nudge her arm in a not altogether subtle way, and then her mother gestured with her eyes in the direction of the women behind them.

Arabella gave a tiny nod of acknowledgement to show that she understood the message.

'So is he still interested in Lady Marianne, Lady Misbourne?'

Arabella felt her blood run cold. Misbourne? An image of the masked bearded man from Vauxhall garden flashed in her mind, and she remembered the anger that had simmered within Dominic at their meeting, and his glib reply when she had asked who Misbourne was. No wonder he was so put out; meeting one's prospective father-in-law with your mistress on your arm was hardly the done thing.

The apothecary returned with the soaps, but Arabella and her mother were still listening intently. Arabella heard Mrs Tatton ask him to unwrap each soap that they might compare the smells, but Arabella could not move. She was frozen, holding her breath while she strained to hear Lady Misbourne's answer.

'Let us just say,' said Lady Misbourne, her voice less friendly than it had been at the start of her conversation with Lady Fothergill, 'that we are expecting an offer in the not-too-distant future. But that little piece of news is for your ears only, Lady Fothergill,'

'Of course,' said Lady Fothergill and there was something in the silky way that she said it that Arabella knew Lady Misbourne's news concerning Dominic and her daughter would be all around London by tomorrow. 'I think I shall choose the jasmine, Lady Misbourne. It is so exotic and so very expensive.'

The apothecary was clearing his throat and she felt her mother give her arm a little shake.

'Arabella, you are wool-gathering.' Mrs Tatton gave a false little laugh and slipped a hand to cover the white shining knuckles of Arabella's hands where she was gripping so tightly to the counter. 'I have come over a little unwell, my dear. Would you mind terribly if we were to come back for the soaps another day?'

Bless you, Mama. Bless your kindness, when her mother did not even know the full extent of the shock.

'Not at all,' Arabella said and then searched in her reticule for her purse to pay the apothecary. Her hands were trembling slightly in her haste to be gone and she set the money quickly down upon the counter, hoping that the apothecary would not notice. With the jar and bottle wrapped up in paper and tied with a handle of string, she took hold of Archie's hand and followed her mother out of the shop.

'Arabella, do not even think about that man. He is not worthy of it. From what I saw in there Dominic Furneaux is moving in all the right circles and most deservedly so I say. I wish him unhappy,' Mrs Tatton said, pure venom in her voice. She tucked Arabella's free hand into the crook of her arm. 'Now, we will not let their words bother us.'

'Indeed we will not,' said Arabella resolutely but she felt numb and chilled to the marrow and her mind was still reeling from what she had heard. Dominic was to marry. It should not have been such a very great shock. He was a duke. It was his duty to beget an heir, but she felt sick at the thought. Sick to the pit of her stomach at the memories those words stirred.

Her mother hurried her along the street and she just wanted to get away from this place and those women.

She heard the shop door-bell ring behind them.

'Excuse me, ma'am.' The girl's voice was tentative and as gentle and unassuming as her mother's was harsh and arrogant. Arabella did not need to turn round to know that it was Lady Marianne who had come out behind them. Lady Misbourne's daughter. The girl that Dominic was to marry.

Arabella did not want to look round. She wanted to keep on walking, to run away from this nightmare. But her mother had already stopped and turned.

Arabella had no choice.

'Your little boy, he left this behind.' There in the

girl's outstretched pink gloved hand was little wooden Charlie.

Lady Marianne was short and slender. A few fair curls that had escaped her pins peeped from the straw of her bonnet. She was dressed in an expensive pink walking dress and pelisse overloaded with lace and ribbon, chosen by Lady Misbourne Arabella guessed. But the outfit did little to detract from the girl's beauty; her sweet face was stunning. Her skin had the smooth creamy opalescence of youth, her features were fine and neat, and her eyes were large and a deep dark brown.

'Thank you,' Arabella said with a smile that would not touch her eyes no matter how hard she tried to make it, and she took the little wooden horse from the girl's hand.

'Thank very much, miss,' said Archie politely so that even given the strain of the situation, she was proud of him and his manners.

Lady Misbourne's daughter smiled at Archie. 'You are very welcome,' she said to him kindly. 'He looks as if he is a very special horse.'

'Oh, he is,' said Archie. 'Gemmell made him for my birthday, and my mama took me to the park and let me and Charlie ride upon a real horse.'

'That is quite enough, Archie. I am sure that the lady is too busy for your stories.'

'Oh, not at all,' said Lady Marianne shyly. 'He is such a sweet boy.'

'Marianne!' Lady Misbourne appeared in the doorway and cast Arabella and her mother a haughty look of dislike.

'Please excuse me,' said Lady Marianne to Arabella and Mrs Tatton, 'but I must not keep my mama waiting.'

She gave Archie a big grin and then she hurried back to where her mother's face was growing sourer by the minute.

Arabella, her mother and Archie walked on along the street.

'I liked that lady,' said Archie and gave a little skip. 'And so did Charlie. I think when I am a grown-up man I shall marry her.' His innocent words drove the blade deeper, right up to the hilt.

'Archie, stop talking such nonsense and walk smartly,' she heard her mother say brusquely.

Arabella's heart was throbbing. And this time she could not force herself to smile. She felt bitter and angry and unbelievably hurt. He had lied to her and betrayed her. He had bought her to keep as another one of his possessions. All of that and yet she was overwhelmed with such a terrible sense of grief, a raw keening agony that gouged at her heart.

The journey home seemed never ending. But, at last, she was able to climb from the coach outside the town house in Curzon Street and make her way in through the opened front door to the welcome of Gemmell, while her mother and Archie stayed hidden in the coach until it drove round to the stables.

Dominic sent a note to say that he could not visit that evening, and Arabella lay alone in bed that night, mulling over the dismal mess of the situation. Everything she had done had been for Archie, everything she was still doing was for her son. She had sold herself, swallowed the humiliation of becoming Dominic's mistress. Worse than that, she had given herself to him in love, because even after everything she could not pretend that her heart was so divorced from him. But now she had to consider the implication of his impending marriage.

He was a duke. Of course he was required to marry. How naïve she had been not to think of it. Once upon a time it was Arabella who would have been his wife. Now she was his whore. The knowledge hurt, as did the thought of him making another woman his wife. And what would it mean for her when he married? Would he still expect their arrangement to continue? Would he come seeking her bed at night before going home to that of Lady Marianne? The thought was anathema to Arabella. She could not bear to think of it.

She climbed from the bed and went to stand by the window, to look out upon the moonlit street. The hour was late and the street was empty except for the night-soil cart that was travelling slowly past and the squat man that walked by its side. She stood and watched, knowing that she was not going to find sleep that night. And in the dark shadowed corners of her mind was the image of the Whitechapel workhouse not so very far from Flower and Dean Street.

Chapter Eleven

Within the drawing room the next evening, after they had eaten and put Archie to bed, Arabella and her mother were darning a pile of Archie's stockings, during which Mrs Tatton was making every effort to cheer Arabella just as she had been doing since they had heard about Dominic Furneaux during their shopping trip. But rather than making her feel better, Mrs Tatton's diatribe on Dominic Furneaux and his failings was making Arabella feel worse.

'If that wretched man had done his duty, it never would have come to this. Why, if I were ever to clap eyes on him again I would tell him exactly what—'

There was an urgent knock at the drawing-room door and then Gemmell hurried in without waiting to be told to enter. One look at the butler's face and Arabella realised that something was wrong. Even Mrs Tatton's heated harangue ceased when she saw him.

'It is the d—' He glanced at her mother and then

amended what he had been about to say. 'The master,' he finished. 'Just drawn up outside this very minute.'

'I did not hear his carriage,' said Arabella.

Her mother paled with fright.

'Come quickly, Mrs Tatton, James here will help you upstairs.' Gemmell gestured to her mother.

Her mother jumped to her feet, forgetting all about Archie's stockings that she was darning so that they tumbled on to the floor. 'Oh, my word! Oh, my word! He will catch me for sure.' Her arms were flapping about in a panic.

'Stay calm, Mama, there is time enough yet. No, leave that,' Arabella said as her mother stooped to pick up the scattered stockings. 'I will see to them. You go with James, quickly now.'

Mrs Tatton half-ran, half-hobbled from the room to take hold of the footman's arm and the last Arabella saw, her mother was being propelled along the passageway on the arm of the footman.

She wasted no further time, for Gemmell was already hurrying to the front door to have it open in time for Dominic to reach the top of the stone stairs that led up to it. Arabella trusted him and knew that the old butler would not open the door until her mother had disappeared from sight, even if it meant he had to do the unthinkable and keep a duke waiting outside his own front door.

She crouched on the drawing-room floor and began gathering up Archie's stockings. The front door opened.

Gemmell's voice.

Then Dominic's sounded. And there was the steady tread of booted footsteps coming along the passageway. She had grabbed the last stockings and was hiding them behind the cushion of the armchair just as Dominic entered the drawing room.

Arabella jumped and looked flustered. There was a hint of colour in her cheeks, some of her hair had escaped its pins to fluff around her neck and face and she seemed a little out of breath.

'I was just darning some stockings,' she said and stuffed the stockings out of sight.

'What need have you to darn anything? Am I not paying you enough to buy new?'

He saw the way she stiffened and the heightened colour on her cheeks and regretted his words immediately.

'I do not like waste,' she said. 'A few stitches with a needle and the stockings are repaired almost as new.'

Make do and mend. And that same unease whispered about him as to the circumstances of Arabella's life that had led her to a brothel.

There was an awkward silence between them and then she said, 'You should have told me about Lord Misbourne's daughter, Dominic.'

So, Misbourne's lies had permeated even this far. 'There is nothing to tell, Arabella.'

'Nothing?' She stared at him and he saw the anger flash in her eyes. 'I know better. Little wonder that you were so displeased to meet him with me upon your arm! I *know,* so you need not pretend otherwise.' She was angry and reckless with it. Her face was pale, her eyes troubled.

'You know nothing other than a false rumour, Arabella.'

'Stop it, Dominic! I heard it from Lady Misbourne's mouth with my own ears.'

He stilled, his pulse suddenly beating fast. 'You have spoken to Lady Misbourne?'

'Not directly. I overheard her conversation with another.'

'And what exactly did you overhear?'

'That you are interested in her daughter as your duchess. That they are expecting you to offer for her shortly.'

He gave a cold hard laugh, although there was nothing of mirth in what he was feeling. 'They may expect, Arabella, but they shall receive nothing.'

'But she is wealthy and an earl's daughter,' and he heard the slight bitterness in Arabella's voice. 'Surely you cannot fault that *she* is a suitable match for you?'

'I have no intention of marrying Lady Marianne Winslow.'

Something changed in her face as if a new thought had only just made itself known to her, and all of the bitterness dropped away to be replaced with concern. 'You have not ruined her, have you, Dominic?'

He gave a cynical laugh that she could believe such a thing of him. Even though he was a rake. And even though everyone knew that fact. 'You need have no fear for the girl's virtue on my score, I assure you, Arabella,' he said coldly.

'At least have the decency to tell me the truth!'

'I *am* telling you the truth,' he said.

'I heard Lady Misbourne's words.'

'She is misinformed, I tell you.'

'No.'

'Yes, Arabella!'

They looked at one another, with only the sound of their breath in the silence.

'I will not marry Lady Marianne for the same reason I will not marry any other.'

He saw the shock, the confusion, the suspicion in her eyes. He should stop now, but he could not. He moved forwards.

'Shall I tell you why there will be no Duchess of Arlesford? Do you want the whole ugly truth of it?'

She backed away a little.

'Of how I have longed for you through the years?' He stepped closer.

She edged back.

'Of how I have relived those last moments a thousand times in my head?' Another step. 'God dammit, Arabella, I loved you!'

'No!' she cried. 'Do not say it. I do not want to hear more of your lies. You never loved me! You only wanted me in your bed and once you had had that—'

Dominic backed her against the wall and placed a hand around the nape of her neck, forcing her to look at him that she might see the truth from which she was so intent on hiding.

'*I loved you,* Arabella,' he said savagely and stared down into her eyes.

'Stop it!' She tried to turn away, but he would not let her. 'Why are you doing this?'

'Because I loved you,' he said again, more gently this time and he could no longer hide the hurt of what she had done to him. 'Arabella,' he said softly, and her gaze moved unwilling to his. 'Arabella,' he said again and looked into her eyes and let her see the truth.

She stopped struggling. Stilled. Stared at him. And the pain that he saw in her eyes was as raw and aching as that in his heart. They stared at one another and everything else in the world ceased to be.

'I loved you too, Dominic,' she said and her voice was thick with emotion.

In the silence he could hear the soft sound of her breath and beneath his fingers he could feel the throb of her pulse.

'Then why did you marry Marlbrook?' It was the question he had waited almost six years to ask.

She opened her mouth to reply, then closed it again and shook her head. But there could be no mistaking the look of anguish upon her face. She looked as tortured as he felt.

His hand moved from the nape of her neck to thread through her hair. He angled her face all the closer to his so close that her lips were within an inch of capture.

'Tell me,' he insisted.

She shook her head again in an infinitesimal motion of denial, but in her eyes he saw something of her resolve crumble and beneath it the flicker of fear.

'You know that I would never hurt you, no matter what,' he said softly.

'You already did, Dominic,' she whispered.

He felt something break apart inside of him at her answer. 'I do not understand. Tell me,' he said again.

She looked deep into his eyes. 'How can you really not know?'

'You married Marlbrook,' he said and knew that he was missing something of monumental importance.

'Yes.'

'Then you did not love me.'

'I loved you more than anything.'

'Then why?' he demanded.

'God, please help me,' she whispered and her voice was trembling. Then she raised her mouth to his and kissed him. Something of that kiss seemed to reach in and stroke against Dominic's soul so that when she withdrew her lips he felt almost bereft. They stared into each other's eyes, and the intensity of the moment was taut between them.

He knew that she was hiding something of the truth from him. And standing here right now looking into her eyes it did not make any difference. He still needed her at every level that was possible. And he knew that whatever else she said, Arabella needed him too. With all of the emotion that was roaring between them it was only a matter of time before she told him what he wanted to know.

His heart was beating in hard steady strokes as he kissed her. His hand slipped around hers and then he took her to bed and made love to her.

Arabella awoke with the early morning light stealing through the curtains to find Dominic still in her bed. He was snuggled against her back, his hand draped against the nakedness of her stomach and her bottom nestled into his crotch.

She lay there for a moment, letting herself revel in the warm strong feel of him before letting reality and all of its worries back in again.

I loved you, Arabella. She heard the whisper of his words running through her head again and knew she should not believe him. If he had loved her so much then he would not have treated her so badly. Words were cheap and so easily woven into a pretty pattern of lies. Actions were what counted. A man's deeds. What he did rather than what he said. And yet even knowing all that, lying here naked in Dominic's arms, her body bearing the scent of his loving, she knew that she wanted to believe him. Her head might know he was lying, yet her heart was a different matter all together.

She craned her neck up to see the clock on the mantel. Five o'clock. Too early, but she knew from the hum in her body that she would not go back to sleep. She was too aware of Dominic and all that was happening between them, the tumultuous peaks of physical ecstasy and troughs of emotional misery. She tried to ease his fingers from her stomach, but the large hand with its long fingers tightened against her.

'Arabella?' His voice was husky from sleep. She felt the stirring of his arousal against her buttocks.

'You are awake.' She rolled round to face him, carefully opening up a small distance between them, not knowing how things would be between them this morning, whether he would probe again into the past, asking questions that were too dangerous to answer.

He smiled and there was about him this morning none of the tension that had been so evident between them last night.

The growth of dark stubble peppered his cheeks and chin. He looked piratical and dangerous and wicked and yet the look in his eyes was loving and velvet and molten. He glanced towards the clock, then smiled again in that way that made her heart somersault.

With an easy, unhurried air he rose from the bed and, without the slightest self-consciousness over his nakedness, made his way over to the pitcher and basin to wash. Arabella sat up, pulling the sheets up high to cover her own nudity, and watched him. His shoulders were broad, tapering down to slim hips. His every movement created ripples in the muscles that defined it. She watched the droplets of water roll down the pale golden skin of his back.

He glanced round and saw her sitting there watching him. She felt her cheeks heat and looked quickly away.

'I will call one of the footman to help you dress.' She slipped from the bed, grabbed up her shift and held it against her to preserve some measure of modesty, then hurried over to the wardrobe to fetch her dressing gown. She opened the wardrobe door using it as a screen between herself and Dominic. The shift dropped to the floor and she slipped on the thin cotton dressing gown, tying its belt around her waist. But when she closed the cupboard door Dominic was standing right there looking at her.

'I do not need a footman.' His voice was husky and his eyes seemed to darken with hunger as he looked at her. She saw his gaze drop lower and watched while he reached a hand across to rub the back of his wet knuckles gently against her breast, wetting the thin white cotton to render it transparent. Her nipple hardened and strained rosy and peaked through the material. He rubbed against it a little longer and she felt desire shimmer right through her. His hand dropped lower to tug one end of her belt so that the loose knot parted and the gown fell open.

'I am not washed,' she said, feeling embarrassed at how wantonly her body was responding to him even in daylight.

He leaned in closer and took her mouth with his, kissing her to make her forget all of her protestations. He smiled again. 'Then let me wash you.' And he lifted the soap.

'Open your legs.'

Arabella stared at him. Her heart was beating very fast. 'You cannot,' she whispered.

'Don't you want me to?' he replied against her lips, then nuzzled kisses against her neck.

She knew that it was wrong, that she should not want any of this. But when he peeled the dressing gown off her shoulders, sliding it down her body to land upon the floor, and kissed her, she wrapped her arms around him and returned his kiss with passion.

Dominic deepened the kiss and ran his hand over her body, stroking her, and caressing her with a touch that was both gentle yet possessive. And then he moved away and she saw him lather up his hands in the water. And her mouth went dry.

He turned to her; there was such a hunger in his eyes that she felt herself tremble. One arm snaked around her waist, pulling him to her.

His mouth was hot against her ear. 'Open your legs,' he whispered.

'Dominic…' she protested.

He kissed her mouth, a long stroking sensual kiss that ended in him biting softly against her lower lip.

Her body reacted independently of her mind; her legs opened for him and she felt him touch her. The water was cold against her heat and she gasped both from the shock of that and the audacity of what he was doing. He massaged her gently, washing her with a thoroughness that made her legs tremble. And then he rinsed her, cupping handfuls of water over her so that it ran it rivulets down her thighs while she gasped with the wanton pleasure of it. Her legs were shaking so much that she collapsed against him. Dominic gathered her up in his arms and carried her to the bed.

She pulled him to her, knowing where this was leading and wanting it all the same, wanting him as if she still loved him. Because when he touched her something inside opened up to him and she could not stop herself from this any more than she could stop her heart from beating or her lungs from breathing. It was more than desire, more than just a physical intimacy. She needed his warmth, his strength, his tenderness. She needed to be able to forget the worry and the pain. She needed to feel this sharing of a heart. Love, even pretended, after all the years of unhappiness, was a balm to Arabella's soul.

'Dominic,' she breathed and felt him move over her and kiss her all the more. She opened to him, wanting him to take her, needing to feel him inside her. And in response the probe of his manhood pressed between her legs. She wriggled her hips, her hands sliding to his firm flank to pull him against her.

'Arabella,' he groaned her name, and she could hear his need in his voice and feel it in the tension that vibrated throughout his body. For all that his movements were controlled she could sense the urgency beneath. His mouth left hers and he adjusted his position to slide lower down her body so that she thought he meant to kiss her breasts, to taste her, to suckle from her. Her nipples hardened with unbearable sensitivity just at the thought of it and between her legs grew even slicker.

But Dominic did not stop at her breasts. When he kept on moving she threaded her fingers through his hair and tried to guide him back to where her nipples ached for his touch. His gaze held hers, all dark and blazing with desire, and as she watched he placed a single kiss just below her ribcage. And then, keeping his gaze locked with hers, he kissed her again, this time lower, in the centre of her stomach…and then a third time, just at the line of her pelvis.

'Dominic!' She tried to close her legs. 'You surely do not mean to—'

But he did.

His warm breath stirred the small patch of golden hair as his mouth touched to her secret woman's place.

She gasped at that first kiss, at the wonder of the sensation that shot through her body. And by the time he was working a magic with his tongue she forgot to bite her lip and groaned her pleasure aloud.

'Dominic,' she whispered, but he did not stop and she was arching her back and driving herself harder into his mouth, reaching for him, needing him with an urgency that obliterated all else. And when his hands closed over her breasts and she felt his fingers pluck at her taut straining nipples she reached her climax, exploding in the sensation, her body soft and pulsing her pleasure against him.

He kissed her thighs, kissed the curve of each hip, kissed his way up to take her in his arms. And then he gently stroked the long wanton curls from where they spilled over her face and looked at her with such love that her heart welled with joy to see it.

'Arabella,' he whispered and she loved him in that moment despite everything, she loved him against all rhyme and reason.

She pulled him closer and felt his hardness press against her leg. She wanted to pleasure him as he had pleasured her. She reached down and touched him.

She stroked the long hard length of his manhood and heard the breath catch in his throat and felt the tremble that racked his body. He lay still and let her take him, giving her the power to do whatever she willed.

She moved back, wanting to see him, wanting to see her fingers as they caressed his member, stroking that silken skin from its tip all the way down to the base amidst the nest of dark hair.

The groan escaped him. She held his gaze and bent her head to taste him…just as a door slammed shut upstairs.

The noise brought Dominic crashing back to reality. He could feel that Arabella had frozen at the sound.

'It is nothing, Dominic.' Her voice was too loud, too desperate, and he saw the flash of fear from her eyes. 'Let it not interrupt us.'

But then the thud of running footsteps sounded through the ceiling above.

Arabella's eyes widened. Her hand gripped tighter to his shaft.

She tried to stop him as he pulled away from her and tugged on his breeches. 'No, Dominic, please!' She jumped up, pulling on her dressing gown and tying its belt quickly around her waist.

They could both hear the tumble of feet on the main staircase.

'No!' She ran in front of him, blocking his path to the door. Her hair was long and wild, her face devoid of all colour and in her eyes was desperation. 'Dominic!' she cried and tried to push him back. 'Do not!' She threw her full weight against him, trying to prevent his continued progress.

The footsteps grew louder as they headed along the passageway towards them.

He grabbed her wrists, secured her hands behind her, resting them lightly against the small of her back so that her breasts were thrust against his chest.

'Who have you hidden in this house, Arabella?' he asked, and even to his own ears his voice sounded harsh. He thought of Marlbrook and a wave of jealousy swept right through him.

'No one!' She struggled against him. 'Please, Dominic, I beg of you!'

'Mama!' a child's voice called and little fists pounded at the door.

The shock stole the words he would have spoken. He released his hold of her wrists. Her eyes were wide with anguish as she stared up at him.

'Where are you, Mama?' the child cried. 'I dreamt that you and Grandmama had gone away and when I woke I was all alone.'

She turned and, opening the door, scooped the child, clad in a long white nightshirt, up into her arms. 'Here I am, little lamb. It was just a silly old dream. I have been here all along, in my bedchamber, as I always am. Now hush, Archie, there is no need for tears.' And she kissed the child and hugged him to her, and soothed a hand against his hair.

Dominic stared and his heart contracted as hard as if a fist had squeezed it, for the little boy in Arabella's arms was the very image of himself.

Chapter Twelve

He watched as Arabella glanced around at the woman puffing breathlessly along the corridor.

'Forgive me, Arabella.' She hurried right up to Arabella and he saw at once who she was. 'He was asleep and I was only gone for a minute to take care of my needs. I am so very sorry.' And then Mrs Tatton glanced anxiously towards him standing there in the bedchamber. Her mouth fell open and she stared with an expression of horror at her daughter. 'Dominic Furneaux! You did not tell me it was him! He is your protector? The one who has paid for all of this?'

Arabella nodded as she rocked the child gently in her arms.

'How could you, Arabella,' Mrs Tatton burst out, 'after what he did to you?'

Arabella made no sign of having heard her mother's words. She spoke to the child again. 'Now, Archie, you must let Grandmama take you back to bed, for it is too early to be up and about.' She kissed the little boy's forehead and smoothed the tangle of his dark locks. 'Be a good boy—I will be up to see you soon.'

'Yes, Mama,' the child said and when she set him back down upon the ground he dutifully took hold of Mrs Tatton's hand, and glanced with curiosity at Dominic as she led him from the room. Mrs Tatton followed the boy's gaze and if looks could have killed the one that the older woman shot him would have had him dead upon the floor. The door closed with a brisk click behind them.

Arabella had not moved. She stood where she was, her eyes hooded and cautious, her face pale.

'He is my son, isn't he?'

She did not answer, just stood there so still yet he could see the rapid rise and fall of her chest beneath the dressing gown and feel the strain in her silence.

'Isn't he, Arabella?' he demanded and he knew his voice was harsh with the shock that was coursing through him.

'Of course he is your son! Why else would I have married Henry Marlbrook in such haste after you left me?' The words exploded from her. 'But do not think, for one minute, that I shall let you take him from me, Dominic!' There was something of the tigress in her eyes, a ruthlessness, a strength, an absolute determination, and he knew that she would fight to her last breath to defend their child.

'I have no intention of taking him from you.' Mrs Tatton's words echoed in his head: *...after what he did to you...* The hostility of the woman's attitude, and of Arabella's own words—*after you left me*—prickled a warning at the nape of his neck. And foreboding was heavy upon him.

'You speak as if it was I responsible for our breaking apart,' he said slowly.

'How can you deny it?' she retorted with eyes that flashed their fury. 'You just upped and offed without so much as a word. Not one consideration for my feelings, not one for what you might be leaving behind. I was nineteen, Dominic. Nineteen!'

His blood flowed like ice. His stomach was brimful with dread. 'What do you mean, Arabella?'

'You know very well what I mean!' she shouted.

'I do not.' He forced himself to remain calm, to carry on despite the dread deep in the marrow of his bones. 'Tell me.'

'John Smith saw us coming out of Fisher's barn that last day. He told my father and my father had the truth from me. He already knew, Dominic, and I could not lie to him. He was angry and disappointed. He went to your father, the duke, and told him that our betrothal must be made formal and the wedding arranged as soon as possible.'

That Mr Tatton had ever visited on such a mission was news to Dominic. He had a terrible premonition of what his father had done.

'Why are you even making me tell you all this?' she cried. 'Was it not cruel enough the first time round?'

'Tell me, Arabella.'

She pushed at him and tried to turn away, but he grabbed hold of her and pulled her back round to face him, knowing he needed to hear every word of the nightmare. 'For God's sake, tell me,' he insisted. 'What did my father say?'

'That the matter would rest with you and you alone.

And like a fool I thought everything would be all right.' The tears spilled from her eyes to roll down her cheeks.

'Arabella,' he whispered and tried to wipe them away, but she struck his hand away as if she could not bear to have him touch her. And then she hit out at his chest, pushing him, trying to free herself, again and again until he captured her wrists and held her still.

'You coward!' she yelled through the tears. 'To send your father in your stead because you had not the courage to tell me yourself!'

The ice spread through his veins. 'You are saying that my father visited you.' It was no question for he could already see the whole horrid story beginning to unfold before his very eyes.

'You know that he did, for you sent him, Dominic!' She ceased struggling, but she was crying in earnest now, the tears streaming all the harder.

'No, Arabella, I did not,' he said, 'I did not send him, Arabella. I did not even know that your father had come to the house.' He felt numb and sick and furious all at once.

'Why are you lying?' she cried. 'Have you not humiliated me enough? Is it not enough that I am your mistress? That you own me? Must you seek to hurt me more with these lies?' She bowed her head that he would not see her crying.

'Arabella, look at me!' And when she would not he took her face between his hands and made her. 'I am not lying.'

She fought against him.

'I am not lying, Arabella.'

And something of his sincerity must have reached her for she seemed to still and hear what he was saying properly for the first time. She looked up into his eyes. And there was such vulnerability there, such hurt that it made everything he had felt across the years pale in comparison.

'I am not lying,' he said for a third time, soft as a breath against her face. 'I swear it on all that is holy.' His hands slid down to her upper arms, holding her in place, supporting her. He could hear the small shudder in her breathing and feel the tremor that ran through her body.

'I do not understand.' Her words were a cracked whisper.

'I think I am beginning to,' he said grimly. 'Tell me what my father said to you, Arabella?'

'He explained it all very carefully. That you did not want me. That young men will be young men and sow their wild oats. And when my own father pointed out that young men must be held responsible for their actions and demanded that you be forced to wed me, he said that he would do no such thing—for surely we could all see that, despite my gentle birth, I was too poor and lowly to be a future duke's wife. He said that such a marriage would be a *mésalliance* and that we had never really been betrothed.'

'That bastard!' The curse could not be bitten back. 'He knew that I loved you and meant to marry you. Hell, he even knew about the locket!'

'My father showed him the locket, and the duke laughed and said that it was no proof of a betrothal and that we could hardly sue for breach of promise. He gave my father money and told us it would go better for us if we kept quiet.' Every word that she spoke was like a cut to his heart. Every word revealing the terrible enormity of what his father had done.

He shook his head, even now hardly able to believe it. 'My own father did this,' he whispered, more to himself than Arabella. The man he had loved and respected and admired. The very foundation on which he had built his life shifted, making a mockery of everything in which he had believed for the last years.

'My God!' There was a sickness in his stomach and he felt chilled to the very core of his being. It took every last drop of his determination to hang on to his self-control.

Arabella could see the strain in Dominic's face, his pallor, the tight press of his lips as he struggled with the magnitude of emotion. In his eyes was such a deadly rage that she almost felt afraid. And she knew from the terribleness of his reaction that he was telling the truth. And if he was telling the truth, then that meant…

The floor beneath her feet felt as unsteady as everything else in her world. She was reeling, floundering with a realisation beyond anything she could ever have imagined. She swayed and felt him clutch her hard against him.

There were a thousand thoughts milling in her head, all of them tearing at the beliefs she had constructed for herself over the years. She felt chilled all the way through, so cold that she could never imagine being warm again. And she knew that she was trembling, but she just could not stop no matter how hard she willed it.

Dominic swept her up into his arms and carried her to the bed where he sat her down on its edge and swathed the covers around her.

'Why would he do such a thing, Dominic?'

Dominic's face was hard and cynical. *'My father,'* and his lip curled with disgust as he spoke the words, 'did not think you a suitable match, Arabella. He said that you were a young man's infatuation. That I would tire of you eventually. That I had a duty to the dukedom to marry either money or status.'

She had known her own unsuitability even then, but Dominic had told her that he would make his own choice and that his choice was her. 'But the old duke was only ever affable to my face. He never so much as suggested a murmur of these thoughts. I believed him understanding of our betrothal.' She shook her head at her own naïvety.

'It was my father who persuaded me to keep the betrothal quiet and informal. He said that if it lasted then he would give it his blessing and make a formal announcement. I never imagined for one minute that he would stoop to such a level.'

'I cannot quite comprehend what you are telling me, Dominic,' she whispered; she felt frozen and numb inside.

'I can barely credit it myself.' His voice was soft, but she shuddered to hear the intensity within it.

He sat down on the bed by her side. And they just sat there in silence.

'Tell me what happened to you,' she said. Every word was torture, but she needed to know. And she knew he needed to tell her. 'You went away.'

'He sent me to my uncle in Scotland. Told me some story of a sudden illness and that he did not feel up to making such a long journey. Could I go in his stead?' His voice was low, his words deadened almost, with a something of a terrible unnatural quiet to them. 'I was forced to leave that very night, but I wrote you a note of explanation and left instructions for its delivery to you. And then I wrote to you every day from Scotland.' He gave a laugh so hard and cynical that it made her blood run cold. 'Little wonder that there was never a reply. You did not receive my letters, did you, Arabella? My father saw to that.'

She shook her head. 'There was no note of explanation. There were never any letters.'

'Was my uncle a part of this ruse? Was he even really ill at all?' He stared into the distance as if he could see the past there. 'Will we ever really know the level of treachery, Arabella?'

She could not answer. She did not know.

He shook his head as if he had his own answer.

'I stayed with him during what I thought was his convalescence and when I returned home you were gone. Married to Marlbrook, they said. A man old enough to be your father.' He looked round at her. 'I thought you had forsaken me for him, Arabella.'

'Never.' Her voice was thick with strain. 'What choice did I have once I realised our child was growing in my belly? Henry was kind. He knew of my situation and was prepared to overlook it.'

'That is why you married him. At last I understand. You thought I had abandoned you.'

'For all these years,' she whispered.

'You were my love, Arabella. My heart. My life.' His voice cracked and she saw the restraint within him shatter and the great storm of emotion unleash. He sprang to his feet. 'Damn my father to hell! Damn him, Arabella. I would kill him myself were he not already dead! He has ruined my life, and your life, and that of an innocent child!' His voice shook with passion. 'I have a son, Arabella, and I did not know! A son!' The words tore from his throat as he turned away and punched his fist hard into the door. His head drooped and in the resounding silence that followed she could hear only the raggedness of his breathing. He turned to her then, and looked at her and the agony on his face was terrible to see.

'Tell me, Arabella,' he said quietly, 'did my father know the truth of that too?'

'No.' She could spare him that at least. 'My own father was a proud man. He said that the duke had already made his feelings clear and he would not go back on his knees and beg. He thought it bad enough that we had taken his money and that it was as if you had enforced the *droit de seignuir* from the old feudal days when the lord thought he had the right to take the maidenhead of his serfs.'

He flinched at the word. He walked to stand before her. 'You moved away so that I would not know.'

'It was one of the duke's requirements. Henry raised Archie as his own even though the truth was so plain to see.'

Dominic looked like he was breaking apart as he stood there. She watched him close his eyes. Heard him murmur, 'My God, Arabella.'

On the door behind him she could see the smear of his blood. Nothing seemed real. Dominic had not left her. He had not abandoned her. And truth revealed only a worse tragedy than any of them could have imagined. For Dominic, and for her, and for their son upstairs.

'You are bleeding,' she said.

He did not even glance down at his hand with his

grazed and bruised knuckles. 'I should have been there to protect you, Arabella.'

'Please, Dominic…' Her voice broke. There were no words that could make any of it better.

'I should have been your husband, Arabella. I should have been a father to my son.'

She began to weep for all that they had lost.

He came to her and sat beside her, scooping her on to his lap as if she were a small child. And then he held her close and rocked her, and she heard his voice against her hair.

'God help us, Arabella. I will do my best for you and for Archie. I swear it.'

And Arabella laid her head against his chest.

Chapter Thirteen

The clock on the mantel was striking two as Arabella watched Archie pretend to groom the little wooden horse that Gemmell had given him.

'You must go to sleep in your stable, Charlie.' She could hear the softness of his voice as he spoke to the toy before hiding it behind the cushion of the sofa and galloping off across the drawing room making neighing noises.

Sitting on the sofa beside her, Mrs Tatton leaned closer and lowered her voice.

'I cannot believe that Dominic Furneaux is behind all of this.' She peered angrily at Arabella. 'You should have told me, Arabella.'

'Mama,' Arabella sighed. 'You must realise why I did not. It was a difficult situation and I knew how you felt about him.'

'I thought you felt the same,' said her mother. 'Lord, but that man ruined your life. He ruined all our lives!'

'Mama, I have already explained that none of it

was Dominic's fault. He suffered as much from this as we did.'

'Nowhere near, Arabella,' said Mrs Tatton. 'He did not have to work his fingers to the bone, or live in a rookery, or go hungry.'

'No, Mama. But he suffered all the same.' When she thought of how much of his son's life he had missed out on she felt terrible.

Her mother gave a snort of disbelief and moved on. 'What are his intentions now that he is aware of Archie and me?'

'He means to do his best for us.'

'And precisely how does he plan to do that?' Mrs Tatton demanded.

'There are no easy answers to any of this. The past cannot be so easily undone.' Lost years could not be recaptured. A little boy's childhood could not be relived. The knowledge broke her heart.

'Nor undone at all, Arabella. How can what happened ever be made right?'

'I do not know, Mama. I need time to think. Dominic needs time to think. There is much to be considered.'

'Much indeed,' muttered her mother. She glanced up to the ceiling and lowered her voice again. 'Why is he still up there? Why does he not leave?'

'He is giving us some time together, and when I feel that we are ready I will ask him to come down. He wishes to meet Archie.'

'I'm sure he does.' Her mother's mouth pressed into a thin line of disapproval. 'Abominable rake! Do you think he will marry you?' Mrs Tatton made it sound ridiculous.

'I know he cannot marry me, Mama. Not now.' The words were bitter in her mouth.

'He is the Duke of Arlesford, Arabella. It would be unimaginable if he were to marry you. Think of the scandal.'

'I know, Mama.' He would keep her here as his mistress and make love to her at night, and pay for everything that she and his son wanted. There would be no more skulking and hiding for her mother and Archie. She should have been glad of it but her heart was heavier and more aching than it had ever been. She sat the teacup and saucer back down upon the table lest its tremor betray her distress.

'Dominic has a duty to the Arlesford seat. No, Arabella, believe me when I tell you that he must marry some rich, well-connected girl, a girl with an untarnished reputation and a father that moves in the right circles.'

A girl like Lady Marianne Winslow.

It was Arabella's unsuitability to be his bride that had caused this whole mess in the first place.

'And when he weds her, what then of you, Arabella? Will he keep you here as his mistress while he begets children on his duchess?' Mrs Tatton shook her head and stared at Arabella with concern. 'And what of Archie? What will become of him when Dominic begins to fill the nursery at Shardeloes with sons who are not born out of wedlock?'

She stared at her mother, appalled at the images she was conjuring.

'He will not be so keen to visit his bastard son then.'

'Archie was not born out of wedlock. I was married to Henry,' she whispered furiously.

'If you think that there is anyone who will believe Archie to be anything other than Dominic's you are fooling yourself, girl! One look at the boy and it is clear. Arabella…' Mrs Tatton sighed again and she took Arabella's hand in her own. 'You must handle this negotiation very carefully indeed both for your own sake and for Archie's.'

'Negotiation? You make it sound like some new arrangement with a protector!'

'Is that not precisely what this is, Arabella? A renegotiation?'

'No! It is not like that.'

'Then what is it like, Arabella?'

Arabella turned her face away, and could give no reply. She did not know herself what it was like, this situation into which they had all been thrust. There were no words to describe what she felt. Confusion and hope and bruising. Love and anger and resentment. And disbelief, an overwhelming sense that this was all some awful nightmare from which she would awaken. She loved Dominic, but her heart was still aching. And there seemed no way to make it better. She loved him, but it was all too late. Because her mother was right. No matter how she dressed it up otherwise, he had bought her from a brothel and made her his mistress. And nothing could change that.

'Mrs Tatton,' Dominic bowed to Arabella's mother.

'Your Grace,' said Mrs Tatton grudgingly and looked at him with daggers in her eyes.

Dominic turned and stared at the little boy; he felt his heart contract and a feeling of tenderness expand through him. Archie was a miniature youthful version of himself. The same dark brown eyes, the same purposeful chin, his hair only a slightly lighter shade of brown than Dominic's own.

'Dominic, this is Archie.' Arabella had a hand upon the boy's shoulder in a gesture to reassure the child.

'Are you my mama's friend?' He saw the innocent curiosity in Archie's eyes.

Dominic's gaze fleetingly met Arabella's before coming back to the child's. He crouched down, so that Archie did not have to tilt his head right back to look at him. 'I am your friend too, Archie.' He was aware of Mrs Tatton sitting in one of the armchairs in the background and the blatant look of dislike upon her face, but he paid her no attention.

'This is Dominic,' Arabella told the child.

Your father, he wanted to say, but knew that he must not. Arabella was right, they must handle this very slowly and gently.

Archie gave a polite little bow. 'I am very pleased to meet you, sir.'

'And I am very pleased to meet you too, Archie.' This was his son, flesh of his flesh, blood of his blood. 'Your mama tells me that you are very fond of horses.'

Archie nodded.

'That makes two of us.' He smiled. And Archie smiled back at him, and at the sight of it Dominic felt a huge wave of emotion hit him and his heart seemed to melt into a pool of overwhelming love. He gave a gruff nod and, suddenly frightened that he was going to start weeping, rose to his full height and cleared his throat.

'I will return tomorrow, Arabella,' he said.

She nodded; there was a look of such tenderness in her eyes when she looked at their son that it made him

want to weep all the more. He made his bow to her and
to her mother, and he left, while he still could.

Dominic waved his secretary away with his diary
of missed appointments. He shut the door of his study
within Arlesford House in Berkley Square and leaned
his back upon it. His gaze wandered around the room,
seeing the papers on his desk, his books, everything,
just as he had left them. And now, less than twenty-four
hours later, everything had changed. Nothing would
ever be the same again. He thought of what his father
had done. He thought of what Arabella had become.
And he thought of the little boy who did not know he
was his son. And he wept.

Dominic did not sleep that night. There were too
many thoughts in his head. Too many conflicting emotions. Rage and bitterness. Betrayal and hurt. Disbelief
and regret. Possessiveness and protectiveness. And love.

By the time the next morning arrived the thoughts
were all still there. He pushed the breakfast plate away
with the kippers and scrambled eggs upon it barely
touched and called for some paper, pen and ink.

Dominic did not go to Carlton House that day to meet
with the Prince of Wales. Instead he went to Curzon
Street—to Arabella and his son.

Arabella watched Dominic with Archie, father and
son, the two dark heads bent together, their faces so
alike, and she felt her chest tighten with emotion and
heard that same whisper of guilt that had been there
before.

Archie's initial shyness had disappeared. He was

laughing and running around the chair on which Dominic was sitting, jumping over Dominic's long legs that were stretched out before him. As she watched, Archie clambered up on to Dominic's knee and with his little hand took hold of Dominic's large one. She saw the depth of emotion that swept across Dominic's face before he hid it. Archie was giggling and Dominic laughed too as he tweaked Archie's nose and pretended that he had captured it from the little boy's face. Arabella had to turn away to stop the tears welling in her eyes.

Father and son played together until Arabella knew that Archie was getting tired and overexcited.

'It will soon be time for dinner, Archie. You must say farewell to Dominic for now and go and get washed and changed.'

'But, Mama,' groaned Archie, 'we are not finished playing the horses game.'

'Dominic will come back another day to play with you.'

'Please, Mama,' Archie pleaded.

'You must do as your mama says,' said Dominic and, lifting Archie to his feet, rose to stand by his son's side. 'I will see you again soon.'

'Tomorrow?' Archie took hold of Dominic's hand and looked up at him.

'Yes, tomorrow,' said Dominic and ruffled Archie's hair.

Archie smiled. 'And we will play the horses game?'

Dominic smiled too, in exactly the same way. 'We will play the horses game.'

'I like you, Dominic.'

'I like you too, Archie.'

Arabella's lips pressed tight to control the swamp of emotion.

She took Archie away to the large bedroom next to her own that had, at Dominic's instruction, been transformed overnight into a nursery. Mrs Tatton sat in there reading, having resisted all persuasions to even be in the same room as Dominic. Her face was sullen as she set the book down and took Archie from her daughter. And when Arabella tried to speak, her mother turned away and would not listen.

By the time Arabella returned to the drawing room Dominic was staring down into the empty fireplace deep in thought. He did not look round until she had closed the door.

There was a poignancy about him, and both an anger and something that looked like disappointment that shadowed his eyes. The very air seemed thick with the tragedy of what might have been.

The question, when it came, hit her harder than she had expected.

'Why did you hide Archie from me, Arabella?'

'You know why, Dominic. I believed the worst of you.'

'Even so, what man, even a scoundrel as you believed me, does not have a care for his own son? You should have told me.' He raked a hand through his hair. 'Hell, Arabella, he is my son! Did you not think I had a right to know?'

Deep in the pit of her stomach was guilt and regret. 'I did not think your right important beside that of protecting Archie.'

'Protecting him from *me?* Damnation, Arabella what did you think I would have done to him?' He looked tortured.

'All of London names you a rake, Dominic, a man who takes what he wants without a care. You are rich and powerful, a duke. I am poor, without connection. You found me in a bordello. I feared you would take him from me.' She squeezed her eyes shut, unable to bear even the thought. 'He is only just five years old, Dominic, a little boy. He needs love, not to be raised by strangers who do not care for him any further than the wage they are paid.'

'I would never have taken him from you.'

'I did not know that.'

'All those times I came here, all those times we made love, and all the while you had our son hidden up in the attic!'

She gasped. 'You make it sound something it was not! I love Archie. I would lay down my life to protect him. Yes, I sold myself for his sake, but you, Dominic Furneaux, are the man who bought me. So do not dare to stand there in judgement of me!'

'If you had told me of Archie it would have changed everything.'

'What would it have changed, Dominic?' she cried. 'That you paid Mrs Silver to have sex with me? That you bought me from her? That you made me your mistress?'

He winced at her words as if it pained him to hear them. But she could not stop; she wanted him to understand.

'I believed you a man who had taken my virginity and my trust and broken my heart. I believed you a man that left me at nineteen, ruined, unmarried and disgraced. A man who was willing to buy me—to use me for his own selfish pleasure.'

Her eyes raked his. 'Would you have me hand Archie over to such a man? Someone I did not trust? Someone with whom I was so angry and did not even like? A man I thought to be ruthless and selfish and arrogant and capable of inflicting such hurt. What kind of mother would that have made me to our son, Dominic?'

'I understand your reasons, Arabella, but—'

'There are no "buts", Dominic.' She needed him to know. 'I did what I had to for Archie's sake. I will always do what I have to, to protect him, no matter what you say.'

They looked at one another.

'Would you ever have told me had not the truth come out?'

Would she?

'I do not know,' she said honestly. 'I felt matters were changing between us. I found that in spite of everything I believed of you that I still had…feelings for you. That perhaps it might have been the same for you.' The words hung awkwardly in the air between them and she wished that she had not said them. Her pride was still too delicate and she did not want it crushed. She turned away, but Dominic took hold of her and pulled her round to face him.

'I never stopped having feelings for you, Arabella,' he said and there was such a strength and determination in his words that she could feel it in the grip of his hands. 'For all that I said in my bitterness, never think it was otherwise.' He brushed his lips against her forehead.

'What are we going to do, Dominic?' It was the question that preyed on her mind constantly.

'I do not know, Arabella. I only know that I will not lose you again, and I will not lose Archie.'

Archie was in a frenzy of excitement the next morning. All he spoke of from the moment that his eyes opened was Dominic's visit.

'We are to play at horses,' he told Arabella and she had not seen him smile so much before.

Mrs Tatton, by contrast, looked pale and tired. She seemed to have aged in the past few days. There were deep lines of worry etched upon her face and shadows beneath her eyes.

'Are you feeling unwell, Mama?' Arabella looked at her anxiously, worried at the strain events were exerting upon her.

'I am tired, Arabella, nothing more. I have barely slept a wink since that terrible night.'

'Mama…' Arabella came to her and rubbed a hand against her arm '…maybe you should go back to bed.'

'What good would it do when I cannot sleep?' Her mother shook her head. 'Oh, Arabella, I wish you would see Dominic Furneaux for what he really is. It pains me that you can so easily believe his lies.'

'What reason would he have to lie about this, Mama?'

'Because he wants the boy without losing you from his bed.'

'Trust me, Mama…' Arabella shook her head '…he is not lying.'

'Forgive me if I find that hard to believe. For all his pretty words, Arabella, his loyalty lies with himself and his title. Once he has found himself a bride he will leave you behind as he did before, taking the child with him when he goes.'

'No, Mama, you have this all wrong.'

'No, Arabella, you are the one whose judgement had gone a-begging. I cannot bear to stand by and watch him destroy you all over again. What will it take to make you realise? Will you wait until he plants another babe in your belly and walks away before you see?'

Arabella stared at her mother, stunned.

'Grandmama, look at me!' shouted Archie. 'I am a horse all ready for Dominic!' He was jumping all around her mother, pulling at her skirt.

'Stop this nonsense, Archie, and go and sit down quietly!' Mrs Tatton snapped, shooing him away. 'I do not want to hear another word about Dominic Furneaux!' Archie's bottom lip trembled and Arabella bit her own to capture the sharp retort she would have uttered to her mother. Instead she turned to her son and spoke calmly.

'Grandmama is tired, Archie. She needs some peace and quiet. Go and find Charlie and we will take him to the park.' And then to her mother, 'We will leave you to your rest, Mama.'

'I am sorry, Arabella,' her mother said softly. 'I did not mean to snap at him. I am just so worried for us all.'

'I know, Mama.' Arabella kissed her mother's cheek. 'Try to rest; it will make you feel a little better. We will not be gone for long.'

Mrs Tatton nodded and watched them leave.

Dominic had not slept again. He had cancelled all of his appointments for the coming week, refused to see Hunter when his friend had called upon him last night, and thought endlessly over Arabella and Archie and the nightmare in which they were all imprisoned. He knew it was too early to call upon them, but he called for his horse to be saddled anyway. Dominic made his way to Curzon Street and in his pocket was a neatly rolled little scroll tied with a red ribbon.

Gemmell showed him in and as he waited in the drawing room he looked behind the curtain where Archie liked to play his games. A little boy's den. He moved away when he heard her footsteps coming down the stairs. Followed them along the corridor. But it was not Arabella who entered the room.

'Mrs Tatton.' He bowed.

'Your Grace.' Mrs Tatton's voice dripped with contempt. 'Arabella and Archie have gone out, but I wish to speak to you.'

He gave a nod and gestured for her to sit down, but she ignored him and stood facing him with undisguised hostility.

'Arabella tells me you have been unwell. I hope you are feeling better.'

'How could I feel better, sir, with what you have done to my daughter and grandson, and with what you are doing to them still?'

'It is a very difficult situation. My father—'

'Oh, do not waste your lies on me. You may fool Arabella, but you do not fool me for a minute. Have you not already hurt her enough? Are you not yet satisfied that you must do it all over again?'

'I would never knowingly have hurt Arabella. I loved her. I love her still.' It was the first time he had admitted the truth even to himself.

'Love? You, who, in her greatest hour of need, bought her as if she was some piece of cheap Haymarketware!

She needed help. Any decent man would have given her just that.'

Mrs Tatton's words confirmed every thought that had taunted him since he had found Arabella in Mrs Silver's. 'You are right and I have regretted my action most sincerely, ma'am. There is no excuse. I should not have allowed myself to be influenced by her circumstance.'

'Which circumstance was that, sir? That of her poverty?'

'I found her in a bordello, Mrs Tatton.'

Mrs Tatton hit out at him, her swollen old hands thumping ineffectually against his chest.

'Do not dare condemn her!' she cried and her breath was heavy and wheezing.

'Mrs Tatton, please calm yourself. I make no condemnation of Arabella. I know she would not have gone there lightly.'

He caught hold of her, worried for her health, and steered her to the armchair.

She sat down heavily, sobbing and clutching her hands to her face. 'I should have known it was such a place. But she told me it was a workshop where women sewed night and day to ready garments faster than anywhere else.'

He remembered Arabella facing him so defiantly that night in Mrs Silver's, and the expression upon her face when she admitted that her mother did not know she was there.

'She wished to spare your feelings, ma'am.'

Mrs Tatton nodded and, wrapping her arms around herself, began to rock. 'She only went there to save me and the boy. After the robbery we had nothing. God knows we had little enough before, but after…' She shook her head. 'Arabella trailed the streets of London from dawn to dusk, looking for honest work. Day after day she walked those streets, walked until her feet were rubbed raw and bleeding, and her shoulders bowed with weariness, and the last of the doors had been shut in her face. She pawned the wedding ring from her finger, the cloak from her back, the shoes from her feet, to keep us from starving. And then there was nothing else left to sell.'

Except herself.

Dominic felt sick to the pit of his stomach. The thought of what she had suffered made him want to cry out against the injustice of it and drive his fist into the wall again and again and again, but he knew that he must control himself. Mrs Tatton was already distressed enough. He passed her his handkerchief and she took it with a murmur of gratitude.

'You spoke of a robbery.'

He saw Mrs Tatton raise her head and look at him in surprise. 'She did not tell you?'

'She told me nothing.'

'I do not understand…'

And neither did Dominic, but he was beginning to. 'Arabella believed the worst of me. It must have been beyond humiliating for her to see me there that night.' He did not tell the old woman sitting before him the full extent of how he had humiliated her daughter, taking her, unknown, masked, to slake his lust upon. The knowledge raked him with agony; he knew it would hurt Mrs Tatton all the more. 'All she had left was her pride.' He took her hands in his. 'Tell me of the robbery, ma'am.'

She looked into his eyes, as if she were seeing him for the first time and was trying to take his measure. She looked and the minutes seemed to stretch, until at last she began to speak.

'Villains broke down the door of our lodgings with a hammer and stripped the place bare. They took every last thing save our mattress from which they had already prised the little money we had hidden there, and that damnable gold locket you gave her. We had already sold most items of value through the years, to make ends meet. But she would not sell the locket for all that it pained her to look upon it.' She looked at him steadily; the fury was gone and in its place was a terrible sadness and exhaustion.

'You have made my daughter your mistress and my grandson your bastard, to be looked down upon and shunned by all society. Set Arabella and Archie and me free, Dominic. Give us enough money to set up elsewhere, to start afresh and at least pretend we are respectable. Please. I am begging you.'

'I cannot do that, Mrs Tatton. I will not lose them again.'

'Then damn you to perdition, Dominic Furneaux.' Her complexion was puffy and grey, and her eyes swollen and red as she looked at him, yet there was about her the same dignity that he had seen in Arabella. 'I have nothing more to say to you, your Grace. If you will be so kind as to leave this house…' The hand with which she gestured to the door was shaking. 'Please leave at once.' She looked ill and trembling with passion. He dared not risk her health further.

Dominic rose from where he sat beside her on the sofa and did as she bid.

* * *

It was later than Arabella anticipated by the time that she and Archie returned to Curzon Street. Mrs Tatton had retired to bed and Dominic had not arrived.

The day wore on and when there continued to be no sign of Dominic Archie's excitement gradually changed to something else.

'Where is Dominic? Why does he not come, Mama?' Archie looked up at her with disappointment in his eyes.

Arabella smoothed his hair into some semblance of tidiness. 'Dominic is a very busy gentleman. I am sure that he will call upon us when he is able.'

'But he said that he would call today.'

'I know he did, little lamb. A very important matter must have arisen to prevent him.' But she was angry at Dominic for dashing a small boy's hopes, and angry at herself for trusting in him.

Archie climbed down from her knee and went off to play behind the curtain.

'Mama, Mama!' He came running up to her a minute later. 'Look what I have found.' In his hand he held a small scroll of paper tied with a red ribbon.

Arabella unfastened the ribbon and looked at the pen-and-ink coloured drawing on the paper before her. And she felt a wave of affection wash through her.

'This is your own little horse drawn by Dominic.' She smiled at Archie.

Archie's eyes widened. 'It is Charlie, Mama!'

'Yes, I think it is.' Arabella smiled, thinking that Dominic must have sent the drawing for Archie because he could not call.

'I cannot wait till I see Dominic!'

* * *

It was only later when Archie had been put to bed and her mother had risen from hers that Arabella learned something of what had really transpired that day.

'You sent Dominic away? But this is his house, Mama.'

'I sent him away, like the rogue he is.'

'Did you speak to him?'

'Oh, yes, Arabella. I told him what you should have.' Her mother looked even more pale and exhausted than when Arabella had seen her last, despite the hours of rest.

A shiver of foreboding moved down Arabella's spine.

Her mother looked at her with the strangest expression. 'Sweet Arabella, with your dignity and your pride,' she said softly. 'Why did you not tell him? And why did you not tell me?'

'What do you mean, Mama?' She had a very bad feeling. 'What was said?'

'I damned him to hell and told him to leave.' Mrs Tatton smiled, but it was the saddest smile that Arabella had ever seen.

'Oh, Mama,' she said softly. And she handed her mother the drawing he had penned for Archie.

Her mother unrolled the scroll and in the silence there was only the ticking of the clock.

And her mother looked at her and knew what she was thinking. 'Do not go to him, Arabella.'

'You know that I have to.' Arabella pecked a kiss on her mother's cheek. 'Archie is asleep. Listen out in case he wakens before I am returned. I should not be gone for long.' And she rang for her carriage and her cloak.

* * *

Dominic glanced round at the commotion that was sounding from his hallway. He raised an eyebrow at the man seated opposite him within his study.

'Please excuse me for a minute.' He set down his brandy and the pile of political papers that had just been handed to him and went to investigate, pulling the door closed behind him.

Out in the black-and-white chequered floor hallway Bentley's frame partially obscured a dark figure with which he was engaged in an altercation.

'I tell you that he will see me!' the voice insisted. Dominic's stomach tightened as he recognised it as Arabella's.

'And I tell you, madam, that he is not at home. Now if you do not leave the premises I will be forced to—'

Dominic stepped quickly forwards. 'It is all right, Bentley. Let her in.'

'Dominic,' she said and slipped the voluminous black velvet hood down to reveal herself, and he smelled the waft of cool night air mixed with the rose scent of her perfume. Her hair had been scraped back into a chignon, but the hood of the cloak had displaced some of the pins enough to let some golden curls escape. She looked beautiful and worried.

'What are you doing here, Arabella?' His voice was hushed as he hurried her into the shadows. His first thought was of the risk she was taking coming here, much more than she realised. And his second was that Arabella would not have come were there not a very good reason. A horrible fear suddenly struck him. His hands tightened around her arms.

'Has something happened to Archie?' he asked and his eyes searched hers.

She shook her head. 'Archie is fine.'

'Your mother?'

'She is well enough, Dominic.'

'Then why are you here?'

'What did you say to my mother today? I have to know.'

'Much as I wish it otherwise, now is not the time to be having this discussion, Arabella. You must leave here at once.'

He saw the hurt flicker in her eyes before cynical realisation showed on her face.

'You are angry that I have come.'

'Very.' He could not lie.

'I see.' Her lips tightened slightly.

'No, you do not.' He hauled her to him, until their faces were only inches apart. He stared down into her eyes, his heart thudding too hard at the danger she was in. 'Arabella, I am not alone this evening. I have visitors, albeit unwelcome ones, in the library—the Earl of Misbourne and his son Viscount Linwood.'

'Misbourne?' Everything about her stilled. 'Lady Marianne's father.' He could see the sudden doubt that flashed in her mind as clear as if she had voiced it aloud.

'Their visit is on a political matter and has nothing to do with Lady Marianne.'

Her gaze was fierce and strong and determined. 'If you mean to marry her, Dominic, please be honest enough to tell me. I understand your position and your obligations mean that you are required to marry and beget an heir—'

But he cut her off, his voice harsh and urgent. 'We

have been through all of this before, Arabella. There has only ever been one woman I wanted to marry and that is you.'

'We both know that is an impossibility now,' she whispered.

'Is it?' His grip was too tight around her arms, but he could not loosen it. 'Do I not already have my heir?'

They stared into one another's eyes and he could feel that she was trembling.

'Return to Curzon Street, Arabella. I am bound into this meeting, but I will come to you tomorrow and we will talk then.' He pressed a short hard kiss to her lips before pulling the hood up over her head and releasing her.

Bentley and a footman appeared and Dominic spoke softly and quickly. 'Help the lady to her coach. Discretion is paramount.'

'Very good, your Grace.' Bentley gave a bow. Arabella was already gone by the time the butler's gaze flitted towards the library door in a warning.

Dominic glanced round to see Misbourne and Linwood standing there.

'Everything all right, Arlesford? No trouble, I hope.'

'No trouble.' Dominic's expression was cold and hard as he made his way back into the library and topped up his guests' glasses. And he wondered just how long the men had been standing there and how much Misbourne had seen. For all their sakes, he hoped that the answer was not very much at all.

Chapter Fourteen

From the minute that Dominic arrived at Curzon Street the next day Arabella could see the determination in his gaze. She thought of what it was he had come to discuss and her heart missed a beat. She was frightened and hopeful and confused all at once.

'Dominic!' Archie ran up, so happy and joyful to see his father that Arabella's guilt at keeping the two of them apart weighed heavier than ever upon her. 'Are we playing the horses game today?'

'Archie, let Dominic come in and at least remove his hat and gloves before you pester him. I told you that he is busy and might not have time to play today,' said Arabella, but Archie was already by Dominic's side looking up at him hopefully.

Dominic smiled and ruffled Archie's hair. 'Of course I have time for the horses game...that is, if your mama and grandmama give us their permission.'

Archie peered across at her and Mrs Tatton.

Arabella glanced at her mother, who was watching

Archie and Dominic together. 'Mama?' she said softly, wanting her mother to be a part of this.

Mrs Tatton nodded. 'Let them spend time together.'

'Thank you,' said Dominic. Arabella knew that he had no need to ask for permission—it was his house and his son. But the fact that he had understood how important this was to her and that he had consideration for her mother's feelings gladdened her more than any fancy words or gifts could have done.

'Hurrah!' Archie shouted and produced a rather crushed and tatty-looking scroll of paper from his pocket. 'I have my picture all ready.'

And when they went through to the drawing room, Mrs Tatton did not make her excuses, but came and sat with them too.

Dominic did not cease to marvel at Archie. The more he came to know him the more he realised that, although the boy had his looks, he had many of Arabella's mannerisms. The way he tilted his head to the side when he was listening, and the way he chewed his lip when he was unsure of himself. Dominic never tired of the wonder of his and Arabella's child.

His tailcoat had long been abandoned, his waistcoat was unbuttoned and the knot in his cravat loosened. Archie insisted on removing his shoes and demonstrating with pride to Dominic how well he could run and slide in his stocking soles across the polished floor. Dominic remembered doing the very same thing at home in Shardeloes Hall when he was a boy.

Dominic took a seat on the sofa and felt something hard jab into his back. He glanced round and found a small carved wooden horse half-hidden by the cushion.

'Oh, you found Charlie sleeping in his stable.' Archie smiled.

'So his name is Charlie,' said Dominic.

'Gemmell made him for me. For my birthday.' Archie smiled even more widely. 'And my mama took us to the park and allowed me and Charlie to ride upon a real horse.' Archie was beaming fit to burst.

'I am sure you enjoyed that.' He slid a gaze to meet Arabella and wondered how all this could have gone on beneath his very nose without him having an inkling of it. Her cheeks flushed and she bit her lip.

'Oh, indeed, yes! It was the best treat ever.'

'So now you know, Dominic,' piped up Mrs Tatton. 'She should have told you of the boy and the rest of it at the very beginning.'

'Mama!' whispered Arabella, scandalised.

'Well, you should have,' said Mrs Tatton to Arabella before turning back to him. 'And you, for all that you can plead your excuses, should have treated my daughter a deal better than you have.'

'You are right, ma'am,' he conceded. 'But I am here today to resolve that matter.'

Mrs Tatton's eyes widened slightly. Her gaze shifted momentarily to Arabella and he saw in it both the question and anxiety before it came back to rest upon him.

No more was said of it, but Dominic stayed for dinner and was still there to kiss his son goodnight when he went to bed.

By the time Arabella and Dominic were alone in the drawing room Arabella was feeling distinctly nervous. She smoothed her skirts and perched on the edge of the sofa.

'Your meeting with Lord Misbourne went well last night?' she asked.

'Well enough.' He was standing over by the fireplace, which was still unlit on account of the warmth of the evening.

There was a silence that she quickly filled.

'Would you like some more tea?'

'No more tea, thank you, Arabella.' His dark pensive gaze came to rest upon hers. 'I meant what I said last night—about marriage—to you.'

'Dominic.' She sighed. It was such a sensitive subject for them both. 'How can we possibly marry after all that has happened?'

'How can we not?' There seemed to be a still calmness about him, yet the flicker of the muscle in his jaw betrayed the tension that ran beneath that stillness.

'I am your mistress, for pity's sake!'

'And have not other men married their mistresses? What of Mountjoy? Besides. I shall hardly be introducing you as such.'

'Too many people know of Miss Noir and Mrs Silver.'

'Maybe, but there is nothing to connect them to Mrs Marlbrook. Rest assured I will take every step to ensure that any such links be taken care of and that your background is nothing but respectable. Are you not the respectable and widowed Mrs Marlbrook recently come to London? They shall think it is a love match.'

Once it really had been a love match. And now... She looked into Dominic's eyes.

'We have to do this, Arabella, for Archie's sake. I have a duty both to my son, Arabella, and to right the wrongs I have dealt you.'

Duty? Her hope, still so new and tender and rising, was crushed. There was no talk of affection, no mention of love.

'This is about duty and appeasing your own guilt,' she said. *How foolish to have thought it could be anything other.*

'My guilt? It was you that hid Archie from me, Arabella.' Her eyes widened as his words found their target.

'What choice did I have? I did what I thought was best for Archie. He is my son.'

'He is my son, too. Do I not also have the right to do my very best for him, or do you continue to deny me that right?'

She turned away to hide her hurt. 'Archie looks so like you that everyone will know he is your son. He will be subjected to their gossip.'

'I care not what they think, Arabella. They may whisper their suppositions, but I am not without power and influence. Besides, unless you mean to keep him hidden for ever they will find out soon enough and I can protect him all the better once we are married—just as I can protect you.'

She knew what he was saying was right, yet she was overwhelmed with a feeling of disappointment and sadness. She should be glad that he had such a care for his son, that he had a sense of honour. And she was. Truly. But she could not help thinking of the first time he had asked her to be his wife, when they had been young and naïve and in love. Everything was different now. Too much had happened. There could never be any going back. And she hurt to know it.

'I am unsure, Dominic.'

'What is the alternative, Arabella? That I keep you here as my mistress with Archie as my bastard? Is that your preference?'

'No!'

'Then there is nothing else other than that we wed.'

She could feel the fast hard thump of her heart against her chest. He was asking her to marry him. The man she had loved; the man she loved still. Yet her chest was tight and she felt like weeping.

'There is another alternative that you have not considered,' she said slowly and it seemed as if the words did not even come from her own mouth. She felt chilled in even saying them, but they needed to be spoken. 'I need not be your mistress. My mother and Archie and I could go to the country. If we had a little money, enough for a small cottage, we could live in quiet respectability and you could—'

He grabbed hold of her upper arms and pulled her close to stare down into her face, eyes filled with fury. 'Is that what you want, Arabella?'

And behind his anger she saw the hurt of the wound she had just inflicted and she could not lie. 'You know it is not.' She shook her head and felt the tears prick in her eyes. 'But this is not about *want,* is it? As you have already said, this is about *duty* and what is best for Archie.'

'And you think it is best to take him away from his father?'

'You could still visit him and—'

But he did not let her finish. 'You may choose to marry me, Arabella, or to remain as my mistress. There is no other choice, for I will let neither you nor the boy go. So what is it to be, Arabella? Will you marry me?'

She felt angry and hurt and saddened. Her head knew his proposal made sense. He was offering what was best for Archie. He was offering what any woman in her situation should have jumped at. But her heart… Her heart was saying something else all together.

'You set it all out so clearly,' she said. And she remembered what he had said that very first night in the brothel: *Whores do as rich men bid.* And part of her revolted against both it and his possession of her.

His gaze held hers, waiting for her answer.

'Yes, Dominic, I will marry you.' *For Archie. Only for Archie.*

He gave a nod, and she felt something of the tension in his grip relax.

They looked at one another and there seemed so much anger and tension and sadness between them.

Then he took a small red-leather ring box from his pocket, inside of which was a ring of sparkling diamonds that surrounded a large square sapphire of the clearest, bluest blue.

'The Arlesford betrothal ring,' he said and slid the ring on to the third finger of her left hand.

She could not say a word, for she feared that all of what she felt would come tumbling out.

'I will make the necessary arrangements.'

She nodded.

Dominic bowed, then he left.

It should have been one of the happiest days of her life, but for Arabella it was one of the saddest. Dominic was marrying her not out of love, but for Archie. They were both doing this for Archie. It was the way it had to be. And she should be used to giving herself to a man who did not love her.

* * *

Dominic knew he had made a mess of the proposal. He was shocked and hurt that Arabella had even suggested leaving. And he was shocked, too, at his resentment at being denied his son. The thought that she could even think of taking Archie away from him brought back all of the anger that he had felt on learning that she had kept the boy hidden from him. He knew that he had done everything wrong by her right from that first night in the bordello. And now he was trying to make it right. But it seemed that it was too late.

She said she still had feelings for him. And he knew what it was he felt about her. He had thought she would have wanted to marry him. He thought she would have been happy. But nothing of the conversation had gone as he had hoped, apart from the outcome, he supposed. Sometimes broken things could not be repaired. Sometimes the damage done was too great. He wondered if there was any way back for them.

He would make Arabella his wife, and see Archie acknowledged as his rightful son, because it was the best thing he could do for them. And as for matters between him and Arabella—well, he could only hope that through time they would improve.

He deadened his heart and set his mind to organising a ball at Arlesford House to announce their betrothal.

Chapter Fifteen

⁓⁂⁓

Two weeks after Dominic's proposal, at nine o'clock on Friday evening, Mrs Tatton was still fussing at the looking glass within her bedchamber when she heard a carriage draw up outside.

'Is it the carriage he has sent, Arabella?' Arabella could hear the anxiety that edged her mother's voice; much as she was feeling nervous herself, she sought to reassure her.

Arabella peeped from the edge of the drawn curtains down on to the road below. 'It is, Mama, but there is time enough yet to compose yourself.'

'Compose myself? I swear that I shall not be composed the whole of this evening. I have never felt so nervous in all my life!'

'You have nothing to worry over.'

'Save the fact I may let us all down before the Prince of Wales.'

'Mama…' Arabella's gaze met her mother's in the looking glass '…you could never do that.'

'But what if they discover the truth of us—that we have not lived so quietly since Mr Marlbrook's death?'

'They shall not discover any such thing; Dominic has taken care of everything. Now take a deep breath, Mama, and let us have one last look at your outfit.'

Mrs Tatton turned back to the looking glass.

Arabella's gaze roved over the purple silk which her mother was wearing. The colour suited her mother's skin and brought a healthy glow to her complexion. It was high necked, the bodice closed over by a line of amethyst buttons that sparkled in the candlelight. On Mrs Tatton's head was fitted a small turban in matching purple silk; the hair beneath had been curled and coiffured to soften the turban's edges. The shimmer of purple silk picked out silver highlights in the grey curls. Arabella had not seen her mother look so well in years.

'You are quite lovely, Mama.'

'Thank you, Arabella.' Her mother smiled, her nerves forgotten for the moment. 'You look lovely yourself. Every bit a duchess-in-waiting.'

Arabella glanced down at the deep blue silk gown. It was plainly, but expertly, cut in the latest fashion to do justice to her figure. In the candlelight her skin looked pale and creamy beside the dark intense colour of the dress. The sleeves were short and sitting off her shoulders and the long evening gloves and reticule were of a shade that exactly matched the dress. Her décolletage was bare and Arabella touched her fingers against the skin and thought fleetingly of the golden locket that had meant so much more to her than the diamond-and-sapphire ring that was now upon her finger. She pushed the thought aside, knowing that she must show nothing of her true feelings, that tonight was all about playing the role of a respectable widow who had captured a duke's heart.

'Thank you, Mama. I shall just have a quick peep at Archie before we leave.'

'He will be sleeping, Arabella.'

'I hope so.' Arabella smiled, but it was all for her mother and there was nothing of happiness inside. 'But I will check so that I am certain. And ensure that Anne knows what to do if he should wake before we have returned.'

Dominic had always thought Arabella a beautiful woman, but the sight of her with Mrs Tatton coming in through the hallway of Arlesford House quite took his breath away. She was lovelier than he could have imagined. Wearing a shimmering silver shawl, under which he could see a plain dark blue dress that was expensive, respectable, and perfectly in keeping with her role as a widow of two years. And yet the dress showed off the curves of Arabella's figure in just the right way. Her hair was an elaborate arrangement of golden curls piled upon her head. Several loose tendrils framed her face and wisped softly around her neck. Even Mrs Tatton appeared to have more colour in her face and was wearing a purple outfit complete with turban, and a purple-and-blue fringed shawl.

He bowed to them both, although it was hard for him to drag his gaze from Arabella for long.

'Your Grace,' she said and curtsied, all formality, just as it had been between them in private these past two weeks.

He could hear the murmur of curiosity amongst the guests that already packed the ballroom.

'And Mrs Tatton,' he said and bowed to her mother.

The hundreds of candles in the three chandeliers in the ballroom sparkled on the sapphire-and-diamond betrothal ring on Arabella's finger as he raised her hand to his lips. The surrounding murmur grew louder.

He spoke to Arabella and her mother in the politest of terms, knowing that their every word was being listened to even above the singing of the violins that sounded so clear and sweet from the musicians up on the balcony.

'You are well, Mrs Marlbrook?' he enquired and his gaze was intent upon hers. He gave her hand that was tucked within his arm a little squeeze as he led her and Mrs Tatton to a small collection of chairs that he had been keeping just for them. He wanted to know how she was bearing up to such pressure, for he knew that beneath that mask of cool tranquillity she would be worried.

He felt the return of the slight transient pressure of her fingers against the muscle of his arm. He gestured to a passing footman carrying a silver salver of filled champagne glasses and passed Arabella and her mother each a glass of champagne. They chatted for a little while, about the weather, about how she and her mother were enjoying London, about horse riding. And then he took Arabella and Mrs Tatton over to where the Prince of Wales was holding court and presented them.

The wave of whisperings and staring was passing right through the room. Dominic was looking forward to making the announcement. He watched Arabella and the prince together and knew that Prinny was giving her his royal approval. No one would dare question her respectability now. He gave a small nod of acknowledgement at the prince and saw Prinny give a nod back.

A royal prince needed his allies every bit as much as a duke. And then Dominic signalled to the musicians to cease playing. It was time.

Arabella was so busy keeping an eye on her mother and guarding her conversation with the prince that she did not notice what was happening until the music stopped. A hushed chatter filled the silence.

Dominic's ballroom was large and there must have been at least a hundred people packed within its glittering splendour. Arabella could see what seemed like the flicker of a thousand candles sparkling against the myriad of faceted crystal drops on the massive chandeliers. The ceiling, the top of the walls and the front of the balcony were decorated with the most pure and beautiful plasterwork. The walls themselves were painted a cool pale green, which lent the room an airy spacious feel. Above the massive fireplace, which thankfully had not been lit, was a huge looking glass that reflected the light from the chandeliers and made the room even brighter. The oak floorboards had been scraped and polished until they gleamed like a rich dark chocolate. Around the room were tables and chairs, and wall sconces that dripped with crystal in a fashion that mirrored their parent chandeliers. It was beautiful and elegant and most luxurious.

And then Dominic's butler was ringing a small bell. 'Pray silence your majesty, my lords, ladies and gentlemen. The Duke of Arlesford wishes to make an announcement.'

She heard the buzz of whispers go around the room. Arabella was standing with the Prince of Wales on one side and her mother on the other. Dominic was on the other side of the prince. Although most of the attention in the room was fixed on Dominic, she could see a few of the gazes upon herself. Every pair of eyes in the room was filled with question. Everyone wanted to know what was so important that the Duke of Arlesford intended making an announcementr.

And then Dominic took her hand and drew her over to stand by his side. And she saw the shock and surprise on some faces and the confirmation of guesses on others. His fingers closed around hers and she felt all of his support flowing through that warm touch.

Dominic began to talk, and her heart gave a little jump, her stomach a little jitter and she realised that this was it.

'I would like to present to you all, Mrs Arabella Marlbrook.'

She could hear him talking and she stood there so still, so calm, facing that sea of faces as if she were the very proper, very respectable widowed Mrs Marlbrook whom Dominic was describing. He was still talking.

'I am very happy to be able to tell you that Mrs Marlbrook has accepted my proposal of marriage. We are to be married as soon as matters can be arranged.'

Which would be in two months' time, at the height of the summer, in Westminster Abbey, if all went according to plan. She would be a duchess, and Archie, his father's son and heir to a dukedom. Her mother would never again go cold. Her son, never go hungry. There would always be enough money for food and medicines and coal. He had made her respectable again. He would make her his wife. But Arabella could not smile.

Dominic raised her hand to his mouth and placed a kiss against it. Every person in the ballroom began to applaud and she could see her mother smiling by her side, and she could see, too, the look in Dominic's eyes when he looked at her—dark and possessive and filled with all they had not said to one another in the past two weeks. She forced herself to smile because it was what everyone was expecting. She smiled as she met the gazes of Dominic's guests. Smiled sadly at the good will she saw in those faces because she knew, if they knew the truth, there would be nothing of good will there. And then her gaze passed over two faces that were not smiling.

One was the grey bearded man whom she had seen in Vauxhall on the night of the carnival—Lord Misbourne—and the other was a taller, younger, dark-haired man by his side. The younger man's expression was filled with such coldness that it shocked her and sent a shiver down her spine. Arabella's feigned smile was all the broader to hide her sudden unease.

Beside her she heard the prince raise a toast to Dominic's and her future happiness. She was obliged to curtsy her acknowledgement to him and take the glass of champagne from the footman who appeared by her side, so that she might raise it in response. And when she looked again to find the face that had so distressed her, it had gone and so had Misbourne's. Her eyes scanned the crowd, searching for the men, but there was not one sign of them.

And then the cheering began, and although Dominic was smiling she could see the darkness in his eyes, and she was smiling even more to hide her unhappiness and discomfort. The band began to play again and people pressed forwards to offer their congratulations. But Arabella's eyes were still searching for the man and, although she took every step to mask it, the unease that he elicited remained. And it seemed that in the background of all the laughter and music that surrounded her she could hear a whisper of foreboding.

Chapter Sixteen

Hunter made no mention of his and Dominic's disagreement over the marriage as the two men rode together in St James's Park a few mornings later.

'How goes the word amongst the *ton?*' Dominic asked. 'Any suspicions?'

'Not a one,' said Hunter. 'There are a few queries as to whether you have rid yourself of Miss Noir or are just being discreet because of your forthcoming marriage. The consensus of opinion seems to be in favour of the latter.'

'I am glad that they think so highly of me,' said Dominic sarcastically.

'You can hardly complain, Dominic, when you have spent the last few years in our dissolute company proving yourself a rake.'

'I suppose not,' he said drily.

'Are you sure that you wish me as your best man? I mean, now that you are trying to clean up your image.' Hunter was not joking, he realised, judging from the serious expression on his friend's face.

'Of course I want you. Who else would I ask?'

'True.' Hunter gave a sniff and a shrug of his shoulders. 'Not much choice when all your friends are rakes. I suppose if you really wanted to be a bastard about it you might ask Misbourne or Linwood. They would certainly get the message that you did not wish to marry their precious Lady Marianne then.'

'I think they already have that message, Sebastian. Why else do you think I invited them to the ball?'

'You should have told Misbourne in no uncertain terms at the very start that you had no intention of marrying the chit.'

'I did, on several occasions.'

Hunter arched an eyebrow.

'But Misbourne is persistent to say the least. He feels his claim is justified and I have no wish to injure his pride any more than I already have. He owns most of the newspapers in London and he is as sly as a snake in the grass.'

'Why you do not cut him dead mystifies me,' said Hunter.

'We are obliged to work together on political matters; besides, you have heard the saying, keep your friends close and your enemies closer still.'

'All the more reason to have called him out and put a ball in the rogue's shoulder,' said Hunter.

'With Misbourne it would have to be a ball in the heart. Otherwise he would just keep coming back. Remember what he did to Blandford?'

Hunter gave a murmur of disapproval. 'Poor old Blandford.'

'And I would not just be able to walk away having murdered a fellow peer.'

'Trip to the Continent called for,' said Hunter.

'A bit more than that. And I will not have Misbourne dictate the course of my life. Besides, the matter is settled now. He might not like the fact that I am about to marry Arabella, rather than his daughter, but there is not a damnable thing he can do about it.'

For Arabella the week that followed Dominic's ball was a whirl of activity and she was glad of it, for it gave her little time to think about the way things lay between them and their marriage that lay ahead. She played a role, went through the motions and was careful to concentrate at all times lest she allow something of their secret to slip.

Arabella, Dominic and her mother attended a musical evening at Lady Carruthers's on Monday, a rout at Lady Filchingham's on Tuesday evening, a showing of Shakespeare's *Hamlet* at the King's Theatre on Wednesday, a ball at Lord Royston's on Thursday, and a visit to the opera on Friday. On top of that she had received three sets of afternoon visitors in Curzon Street. It was now Saturday morning and they were due to attend yet another ball that evening.

Mrs Tatton was yawning and half-dozing in the armchair by the fire, while Arabella was teaching Archie a card game at the little green baize covered table.

'I win!' Archie shouted triumphantly and spread his cards for Arabella to see.

'Hush, you rascally boy,' she whispered with a laugh. 'You will wake your grandmama.'

'I am not sleeping,' Mrs Tatton muttered, 'just resting my eyes for five minutes while I have the chance.' Her voice trailed off and her breathing reverted to the regular heavy breaths of sleep with the slight snore that her mother always made.

Archie giggled. 'She *is* sleeping. Listen, Mama.' And then he laughed again as Mrs Tatton made a soft snoring sound right on cue.

The rat-a-tat-tat of the brass knocker on the front door sounded loudly, making both Arabella and Archie start and wakening Mrs Tatton.

'Is it Dominic come to see me again?' Archie asked. 'I hope so for I do like him, Mama.'

'I am glad of that,' said Arabella and she truly was, no matter how matters lay between her and Dominic, for as the days passed she was coming to see that even if Dominic did not love her, he loved his son.

'Is it Dominic? Are we expecting him at this time of the morning?' Mrs Tatton rubbed at her eyes and sat up straight. 'Dear Lord, I do not know why I am so very tired these days.'

'Too many late nights, Mama,' said Arabella with a smile. 'And, no, we are not expecting Dominic or any other visitors at this hour. Gemmell will deal with it.'

But less than five minutes later Gemmell appeared in the drawing room. 'Excuse me, madam, but there is a gentleman at the door who is most insistent that he speak with you, a Mr Smith.' Quite what Gemmell thought of a gentleman caller bothering his mistress, particularly at this time of the morning, was written all over his face, as if she were the respectable Mrs Marlbrook she was pretending to be. Arabella felt a rush of affection for the elderly butler.

'I tried to send him away but he is refusing to leave until I pass you a message. I could have him thrown down the steps on to the street, out I thought that such a drastic action would attract attention of an undesirable nature.'

'You are quite right to come to me, Gemmell.' Arabella did not know any gentleman by the name of Smith, and, moreover, she was anxious not to receive any gentleman callers other than Dominic, but neither did she wish to be creating gossip and scandal by having the caller manhandled from her front door. 'And the message is?' she asked Gemmell.

'The message is…' She saw Gemmell's cheeks colour in embarrassment. He cleared his throat. 'Miss Noir.'

The name seemed to echo in the silence that followed his words. Arabella could not prevent her eyes widening in horror. Her heart's steady rhythm seemed to stumble and stop and she felt a chill of dread spread right through her.

Miss Noir. An image of herself as she had stood before the looking glass in Mrs Silver's house flashed in her head. Of the black translucent dress that showed hints of what lay beneath, of the indecent way it clung to her every curve. Of the black-feathered mask that hid the top of her face.

Someone had seen her.

Someone knew.

'Miss *Noir?*' Mama repeated and looked confused. Fortunately Archie was playing with the cards, oblivious to what else was going on in the drawing room.

Arabella's heart began to beat again, each beat resounding after the other in a series of rapid thuds so heavy that she could feel them reverberate in the base of her throat.

'I will deal with this, Mama, then the gentleman will

leave us in peace.' Then to Gemmell, 'Show him into the library.'

Gemmell cleared his throat awkwardly as if even he had heard of the infamous Miss Noir.

Arabella rose, smoothed out her skirts, checked her appearance briefly in the peering glass to ensure that she did not look as frightened as she felt, and then, taking a deep breath, she walked out to face the gentleman caller.

She closed the library door quietly behind her.

The man was standing by the bookshelves, with his hat and gloves dangling from one hand, browsing the titles of the leather-bound books arranged upon it, and when he looked up at the sound of the door she saw at once who he was.

He was of medium height with a lithe lean build, and the lazy loose way he was holding his hat and gloves belied the tension that seemed to ripple through the rest of his body. His hair was a raven black against a face that was of pale olive complexion. But it was his eyes that she noticed the most, for they were black and dangerous and filled with fury. And he was looking at her with cold dislike, just as he had looked at her from his place upon the crowded floor beside the Earl of Misbourne on the night of Dominic's ball.

'Mrs Marlbrook,' he said in a smooth voice. 'I thought that you would see the sensible course and respond to my message.'

'Mr Smith.' She gave the smallest inclination of her head and attacked first, hoping to call his bluff with a confident assault. 'I will speak bluntly and with the same lack of consideration that you have shown in coming to my door bandying such a name. I do not know who you are, or why you have come here on such a malicious mission, but I will tell you, sir, that if you are seeking to make mischief between the Duke and myself, then you are wasting your time. I am a widow, sir, and not completely ignorant of the workings of the world. What his Grace has done in the past and with whom is no consideration of mine. You have had a wasted journey, Mr Smith. So, if you will be so good as to leave now.' She kept her head high and her gaze level with his.

Mr Smith clapped his hands together in a slow mockery of applause. 'A performance worthy of Drury Lane, Mrs Marlbrook,' he said.

'How dare you?' Her cheeks warmed from his insolence. 'I shall have my butler escort you out.'

'Not so fast, madam. Unless you want it known that the respectable widow to whom Arlesford is betrothed is the same woman who visited his house alone at night a matter of weeks ago. And the same woman who bears a startling resemblance to the whore that he bought from Mrs Silver's bawdy house and took with him to the masquerade at Vauxhall. I guarantee you that I can have the story published in more than one of London's newspapers. People will draw their own conclusions, but I would warrant that you will not be so warmly received then, for all of Arlesford's connections.'

'I have never been so insulted in all my life!' Truly the performance of an actress, just as he had said. 'I will not even deign to reply to such scurrilous and ridiculous accusations.'

'You may protest all you like, madam, and indeed I would expect nothing less from a woman like you. I might even believe you had I not seen you with my own eyes,' he said. 'From doxy to duchess in a few weeks. That is quite an achievement.'

'Get out!' She pointed to the door, showing all of her anger and none of her fear. 'You can be very sure that I will inform the duke of your interest in the matter, Mr Smith.'

'Please do, Mrs Marlbrook. And tell him also that although he was very careful in fabricating a cover for you, with Mrs Silver, Madame Boisseron and your landlord at Flower and Dean Street, there are always those in the background who are missed. He cannot catch every faceless soul upon the street, every witness to the truth. And you would be surprised at what some people are willing to do for money, Mrs Marlbrook. But then again, madam, perhaps not that surprised after all. I know quite conclusively that you are Miss Noir.'

'You have a villain's tongue in your head, sir! Be gone from here. I will not tolerate your presence for a moment longer.'

He cocked his head to the side. 'Not even to hear what it is that I want in order to keep your secret from the newspapers?'

The fear was pumping through her veins, the scent of it filling her nose, the taste of it churning her stomach. Yet still she faced him defiantly, keeping up the pretence to the end. 'Publish your lies if you will, Mr Smith. Now, leave my house, sir.' She strode towards the door and, opening it, stepped out into the hallway, intending to have Mr Smith escorted out. And the sight of what greeted her eyes made her stop dead in her tracks and snatched all of the wind from her sails.

There was a light drumming in her head and she felt sick.

'Mama?' the little voice uttered quietly. For there, sit-

ting on the floor at the side of the library door, his back
leaning against the wall, playing cards spread out on the
floorboards around him, was Archie. 'Grandmama fell
asleep again and I was bored waiting for you to return.'

'Well, how very interesting,' said the gentleman's
voice from directly behind her, although he had not yet
crossed the threshold from the library. 'You might not
have a care how your own name is discredited within
the newspapers, Mrs Marlbrook, but your son—and
Arlesford's, if I am not mistaken—well, I fancy that
might be a different matter all together. Only think of
the interest that the duke and his bastard will arouse.
Even with Arlesford to smooth the way for him the boy
would never completely escape the scandal. He, as well
as you, would be the talk of the *ton.*'

Gemmell appeared just at that moment, barely con-
cealing the scowl he directed at Mr Smith. 'Madam?'
he enquired.

Somehow Arabella found the strength. She looked
at Gemmell quite calmly. 'If you would be kind enough
to take Archie through to my mother, and see that he is
entertained with a game of cards.'

'Very good, madam. And shall I then return to escort
Mr Smith out?' He eyed the gentleman with disdain.

'No, that will not be necessary, thank you, Gemmell.
Mr Smith and I have not yet concluded our discussion.'
And, walking back into the library, she closed the door
behind her.

'What do you want?' She faced him squarely, keeping her face as impassive as she could, although she
knew full well that her disgust of him must have been
blazing from her eyes. They stood as if they were two

opponents in a fight, sizing one another up for strengths and for weaknesses.

'For you to leave Arlesford. Break off your betrothal and go, I do not care where, as long as it is not London.'

'Why should it matter to you whether I marry him?'

'That is my business. You will not marry him, nor will you remain here as his mistress.' He slipped a hand into his pocket and produced a cloth-wrapped package. 'There is five thousand pounds here. Admittedly a good sum short of what Arlesford could give you, but enough to pay for your expenses to set up elsewhere and find yourself a new protector.' He held out the package to her.

It was all she could do not to dash the package to the floor, such was her contempt for his offer. But she restrained herself and just turned away. 'You are under a gross misapprehension as to my character, sir.'

'I do not think so.' He held the money out for just a moment longer, then, when he realised she had no intention of taking it, he sat it down on the closest table.

'No one would print your lies. It is all of it an idle threat,' she taunted, but even as she said it she knew that it was not. Just one whisper of his accusations would be enough. Once word of Archie was out, the press men would be peeping in their windows, stalking their every move. She could run their gauntlet, but she could not risk subjecting her son to any such torture.

'I assure you most solemnly that I can have the story in print and on the front pages by Monday morning.' He looked at her with an expression upon his face that told her what type of woman he thought her.

'And do not think to go running to Arlesford with a tale of this meeting or of me. If he hears one word

I will know and not only will I publish, but...well, let us just say that London can be a dangerous place, Mrs Marlbrook, even for a man such as Arlesford.'

'You are threatening his safety?' She stared into those black eyes, reeling at the ruthlessness she saw there.

'Take my words in whatever way you will.' He smiled the coldest smile of promise she had ever seen and she knew with an absolute certainty that this man would have no qualms about executing all that he threatened. Arabella shivered and felt goose pimples break out over her skin.

'If you have not left Arlesford by tomorrow I will go ahead and make good on my promise to publish. Do you understand, Mrs Marlbrook?'

'I understand, sir, and I will do as you ask.' The gall was rising in her throat. 'Take your money. I do not want it.' She lifted the packet of money from the table and handed it to him.

'If you insist.' He smiled and slipped it back into his pocket. 'Do not bother calling your butler. I will show myself out.'

When the front door shut after him she went to the window and saw him walking along the street. There was no horse; there was no carriage. Mr Smith vanished as quickly as he had appeared.

She leaned heavily against the table, trying to smooth the unevenness of her breathing, trying to calm the anger and the fear that had set her whole her body trembling.

What choice did she have? He had threatened to expose Archie and end Dominic's life. Arabella dared not risk either. There was no one she could tell. No one who would help her. She did not want to panic and frighten her mother. She knew this was a decision she would have to make on her own. Except that there was no decision to make. How could there be when it came to those whom she loved?

One more deep breath and then she stood up straight and walked through to tell her mother to start packing.

Arabella heard Dominic's carriage come to a halt outside Curzon Street at nine o'clock that evening. He had come to collect her for the ball. Arabella was sitting alone in the drawing room, dressed not for the ball but in a plain day dress with a shawl wrapped around her shoulders. The curtains were drawn; there was no fire upon the hearth, and only a single candle had been lit. The room was in semi-darkness, just as she wanted it, for she did not want him to be able to see the truth upon her face when she told him.

She heard the closing of the front door and the steady sound of his footsteps as he approached the drawing room. Her stomach clenched with the dread of what she must do.

'Arabella?' She could see the surprise upon his face. 'What is wrong? You are not ready for the ball.'

'I am not going to the ball.' She rose from the chair and stood very still facing him. She felt chilled, so chilled that her legs were trembling. 'Dominic, I have to speak to you.' It did not matter how many hours she had spent rehearsing the words, now it came to speaking them they would not come to her lips. She felt sick to the pit of her stomach, so sick that she wondered if she was going to be able to go through with this.

'What has happened, Arabella?' The growing concern in his eyes made it impossible for her to look at him. And she wanted to tell him the truth so much, all about Smith and his horrible threats. But the promise of what that villain would do was too clear in her head. Smith would ruin Archie and God only knew what he intended for Dominic. She thought of the night Dominic had come here with the mark of a blade across his ribs, and she wondered if that, too, had been Smith's handiwork. She was shaking so much at the thought she feared Dominic would see it. She thought of how much she loved both Archie and the man who was his father, and knew she had to do this, for both their sakes. She forced herself on.

'Matters have changed. I…I have reconsidered my situation…' She gripped her hands tightly together.

He came towards her and she knew he meant to take her in his arms and she knew absolutely that she could not let that happen. 'No!' She put out a hand to stay him and backed away. 'Please come no closer.'

He stopped where he was. 'Arabella, are you going to tell me what this is about?'

She took a breath. And then another. There was no excuse she could give.

'I…' There was nothing that would make it any easier for either of them.

'I cannot…' She must say the words.

'Dominic…' She must say them no matter how like poison they were on her tongue.

'I cannot marry you. I am breaking our betrothal.'

He gave a half-gasp half-laugh, but his eyes were serious and tense. 'Is this some sort of jest?'

'It is no jest.' She could not bring herself to meet his

gaze. She willed herself to think of Archie, not of what she was doing to them all.

There was a moment's silence as he absorbed what she had said.

'Why?' It was the question she had known he would ask and the one she could not bear to answer. She shook her head.

'Have I pushed you too much into the public eye? If all these outings are too much we can reduce them. Spend some evenings more—'

'No,' she interrupted him. 'No,' she said again.

'Is it the wedding? We can make it a small quiet affair if that is what you prefer.'

'No, Dominic.' It was harder even than the worst of her imaginings. 'It is none of that, nor anything that you have done. Please believe me.'

'Then what?'

She shook her head again.

'I love you, Arabella.'

The words hung in the air between them. Words that, had he uttered them yesterday, would have filled her with such joy. Now they broke her heart.

She gave a strangled breathy laugh at the irony of it and squeezed her eyes shut to stop the tears. '*Now* you tell me.' She felt a tear escape to trickle down her cheek and wiped it away with the heel of her hand.

'I've never stopped loving you,' he said.

'You never told me. You never said it.' Her self-control was stretched so thin she could not think ahead, could only handle the awfulness of the situation one second at a time.

'I am sorry that I made such a hash of the proposal.'

He raked a hand through his hair. 'But why else did you think that I asked you to marry me?'

'For Archie. Out of duty.'

'That is only a part of it. I am marrying you because I love you, Arabella. I should have told you.'

'Oh, God,' she whispered. 'Please do not make this any harder than it already is. I cannot marry you, Dominic.' The tears were running down her cheeks now and she could not stop them. 'I cannot.'

He moved to her.

She backed away, stumbling, as she bumped against an armchair. Dominic caught her and pulled her to him, his hands gripping her upper arms tight as he stared down into her face.

'I know that you love me too, Arabella.'

She shook her head, but could not say the words to deny it. 'I cannot marry you,' She clung to the mantra, knowing that she dare not trust herself to say much else.

'You are out before all of society. Fading into the background to be my mistress once more is not an option.'

'I cannot marry you and I cannot be your mistress. I have to go away, Dominic, away from you and away from London. Tonight.'

He gave a hard-edged laugh that rang with incredulity. 'And you think I will let you go, just like that?' He shook his head and she could see the determination in his eye. 'I do not know what this is about, Arabella, but I told you before and I meant it, I have no intention of losing you again. And I have no intention of losing the son that I have only just found.'

And she was more afraid than ever because she

recognised that implacable look on his face. 'You have to release me and Archie, Dominic.'

'No, Arabella, I do not.' His jaw was set firm.

'Please.' She looked directly into his eyes for the first time. His life and that of their child hung in the balance. 'I am begging you, Dominic. Believe me when I tell you that it is better this way.'

'Better?' His eyes held hers with possession and fierce protectiveness and suspicion. 'You know that I love you. I would make you my wife, my duchess. I would give you and Archie everything you desire. And I know that you love me. So what are you running from, Arabella?'

He was coming too near the truth without even knowing what it was he was risking. She looked at him, this man that she loved so much, and she knew what she had to say to make him release her. To say it would kill a part of her for ever. But it would save him. And it would save Archie.

She looked into his eyes, so like those of their son. Inside her chest she felt the slowing of her heart. And inside her mind she felt a shutter close.

'You are mistaken, Dominic. I do not love you.' The words slipped from her mouth, slowly, quietly, to lie in the room between them. She felt as if she had screamed them at the top of her voice. She saw the shock in his eyes, the hurt, the pain, the disbelief. And it was as if she had taken a knife and plunged it into her own heart, and twisted that blade as cruelly as she could.

The clock on the mantel marked the seconds.

Tick.

Tick.

Tick.

'I do not believe you,' he whispered.

'I do not love you,' she said again, and her heart beat once…and twice…and a third time. There was nothing of warmth left in her. Where once blood had flowed in her veins there was only ice.

He stared down into her face and she saw the depth of the wound she had dealt him. She realised that in hurting him so badly she was destroying herself.

And still she stood there, so still, so immobile, and she did not allow herself to think, only to speak the lies.

'And you have only just decided this?' She saw the dangerous darkening of his eyes and the slight raising of one of his eyebrows. The hurt was still there, but there was anger before it, vying with incredulity. If she weakened in the slightest, if she gave him one sign of the truth… She grasped the handle of the knife that was already within her heart and stabbed it even deeper.

'I should not have pretended otherwise.' Her heart broke apart. She looked away because she could not bear to see the raw pain in his eyes.

'You *pretended?*' She could hear his anger. But she could bear his anger better than his hurt.

'Yes,' she said and forced herself to meet his eyes.

'When we were making love? When you cried out your pleasure as I spilled my seed within you? When I lay with you all the night through?' he demanded savagely.

'Yes,' she said again. And it was easier now that she could see his fury was taking over. She had to make him believe her.

The silence hissed between them. The seconds seemed too long. She stood there and waited, waited and waited, beneath the blast of his scrutiny, until at last he said,

'Then I will not bind you against your will.'

'Thank you.' The words sounded distant as if it was not Arabella who had spoken them, but someone else far away. She did not even feel like she was really there in the room, but was standing outside of her body watching a tragedy unfold before her.

His eyes were glacial, but she knew they only masked a hurt deeper than her own. 'Then let us sort the practicalities of this separation.'

'There is nothing to sort. We will leave tonight and go to the village of Woodside; we lived there for a while when Henry was still alive."

'Oh, no, Arabella. You will wait until morning and then you will go to Amersham, to the cottage you once shared with your family.'

'I—' she started but Dominic cut her off.

'The deeds of the cottage are already in your name, Arabella. It was to have been one of my wedding gifts to you. And do not refuse me, for I tell you that this is one of the stipulations by which I will release you.'

He had bought her the cottage. She batted the thought away, knowing she could not afford to let it in, not yet. Her mind felt frozen, but she could feel the great cracks that were spreading across the ice and she knew the barrier would not hold for much longer.

'And your other stipulations?' Second by second. It was nearly done.

'Archie is my son and I mean to provide for him and keep both him and his mother safe. You will never go near a bordello again. Do you understand, Arabella?'

'Yes.' She understood what he still thought. She had

never told him the truth. That there had only been that one night. That there had only ever been him.

'I will provide you with an allowance and I will visit Archie regularly. A boy needs a father, Arabella.'

'But—' *What would Mr Smith say to that?*

'But nothing. These are my conditions. I will agree to nothing less.'

His eyes were hard as flint. His jaw was clamped and resolute. She knew he meant exactly what he said. Smith had specified that she must not marry Dominic nor be his mistress, and that she must leave London. There had been no mention of anything else, although she did not trust what the villain would do if he came to hear of it.

'It will be as you say.' She could not hurt him or Archie any more than she had to. Hurting them to save them. Breaking Dominic's heart to save his life. Such cruel irony.

'Take the coach and what servants you will. I will close up this house when you are gone.'

She lifted the little red-leather box from beside the candlestick on the table and opened the lid to reveal the Arlesford betrothal ring nestled inside upon the cream velvet. In the dim light of the drawing room the sapphire had turned from a clear sky blue to a deep inky black as if it was in mourning. The diamonds glittered and winked in the flickering light of the solitary candle. She held the box out to him.

He hesitated for just a moment before taking it from her. The lid shut with a snap and he slipped it into his coat pocket.

'Goodbye, Arabella.' His eyes met hers and what she saw in them broke her heart into a thousand pieces. She did not trust herself to speak as she stood there barely hanging on to the shreds of her self-control.

He turned and walked away. And she just stood there, facing straight ahead at the paintings on the wall. She heard the click of the door shutting. Heard him speak to Gemmell and then his footsteps receding along the passageway. The front door closed with a slam that reverberated throughout the whole house. Only then did the ice barrier shatter as the great tide of raw emotion swept right through her, ravaging her with its ferocity. And she felt, absolutely felt, every last bit of what she had just done.

Arabella fell down to her knees and began to sob. She had saved the man she loved and their son, but at a cost so great she did not know if she could bear it. Arabella put her head in her hands and wept all the harder.

Chapter Seventeen

Dominic was in his study in Arlesford House sitting at his desk with all of the paperwork pertaining to Curzon Street open before him. He knew he should be checking through the details. But he barely noticed the letters. He was thinking of Arabella and that terrible last scene between them.

Over the subsequent days the shock and initial flare of reaction had diminished enough for him to at least begin to think straight. He was still hurt and angry beyond words, but he was also aware of an underlying feeling that something was not right. Not that anything could be right about her jilting him, again, or looking him in the eye to tell him that she did not love him. But he could not rid himself of the notion that there was something else, something that held the key to why Arabella had suddenly changed her mind. He revisited the scene in his head for the thousandth time, hearing her words again.

I cannot marry you. That same expression repeated

again and again, so stilted, and with nothing of an explanation even though he had pushed for it. She refused to be either his wife or his mistress.

I have to go away, Dominic, away from you and away from London. Tonight.

The words had made his blood run cold, but now that he analysed them stripped of all emotion, he could see that they were all wrong.

He thought of her response to his baring his heart. She had wept as if her heart was breaking, yet she had not backed down.

And when he had told her he would not let her go she had begged. Arabella, who had led him to believe she was in a brothel out of choice, rather than reveal her dire circumstances. Arabella, who had suffered so much for the sake of her pride. Arabella, who had not begged even in the worst of her situations.

And as he listened again to that conversation, without letting the hurt and the anger cloud his mind, it dawned on him that only when she had realised he was serious about not releasing her had she said that she did not love him. It smacked of a woman lying out of desperation.

What are you running from? He heard the echo of his own question and remembered the sudden flicker of fear and panic in her eyes.

And he shivered at the realisation.

A knock sounded on the door and Bentley showed in Gemmell.

Dominic was barely listening as the elderly butler detailed how all that Dominic had bought had been packed away and removed from the Curzon Street house. He was aware that he had been so selfishly

caught up in his hurt and his anger and his righteous-
ness that he had missed what was before his very eyes.

Gemmell stood on the opposite side of the desk.
'Everything is recorded in the list drawn up in the
housekeeping book.' The butler gestured towards the
open book on the desk before Dominic. 'The furnishings with which the town house was rented are all back
in place. All is in order, your Grace, and the servants
that did not accompany Mrs Marlbrook have been paid
off. Several are asking if your Grace would be so kind
as to furnish them with a character.'

'Of course.' Dominic gave a nod. 'Who did Mrs
Marlbrook take with her?' He looked at Gemmell and
it occurred to him that that the old butler, and indeed all
of the staff of Curzon Street, had always behaved as if
Arabella was their employer rather than Dominic. Not
a single servant had told him of the presence of Archie
or Mrs Tatton in the house for all of those weeks. In a
matter of loyalty Gemmell would do what he thought to
be best for Arabella. He wondered what else Gemmell
might not have told him.

'A manservant and two maids.' As if to prove the
path Dominic's thoughts were taking, Gemmell added,
'Madam asked me to move to Amersham with her, but
unfortunately I had to decline. I have family commit-
ments in London. Thirteen grandchildren to be precise,'
he said with a note of pride. Gemmell handed him the
keys. 'The house is locked up secure, your Grace.'

Dominic took the keys. 'Thank you.'

Gemmell gave a nod. 'Will that be all, your Grace?'

'Not quite.' Dominic met the old man's eyes. 'Did
anything unusual happen between Mrs Marlbrook's

return from the opera on Friday night and my visit on Saturday?'

Gemmell's gaze shifted away and there was about him a slight uneasiness. He gripped the hat and gloves in his hands a little too tightly.

'Any messages delivered? An unusual letter, perhaps? A visitor?'

He saw Gemmell's mouth tighten slightly, and felt his own expression sharpen at the small betraying gesture. Yet still Gemmell hesitated as if, even now, he thought that to tell Dominic would be to compromise his loyalty to Arabella.

'Gemmell,' said Dominic quietly, 'I have only Mrs Marlbrook's welfare at heart.'

Gemmell looked at him and Dominic saw the old man wrestle internally with the dilemma before he gave a nod.

'There was something, your Grace. A visitor called on Saturday morning. A...' the slightest of hesitations '...gentleman by the name of Mr Smith.' Dominic could sense his discomfort and understood that Gemmell had been trying to protect Arabella.

'Go on,' he encouraged.

'They spoke in the library for some twenty minutes and then I heard the door open and I thought that the gentleman meant to leave, but when I arrived there, Master Archie had escaped Mrs Tatton and was playing outside the library. Mrs Marlbrook told me to take Archie to her mother and she went back into the library with Mr Smith.' Gemmell must have been aware of how bad it sounded, for he looked as if he wished the ground would open up and swallow him.

Dominic was thinking fast. 'Did Smith see Archie?'

'He did, your Grace.'

'And when he departed, did Mrs Marlbrook ring for anything?'

'Indeed, sir. Immediately that the gentleman was gone Mrs Marlbrook and Mrs Tatton started packing for a journey.'

There was a silence after the butler's words during which Dominic digested what Gemmell had just told him.

There was some measure of foul play at work; Dominic knew it.

Words that Arabella had once uttered played again in his mind: *I did what I had to for Archie's sake. I will always do what I have to, to protect him, no matter what you say.*

And Dominic knew that whoever Smith was and whatever hold he had over Arabella, this was somehow about Archie. The significance of the man seeing his son made Dominic's blood run cold.

'Mrs Marlbrook received Smith's visit without question?'

'No, your Grace. He gained admittance by means of a message.'

'What was the message?'

The hint of a blush crept into the butler's cheeks. 'It was the name, your Grace…of a lady.' Gemmell cleared his throat and shifted his feet and did not meet Dominic's gaze.

'And the lady's name?'

'Miss Noir.'

The words fell into the silence and the study seemed to echo with their significance. Dominic felt everything in him focus and define. Arabella had done none of this of her own accord. He felt sure that the man calling himself Smith had threatened her. What he did not understand was why she had not just come to him and told him.

He rose abruptly and walked away to look out of the window until he was sure the emotions were schooled from his face. He felt his resolve harden and he knew he would find who this man was and just what dangerous game he was playing.

'Smith—what did he look like?' Dominic glanced round at Gemmell.

'He had dark hair and was well dressed. He carried a cane and was well spoken.'

Just like a hundred other gentlemen in London, thought Dominic.

'Tall, short? What of his build?'

'I am afraid I did not notice.'

'There was nothing else to distinguish him?' Dominic needed every scrap of information Gemmell could give.

'Nothing, your Grace.'

'And what of his carriage?'

'He travelled on foot. I am sorry I cannot be of more help.' Gemmell looked worried.

'Thank you for telling me, Gemmell.' Dominic sought to reassure the old man.

When the door closed quietly behind Gemmell Dominic rang the bell for his horse to be readied.

If 'Smith' had known that Arabella was Miss Noir, there was only one place he could have learned that information.

Mrs Tatton was settling back into life in Amersham just as if she had never been away. Arabella was not.

Dominic had had the cottage refurbished but, aside from that, the little house and its long garden were as Arabella remembered, except that now there was no need to scrimp over coal or count the pennies for food. The generosity of the allowance that Dominic had settled upon her made the misery weigh all the more heavily in her heart.

Dominic. She tried to turn her mind away from consciously thinking of him. She had to survive for Archie's sake, but if she allowed herself to think of Dominic and of the extent of the hurt she had been forced to deal him, she was not sure she could make it through the rest of this day, never mind the next.

He would come to visit Archie, and Arabella dreaded to see him. But she longed for it too.

She toyed with the food on the dinner plate before her.

'Eliza Breckenbridge invited all three of us for dinner next week,' her mother was saying with an excited air. 'And Meg Brown could scarce believe what a fine boy Archie was.'

The country air had been good for her mother's lungs, Arabella thought as she glanced across the kitchen table at her. Mrs Tatton's appetite had improved and Arabella had not seen such a healthy colour in her cheeks in years.

'Are you even listening to me, Arabella?'

'Of course, Mama. You were telling me of your friends.'

'And not one bad word have they said, not one slight, though they must have guessed by now the truth of Archie's parentage.' Mrs Tatton added a little more butter to her potatoes before finishing them off. 'It is good to be back here, Arabella; I had not realised how much I missed the village.'

'I am glad that you are happy, Mama.' Arabella forced her lips to curve in the semblance of a smile. But it felt as dead and wooden as the rest of her.

'Dear Arabella.' Her mother sighed and reached across the table, taking Arabella's hand in her own. 'You are so brave in light of what that man did to you.'

'Please, Mama. Let us speak of it no more.' She was not proud of the lie she had told her mother, but she knew Mrs Tatton understood her too well to believe that Arabella had just changed her mind over the marriage. And she did not trust that if she had explained about Mr Smith and his threats her mother would not have gone straight to Dominic and told him of it. And she could not risk that. Not when Dominic's life and her son's welfare hung in the balance. Any thaw in relations between Mrs Tatton and Dominic had ceased with Arabella's lies. In her mother's book Dominic Furneaux was akin to the very devil himself.

'Abandoning you for a second time. I knew I should not have trusted him for a minute. Such untruths, and about his own father!'

'Mama,' she said firmly, 'I have asked you not to discuss these matters in front of Archie.'

'You are right, Arabella.' Mrs Tatton had the grace to blush. 'I beg your pardon.'

Arabella turned her attention to Archie, who was sitting listening with a worried expression upon his face. She reached across to Archie's plate and cut the chicken breast that lay there untouched into small tempting pieces. 'Now come along, slowcoach. You have not eaten your chicken. And you have not told me how school was today.' Archie was a new attendee at the village school.

He seemed unusually quiet this evening, and he had eaten little of his dinner.

'I am not hungry, Mama.' He kept his face downcast and did not meet her gaze.

'Archie?' Arabella looked more closely at her son's face, placing her fingers on his chin and angling his face in the light to peer at the faint beginnings of a bruise around his eye and a slight swelling upon his lip. 'Is there something that you wish to tell me?'

'No, Mama.'

'Have you been scrapping with the other boys?'

'The bigger boys said bad things about you, Mama, so I hit them and they hit me back.'

She felt her heart turn over. 'Well, I thank you for your defence of my good name, Archie.' Arabella stroked a hand to his hair. 'But they are just silly boys and they do not know what they are saying. Stay away from the big boys and play with the little boys who are more your age.'

'What is a bastard, Mama?'

Mrs Tatton gasped with the shock of it, inhaled the mouthful of food she was chewing and started to choke and cough. By the time Arabella had dealt with her mother and the coughing fit was over, Archie had run off to play in the garden, and there was no need to answer his question. But Arabella knew she could not avoid it for ever, even if Archie was not illegitimate in the strict sense of the word.

Arabella stood that night at the window of the little room she shared with her son. Archie's soft breathing sounded from the truckle bed behind her, regular and reassuring. She stared out at the darkening blue of the sky and the tiny pinpricks of stars that twinkled there. A crescent moon curved its sickle amongst the stars and she knew that soon the sky would wash with inky blackness. Her heart was heavy and aching as she stood there and watched the night progress. No matter how bad she had thought it when she believed Dominic to have left her all those years ago, nothing compared to how she felt now. A part of her had died. She wondered if she would ever feel alive again.

It did not matter what she did, she could not protect Archie from every hurt. She was all that stood between him and the world, and she thought of how she had deprived Archie of his father and Dominic of his son. And for the first time she wondered if she had done the right thing over Mr Smith's blackmail. Maybe she should have gone to Dominic and told him of the man and his threats. Maybe Dominic would have dealt with Smith...and maybe Dominic would have been found dead in an alleyway with a knife between his ribs.

She could not risk his life because of her own weakness. She stood and watched the night and she knew that, were the choice laid before her again, she would make the very same decision. The knowledge did not make her feel any better. She dropped a kiss to Archie's forehead and silently slipped from the room.

'I paid you most handsomely, madam, and now I find that you have been less than discreet.'

Within the drawing room of her House of Rainbow Pleasures, in which they both were standing, Mrs Silver paled beneath the cold raze of Dominic's gaze. 'My girls and I took your money, your Grace, and we kept our side of the bargain. We have spoken not one word of Miss Noir to anyone else. Of that I give you my most solemn word.'

'You cannot be so certain of your girls.'

'I am certain enough, your grace.' The dark coiffure of her hair made her skin look almost bloodless. 'I trust them.'

He was thinking fast. Smith had to have recognised Arabella somehow. There were possibilities about which he did not want to think, and yet he knew that he had to.

'Was there ever any trouble between Miss Noir and any of her...' he forced himself to say the words, '...gentlemen customers?'

Mrs Silver looked at him with a strange expression. 'There was no one else, your Grace.'

'Think back very carefully. It is important. Maybe there was someone she made mention of as—'

'No, your Grace,' Mrs Silver interrupted him. 'When I say that there was no one else, I mean exactly that. Arabella only came to me on the day of your visit. She had sold herself to no one before you. I thought you knew.'

Dominic was reeling. Arabella had not been a whore, until he had made her one. He felt the chill ripple right through him and with it the magnitude of the guilt of what he had done to her. No wonder Mrs Tatton had thought him a scoundrel. No wonder Arabella had balked at him making her his mistress. He had spent the last few weeks blaming it all on his father. But he knew now that he was as much to blame as the late duke.

It was even worse than he had thought. Mrs Tatton had been right; had he been a better man he would have helped Arabella without making his own selfish demands. He would have given her the money to leave the brothel and set her up without making her his mistress. And it should not have mattered if she was already a whore or not. But Dominic knew he was not a good man. He had wanted her…and he had taken her. And now he must live with the knowledge of the terrible thing he had done to her for the rest of his life.

And he had wondered why she had not told him of Archie!

Mrs Silver was staring at him and he knew he had to pull himself together. He composed his thoughts.

'How did she come to be here?'

'I saw her in a dressmaker's shop when she was seeking employment. Times are lean; there is not much work to be had. She looked tired and down on her luck.'

She had been desperate.

Dominic remembered what Mrs Tatton had said of her selling her shoes. She had sold herself to him to save their son. And he, like the bastard he was, had bought her.

'But, even so, she was a beautiful woman, and I knew she would be an asset to my rainbow. So I told her of the money she could earn and gave her my card. And she came here the very same evening as you.'

Hell! He clenched his teeth to stop the curse escaping. 'And the dressmaker in whose shop you found her?'

'Madame Boisseron.'

Dominic closed his eyes and bit down even harder. He wondered if he had done anything right by Arabella in all of this time.

'She has a shop in—'

But Dominic was already on his way out to find the woman he had employed to dress Arabella as his mistress.

In Amersham Archie was suffering from another sore stomach.

'This is the third time this week that the boy has been in this state, Arabella.' Mrs Tatton's face was creased with worry.

Archie was moaning and tossing and turning within the bed. A faint sheen of sweat was moist upon his brow and his face was pale. Arabella placed a hand over his forehead to feel how hot he was, and found the skin beneath to be surprisingly cool. She peered anxiously into his face.

'My tummy is sore, Mama,' Archie moaned.

'We have sent for the doctor to come and examine you.'

Archie began to cry. 'I do not want the doctor.'

'What nonsense is this?' said Arabella gently. 'He is a kind old man who will make you better.'

Archie said nothing, just closed his eyes.

There was a knocking at the front door of the cottage and Arabella hurried down to let in the elderly Dr Phipps whom she had known all her life, and indeed who had delivered her into this world as a baby. But when she opened the front door it was not Dr Phipps standing on the step.

'Mrs Marlbrook?' The man was as young as Arabella, and had striking blue eyes that held a tinge of green. His hair was muddy blond and he was smiling a very pleasant smile. 'I am Doctor Roxby, Doctor Phipps retired last year, I am afraid. You sent a message that your son is unwell.'

Arabella invited the young doctor inside. 'Archie has been complaining of a sore stomach, twice last week and three times this week. The pains are severe enough to keep him bedridden and they seem to be getting worse.'

Arabella and the doctor climbed the narrow spiral staircase of the cottage to reach the bedchambers upstairs.

Doctor Roxby ducked his head to enter the bedchamber that Arabella and Archie shared. 'Rest assured, ma'am, I will do everything that I can for him.'

The doctor examined Archie carefully while Arabella and her mother looked on. His manner was kind and reassuring. And while he worked he spoke to Archie telling the boy what he was doing and asking Archie questions. Did it hurt when he pressed here? Was this worse? Or better?

'Is he using the chamber pot regularly, Mrs Marlbrook?'

'He is.'

'And eating as normal?'

'His appetite has been impaired of late.'

'Nothing that we cannot sort, young man,' said the doctor, smiling down at Archie.

Arabella and her mother went downstairs with the doctor, leaving Archie to rest.

'I can find nothing wrong with him, ma'am. Perhaps it is more a problem of his sensibilities. Archie tells me that he has recently started at the village school. Might there have been any associated problems?'

Arabella saw her mother throw her a meaningful

look, and thought of the fight that Archie had got into during his first week there.

'I will look into it, Doctor,' she said, not wishing to reveal the details of the affair.

Mrs Tatton, who had been standing quietly listening to all that the doctor had to say, stepped forwards. 'My daughter has been a widow these years past, Doctor, and the boy suffers for the lack of a man's influence.' She looked pointedly at Arabella as if to remind her that it was all Dominic's fault.

Arabella looked away, feeling the sting of guilt at blaming Dominic for a crime of which he was innocent.

'I will call again in a few days to check upon Archie.' Doctor Roxby accepted his payment and took his leave of them.

As soon as the door shut Arabella leaned her back upon it.

'Well, I have never heard of such a thing in all my life,' said Mrs Tatton.

'Now that he has said it, I begin to see the signs,' said Arabella. 'Archie is better on the days he does not have to go to school. After only one day back there he is ill again. He speaks so very little of it. And never makes mention of the other boys.' She felt quite sick at the thought that the bullying had continued. 'Why did he not tell me, Mama?'

'Maybe he did not wish to cause you worry or perhaps he has been threatened into silence by the bullies.'

How could she not have realised?

'We can guess the cause of the bullying. You heard what he asked at the dinner table the other week.' Her mother lowered her voice. '*Bastard,* indeed! You see what *he* has done to the boy, Arabella? Why could he not have just married you, and been done with it? And then none of this would have happened. But, no, he decides that you are not good enough for him— again—and now we are come to this, with your son lying upstairs afraid to go to school for fear of what the other boys are saying about his parentage.' Mrs Tatton sat down heavily and placed her trembling hands upon the parlour table.

'There is no good to be had going down that route, Mama. Let us just deal with this the best we can. Please be kind enough to check upon Archie while I visit the schoolhouse.' And Arabella left before she could no longer stopper her tongue and the terribleness of the truth burst out, revealing to her mother the whole mess of it.

Dominic's visit to Madame Boisseron's shop had convinced him of her innocence. The woman was honest and he believed her assertion that, such was the delicacy and secrets involved in the affairs of her clientele, for her to talk of any of her customers would be to lose her business.

That evening he was sitting alone in his study trying to think of how on earth he was going to trace the man calling himself Smith, when Bentley showed Hunter in.

Hunter sat down in the wing chair on the other side of the desk from Dominic.

Dominic poured his friend a large brandy using the crystal-cut decanter and glasses on the silver tray by the window.

'Not having one yourself?' Hunter took the glass with thanks and lounged back in his armchair.

Dominic shook his head.

'Misbourne has been asking around about you at White's.'

'Just what I want to hear,' said Dominic. 'Did you come over to tell me that?'

'No. I came to see how you are.' Dominic could feel Hunter's watchful gaze.

'I take it you know?' Dominic could tell from the compassion on his friend's face that he did.

'All of London knows. It makes no sense, Dominic. Arabella has even more reasons than you to want this marriage. Why would she break the betrothal?'

'I believe she was acting under duress. Someone got to her, Sebastian. Someone who knew that she was Miss Noir.'

Hunter's face sharpened. He sat up straighter in his chair. 'I think there is something you should hear, concerning Miss Noir, Dominic. I paid another little visit to Mrs Silver's house the other night, to see Tilly, Miss Rose. In the course of things she mentioned that there have been quite a few enquiries about Miss Noir.' Hunter met Dominic's gaze.

'It is not unexpected. They were well paid to stay quiet. And Mrs Silver is adamant they have not talked.'

'And I think she is correct for Tilly would not speak of Miss Noir to me. But she did let slip that there was one gentleman who offered serious gelt—I mean hundreds of pounds—for the smallest scrap of information concerning Miss Noir. Tilly thinks that one of the footmen may have been tempted to break his silence. Apparently the servant has recently disappeared. And there were whispers that he was experiencing financial difficulties of a nature similar to my own.'

'Gambling debts?'

Hunter gave a nod.

'And what of the gentleman asking the questions?'

'A Mr Smith, apparently, although I doubt he would have been fool enough to use his real name.' Hunter gave a grim smile, which soon faded as his eyes met Dominic's.

Dominic's gaze narrowed. 'Smith?'

'Indeed. I see it has some significance for you.'

'Did the girl tell you anything else other than his name?'

Hunter smiled again. 'Oh, yes. Very observant is Tilly. She described him right down to his "dark dangerous eyes", and his walking cane with a "monstrous silver wolf's head" as its handle. She noticed it because it had tiny emerald chips for eyes.'

A wolf's head on a walking cane? There was something familiar about that. Dominic had seen such an item before, but he could not remember where. 'Cannot be too many of those around.'

'No,' said Hunter with a meaningful smile. 'I see your mind follows the same path as mine. I suppose now you will be off hunting down this Smith character tonight rather than hitting the town with young Northcote and Bullford and a few of the others?'

The two men exchanged a look.

'Damned shame. Thought you might have changed our present run of bad luck on the tables.'

'Another night, my friend,' Dominic said and gave Hunter a light thump on the shoulder. 'After I have found Smith.'

Chapter Eighteen

Dominic was becoming increasingly frustrated with the slow progress of the investigation. It had been half an hour since the ex-Bow Street runner had left his study in Arlesford House and Dominic was musing over the scraps of information the man had delivered. Despite five days of intense questioning, tracking and bribing, it had proved impossible to find the silversmith who had crafted the unusual head of the walking cane. And all enquiries to discover its owner had so far met with a wall of silence.

Dominic's other lines of enquiries had been more fruitful. He knew that Smith had attempted to buy information concerning Arabella in her guise as both Miss Noir and Mrs Marlbrook from a variety of sources, including the servants both in his and Arabella's households. He knew that enquiries had been made concerning who was paying the rent on the town house in Curzon Street, who had ordered and paid for the furnishings and who had arranged for and paid the servants.

The missing manservant from Mrs Silver's had been found in a gaming house in Brighton, frittering away the last of his enormous bribe on the tables, with not a one of his debts cleared, and a very ugly posse of creditors at the door. Five hundred pounds was an extraordinary sum to have been paid for a description and confirmation of the fact that the Duke of Arlesford had bedded Miss Noir on her first night in the place and bought her the next evening from Mrs Silver. And although Dominic did not yet know the identity of Smith, he did know that someone very rich had gone to a lot of trouble to find Arabella.

The obvious next step was to go up to Amersham and speak to Arabella, but there was a risk that if he did she would tell him nothing, Smith would get word of it and then would discover her whereabouts. He needed to find this Smith first. And he wondered again why the hell Arabella had not come to him for help. No matter the threats Smith had made about revealing her identity, Dominic knew he could have protected her. He massaged the tightness from his temple and poured himself a brandy.

There came the sound of the front door being opened and then quietly closed again. Dominic barely noticed it. What he did notice was the light running footsteps that pattered quietly across the marble flags of his hallway. He felt the warning whisper against the back of his neck and goosepimple his skin. Dominic stopped lounging, sat upright and set his glass down on the desk. His hand was slipping within his desk drawer just as the door burst open and a small dark cloaked figure rushed into his study to stand before him.

She gave a small scream when she saw him sitting behind the desk. 'They said that you would not be—' The woman bit off what she had been about to say. 'That is, I—I….' She twisted her small black gloved hands tight together.

Dominic's fingers relaxed around the handle of his pistol for he recognised the voice and he knew who it was standing there before him. 'What are you doing sneaking into my study, Lady Marianne?' He raised one eyebrow and looked at her with his sternest face.

'Then you know that it is me,' she said softly and slipped the hood back to reveal her fair hair scraped back in a severe chignon. Lady Marianne Winslow stood there, her cheeks flushed with embarrassment, her eyes huge and frightened. She clutched the cloak to her as if he were a beast about to ravish her.

'You have not answered my question,' he said without the flicker of a smile.

Lady Marianne's face drained of all colour. She began to edge towards the door. 'I fear there has been a dreadful mistake,' she said and he could hear the slight tremor that shook her voice. 'I should not be here.'

'No, Lady Marianne. You should not.' He rose and in one swift motion was across the floor to block her exit.

Lady Marianne gave a gasp and stopped where she was. 'Please, your Grace. Let me leave unaccosted.'

'You may leave once you have told me what you are doing here.' His words were so cold and hard that she actually shivered.

She nodded her submission. 'I was told that you

would not be here, that I was to steal in unnoticed and
leave a letter upon your desk. After which I must leave
again as quietly as I had entered.' She slipped a hand
into her pocket and held out a neatly folded letter. He
could see the paper shaking between her fingers.

He took it from her, noting that the front was
addressed to his name alone. 'Who sent you?' he asked
as he broke the sealing wax.

Lady Marianne gave no answer.

He began opening up the letter. 'Spit it out, Lady
Marianne, or rest assured I will keep you here until you
do.'

The girl shook her head. 'I will not tell you,' she
whispered.

He opened the last fold of the letter. And he knew
then who had sent her and what this was about. For the
paper was blank.

He moved swiftly to the bell and rang it. His butler
appeared almost immediately.

'Escort this young lady out via the back door, Bentley.'

Bentley was experienced enough not to reveal anything of his surprise at finding a young woman alone in
his master's study. 'Shall I summon a hackney carriage
for the lady, your Grace?'

'No.'

Bentley glanced up at Dominic, the question clear
in his eyes before his lowered them again.

'I am sure that she has her papa awaiting outside this
house even as we speak,' he said to the butler, and then
to Lady Marianne, 'Am I not right?'

Even if she spoke not one word, she was betrayed by
the blush that stained her cheeks.

'Get her out of here as quickly as you can, Bentley,' he commanded, knowing that he was right about what had been planned for this night.

But it was too late.

Already he could hear the hammering of fists upon the front door and heard the men enter the house without the decency of waiting for an invitation.

'I will fetch Hillard and Dowd immediately, your Grace.' As Bentley opened the study door two men rushed in.

'There is no need, Bentley. I will deal with this. Leave us.'

The butler looked unconvinced, but he left all the same just as he had been told.

Dominic moved back to resume his seat.

'Good evening, gentlemen. I have been expecting you,' said Dominic as he surveyed the Earl of Misbourne and Viscount Linwood who were standing between him and Lady Marianne. 'What a nice family reunion.'

'Papa! Francis!' She cried and hurried to her father and brother. 'Thank goodness you are here. It has all gone horribly wrong!'

'No, Lady Marianne, I suspect it has gone entirely according to plan,' said Dominic grimly. He gestured to the two chairs on the other side of his desk. 'Do take a seat, gentlemen.'

Misbourne ignored him and stayed where he was. He puffed out his chest. 'Look here, you scoundrel, Arlesford. What do you think you are doing with my daughter? You have abducted her with the intention of seducing her.'

'What are you saying, Papa? You sent me here to deliver—'

'Silence, Marianne! Do not dare to utter another word, you foolish chit!' roared the earl.

The girl's face paled and she rapidly closed her mouth and backed away to stand by the door.

'Well, Arlesford?' demanded the earl.

'Well?' echoed Dominic.

'You must know that she is ruined just by being here—a gently bred innocent alone in the house of one of London's most scandalous rakes.'

'If it becomes known that she is here, then, yes, I agree, your daughter's reputation would not remain unscathed.'

'Then you will do the gentlemanly thing and save both her honour and your own by offering for her hand?' Misbourne's eyes glittered as he said the words. He could barely keep the smile from his face.

'Indeed not, sir. As you have already pointed out, I am known as a rake. Why should I care that Lady Marianne is ruined? She is *your* daughter.'

'Good Gad! Where is your sense of honour, sir?'

'In the same place as yours, Misbourne. I care not if you strip her naked and sit her upon my doorstep for all the world to see.' From the corner of his eye he saw Lady Marianne clutch a hand to her mouth and he felt sorry that she had to witness this. 'You may publish the story in every one of your newspapers and still I tell you most solemnly, sir, I will not marry her.'

Misbourne's face turned an unhealthy shade of puce. And then paled to an ashen shade as he realised his plan had failed. 'You have reneged on a contract that was agreed by your father. This betrothal has been in place since before my daughter was in her cradle.'

'As I told you before, Misbourne, I will not be bound by a contract that never existed. I thought that we could maintain some degree of civility between us because of our political association.'

'You led me to believe that you would consider taking her as your wife.'

'If I did, then I am sorry, sir, for it was never my intention.'

'You have made us a laughing stock before all of London, you damnable cur!' the earl growled. 'I should call you out!'

'I would be only too happy to oblige you, sir,' said Dominic coldly.

'No, Papa!' he heard Lady Marianne cry in the background.

'A moment, sir.' Viscount Linwood laid his hand upon his father's shoulder. 'We have not concluded our negotiation with his Grace.'

'On the contrary,' said Dominic, 'I consider the matter closed.'

'But we have not yet touched on Mrs Marlbrook, or should I call her Miss Noir? And then there is the consideration of the boy. I believe his name is Archie. What a startling resemblance he does bear his papa.' Linwood smiled a dark dangerous smile, and Dominic's gaze dropped to see the tiny glint of emeralds and the shape of a wolf's head in the handle of the walking cane beneath Linwood's palm.

Dominic's stomach turned over. He felt his blood turn to ice. 'It was you,' he said, hardly able to believe it. Smith. And in that moment all the answers slipped into place. Linwood part-owned his father's newspapers. He had journalistic connections. He had money in plenty. And an interest in seeing that Dominic did not marry Arabella.

'Think of what it would do to the boy were the truth of his mama and his most famous papa to be published throughout the capital. The duke, his doxy and their bastard—what a headline that would make!'

Dominic reacted first and thought later. His fist smashed hard against Linwood's jaw. It happened so fast the viscount did not see it coming and was left staggering and clutching a hand to his bleeding lip.

'That is what you used to threaten Arabella when you went to Curzon Street, is it not?' Dominic grabbed at Linwood's lapels and backed him against the wall.

'That and the threat of violence against your person if she told you. Did you think that I would just let you get away with how you have treated my sister?' snarled Linwood. 'The snub you have dealt us? You arrogant villain, Arlesford! Marry Marianne or I swear to you I will print every damn word of it.'

Dominic looked Linwood straight in the eye and watched the viscount pale. He allowed the deadly intent to show for the briefest of moments before masking it once more. And when he looked again at Linwood he was more under control and ready to play the biggest game of bluff of his life.

'Sit down, gentlemen. Let us discuss the matter.' He gestured once more to the chairs by his desk. 'I am sure you will forgive my outburst…given the provocation. The urge to protect one's blood is strong. I think we, all of us in this study, understand that. You have seen what young Archie's mother was prepared to sacrifice.

Can you expect his father to be any less protective?' He resumed his seat behind his desk.

Both Linwood and Misbourne still looked wary, but Dominic could see that they thought victory was at hand. This time they sat down as they were bid.

'A father has a duty to his son…and his daughter,' said Misbourne. 'By marrying my daughter you would be protecting your son. Only think if the scandalous story were to come out, what it would do to the child.'

'I do, sir, and thus I will do all in my power to avoid its publication.'

Misbourne nodded and could not quite hide the triumph in his smile. 'I am glad you begin to see sense, Arlesford.'

'Indeed.' Dominic returned the smile, but it was a smile that would have frozen the Thames. 'However, it does occur to me that the story Lord Linwood outlined is perhaps not the best one to fit the facts.'

'How so, sir?' Linwood's eyes narrowed slightly.

Dominic smiled again. 'Let us review the facts: firstly, there is the blonde masked courtesan, Miss Noir, whom, in contrast to my previous custom, I have gone to great lengths to keep secret. Secondly, there is the Earl of Misbourne's desperate insistence that I marry his daughter, his *blonde* daughter. And finally, there is the small matter of his daughter's presence here, at Arlesford House, the home of a dissolute bachelor, late at night.'

'What are you saying, Arlesford?' Misbourne demanded.

'Why, that the woman behind the mask of Miss Noir is none other than Lady Marianne Winslow, your daughter, sir.'

'Damnable lies, sir!' The words exploded from Misbourne as he jumped to his feet.

'So you say, but what would the *ton* make of it, I wonder?'

Linwood got to his feet too, staring daggers across the desk at Dominic. 'We have a witness to place Arabella Marlbrook as Miss Noir in Mrs Silver's brothel.'

'Do you? Have you tried to contact him lately?' Dominic's gaze was glacial and deadly. He rose and stood taller than the other two men. 'It seems you did not pay him quite enough for his creditors to be completely forgiving. I fear for his health. And as for the rest of Mrs Silver's household, I am sure that they will back my account of events.'

'People will see that you paid for their lies,' said Misbourne.

'People already know why a notorious rake would pay Mrs Silver and her girls. But why would an upstanding gentleman like Viscount Linwood be paying Mrs Silver, other than for her silence over his setting up his own sister as a doxy to trap a duke.'

Misbourne shook his head. 'That is too far-fetched for anyone to believe.'

'On the contrary, sir, people will see it as a bold and ambitious plot that will only enhance your already formidable reputation. Your daughter's reputation, I fear, will not fare so well.' Dominic smiled a cold hard smile. 'No, Misbourne, it is you who will be seen as the liar. And the blackmail of a respectable widow as a final act of desperation on your part.'

'Damn you, Arlesford!' Linwood's knuckles gripped white against the wolf's head handle of his cane.

Dominic glanced across at a white-faced Lady Marianne and felt the sting of his conscience. 'Thank you, gentlemen, I see that this business is now concluded. You may use the back door if you care to save the girl from further scrutiny.'

He watched while Bentley and two footmen escorted his unwanted guests away. The door closed behind them and Dominic relaxed back down into his chair. He would weather the storm if he had to, to protect Arabella and his son, but he doubted it would come to that; instinct told him that Misbourne and Linwood now realised they had overplayed their hand.

Dominic stared at the glass of brandy on the desk before him, the tawny amber of the liquid burnished red by the warm glow from the fire. He knew now why Arabella had refused to marry him. He knew now why she had lied and said that she did not love him. And he knew why she had not come to him and told him of Smith's threats. She had sacrificed herself to save him and their child.

He lifted the glass, and took a sip of the brandy, breathing his relief as the heat and strength of the alcohol burned his throat. He resisted the urge to run out to the stables, climb upon his horse and gallop off in the direction of Amersham. There were matters to be dealt with before he left London, matters that he would attend to at first light. He schooled his impatience and let his mind run to thoughts of Arabella.

'Archie is in fine health this morning, Mrs Marlbrook,' Doctor Roxby smiled.

Arabella was just about to speak when her mother rushed in there before her.

'Indeed, Doctor,' agreed Mrs Tatton. 'Your visits have made all the difference to my grandson's health.'

The doctor glanced away, slightly embarrassed. 'I am sure the improvement is down to Mrs Marlbrook's intervention at the school.'

'Miss Wallace is keeping a close eye on Archie and the boys who were taunting him.'

'Archie certainly seems to have taken a shine to you, Doctor,' said Mrs Tatton.

'And I, to him. He is a pleasant child, ma'am,' said Doctor Roxby politely. 'And a credit to his mother.'

'Would you care to stay for dinner, Doctor?' Arabella heard her mother ask and could have cringed in disbelief.

Doctor Roxby's eyes met Arabella's and she saw in their clear blue-green gaze both question and interest. She looked away, not wishing to encourage him.

'Thank you for your most kind offer, Mrs Tatton, but I am afraid I must decline upon this occasion. I have other patients to call upon and the hour grows late.'

'Perhaps another day, Doctor.' Mrs Tatton smiled.

'Indeed,' said Doctor Roxby and he smiled as his gaze once more went to Arabella. He gave a bow and, lifting up his black leather bag, he left.

Arabella waited until she heard the creak of the garden gate before she rounded upon her mother. 'Mama, what on earth did you think you were doing inviting him to stay for dinner?'

'It was a simple enough offer, Arabella,' her mother protested.

'I do not wish to give him the wrong impression.'

'Nonsense, Arabella,' said her mother brusquely. 'He is a respectable gentleman. I can see in his eyes that he is kind, and look how well he takes to Archie, and Archie to him.'

'He is only doing his job. Do not read more into it than there is.'

'Oh, stuff, Arabella. I am not yet in my dotage. I see the way he looks at you, and why not? You are still a young and comely woman. As a doctor within our community, young, handsome, and not yet married, he must be in want of a wife.'

'Mama, it is just a matter of time before he hears the village gossip about…' She could not bring herself to say Dominic's name. The pain was still too intense. 'About Archie's parentage. Indeed, I am surprised he has not heard already.' She knew she sounded bitter, but she could not help it. She just felt so miserable.

'You imagine the gossip to be something it is not,' chided her mother. 'And have I not already told you the truth? Of course there are whispers, but the villagers are our own people, and it was not as if you were left unwed with a child. They know you married Mr Marlbrook, and would have accepted you and Archie just the same. And, yes, it is unfortunate that the boy is the very image of…' her mother's voice hardened as it always did when she spoke of Dominic '…*that man,* but it was the old duke who forced us from this village, and nothing else.'

'Perhaps you are right, and indeed I pray that you are, for I want more than anything for Archie to be happy here.'

'And he will be.' Her mother patted her hand. 'The children will soon tire of their taunting.'

'I hope so,' said Arabella.

Her mother looked into her face. 'I can see that

you are unhappy and I do not blame you after all that you have been through with that villain Arlesford. But you must move on, Arabella, both for your own sake and for Archie's. The boy needs a father and you, a husband.'

'No, Mama,' Arabella objected. 'We are fine as we are. We do not need another man.' She knew her mother meant well, but Mrs Tatton did not know the truth. She did not know the terrible lies that Arabella had told. She did not know the guilt and the misery that weighed heavy on her heart.

'Will you hide yourself away here in this cottage for the rest of your life because he broke your heart? That is not you, Arabella. You have pride. You have spirit. You are a strong woman. A woman not unlike myself when I was younger.'

Her mother smiled at her, but in the smile was sadness and her eyes were filled with worry. Arabella felt all the worse, because it was her own fault. One lie upon another, and too many of those that she loved were suffering because of it.

'You must do what is best for Archie,' said Mrs Tatton.

'I always have,' said Arabella, 'and I always will.' No matter how hard that would be. No matter what it cost them all.

'And I am glad of it. I know you do not believe me when I tell you there will come a time, not so very far in the future, when the affection of a good and kind gentleman will heal your heart, Arabella, and make you forget all about Dominic Furneaux.'

No one and nothing would ever make her forget Dominic. She would never stop loving him. But she knew it would be a mistake to say this now to her mother. She did not want to talk any more about such a tender subject, especially one about which she could not tell her mother the truth. So she just smiled and gave her mother's hand a gentle pat.

'I know you have ever had my best interests at heart, Mama, and I thank you for it, but matters are still too raw. It needs to be just you, me and Archie for now.' And then she rose from the table and went to check on her son.

Dominic dealt with matters as speedily as he could the next morning. He visited the Archbishop of Canterbury, Moffat, his man of business, and finally Hunter, who, despite the afternoon hour, was only just up following an 'all nighter' at the gaming tables, but who nevertheless rallied to Dominic's request.

'And so Smith was really Linwood all along,' said Hunter as he stood there in his bedchamber with his chin up, letting his valet tie his cravat in some wonderful new knot. 'Damn the man. You should have run the villain through.'

'No doubt,' replied Dominic drily. Around them was a flurry of activity, as servants hurriedly took Hunter's clothes from their drawers and wardrobe and packed them in a travelling bag.

'Does Arabella know you are coming?'

'No. A letter would not arrive significantly before we do, and besides, I think what has to be said would be better in person.'

'I'll say,' said Hunter with a grin. He glanced at the coat that was being folded into his bag and spoke to

his manservant. 'No, no, Telfer, my best one, man, the
black superfine from Weston.'

In a matter of fifteen minutes Hunter was ready in
his riding coat and breeches, his fully packed travelling
bag strapped behind his saddle, and the two men geeing
their mounts out on to the Aylesbury road.

Dominic waited until they had left London behind
and were trotting along in the countryside before he
spoke again.

'There is one other thing that I ought to tell you
before we reach Amersham, Hunter.'

'What is that?' Hunter glanced across at him.

The small matter of his son. And Dominic told his
friend all about Archie.

'Hell, Dominic, I had no idea. So Arabella married
Marlbrook because she was—' He stopped himself just
in time.

Dominic raised an eyebrow and drew him a droll
look.

Silence, and then Hunter asked, 'Did Linwood know
of the boy?'

'Most definitely.'

'Ah, I think I understand your feelings towards Linwood. Bad enough threatening your woman, but your
son too?'

Dominic's eyes darkened at the memory. Linwood
was lucky to have walked out of his house alive.

'Anything else you have not told me?' Hunter asked
with a grin.

'Nothing you need know,' said Dominic, and smiled.
'Now, you'd better get that horse moving if we want to
reach Amersham before midnight.'

Hunter laughed and kicked his horse to a canter. And Dominic thought of Arabella in the little Tatton cottage in Amersham, and he raced his mount past Hunter.

It was late by the time they reached Amersham. A waxing moon near to fullness hung high in the dark night sky and helped guide their way. The glow of light from the edges of windows shone in some of the cottages down in the village, but all was silent, all was still. Dominic glanced in the direction of the Tatton cottage, and although he was tired, travel stained and saddle sore he was restless to spur his horse down there and knock upon Arabella's door. Was she awake? Was she thinking of him as he thought of her?

'Do not even think it,' warned Hunter's quiet voice by his side. 'You want her to see you in your best light, Dominic, not when you are in need of a bed, a bath, a shave and some fresh clothes. Besides, I need a drink, very, very badly. I hope you have got some of that rather fine brandy of yours up here.'

Hunter was right. Dominic wanted everything to be readied and perfect when he saw Arabella again. He wanted to take her in his arms and tell her that everything was going to be all right. 'Come on then, five minutes to the Hall. And then you may have your brandy.' With one last longing glance towards the Tatton cottage he turned and spurred his horse along the road towards Shardeloes Hall.

At half past six the following evening Arabella bathed Archie. Once he had been dressed in his nightclothes with his hair dried by the fire and his supper of honeyed toast and warm milk long since eaten, she settled him in his little truckle bed. Then she drew the curtains across the small bedchamber window to block out the light, which was still bright. With the curtains closed the room felt dim and safe. Archie yawned as he snuggled down beneath the covers.

She bent to give him his goodnight kiss. 'Sleep tight, little lamb,' she said as usual, determined not to let her son see how miserable she felt.

'Mama,' he said quietly, 'I miss Dominic.'

'I miss him too, Archie.' She stroked his hair and kept her voice light.

'Will he come to visit us soon?'

'I do not know.' She forced the smile to her face. 'No more questions, my darling. You must go to sleep like a good boy, for it is Sunday tomorrow and we have church.'

'Not church, Mama,' he grumbled, but snuggled down and closed his eyes just the same.

Arabella walked down the stairs to the parlour, where her mother was sitting waiting for her.

'How is he?'

'Fine, because there is no school. I only hope he is well enough come Monday.' Arabella pinched the bridge of her nose and curbed the rest of her worries for Archie and his future.

'That Dominic Furneaux has much to answer for.'

Arabella did not feel strong enough to withstand another argument with her mother over Dominic. Her confidence felt shaken and her normal calm disposition ruffled. She was tense and anxious. 'Mama, please let us speak no more of Dominic.'

'No more? We have not spoken of him at all for

the sake of the boy. And I have held my tongue long enough.'

Arabella gave a sigh and sat down in the armchair by the window. She lifted her needlework. 'Mama, there is nothing to be gained by this.'

'He abandoned you, not once but twice, Arabella, and in the worst possible of ways. Publicly announcing a betrothal only to break it off again. Of all the cruel most humiliating ways that he might—'

'Mama!' Arabella said quickly. It had been cruel. It had been humiliating. But for Dominic, not for her. 'Remember that it is Dominic who gifted us this cottage and Dominic who is paying us an allowance that we may live a comfortable existence.'

'It is only right that a man should pay for his own child, Arabella. Especially a man who is now as rich and powerful as Dominic. Archie is his son; heaven knows he has done precious little else for the boy. Casting him off without a care—it breaks my heart to see it. The boy should be heir to a dukedom, not suffering the taunts of illegitimacy or begging for the crumbs Dominic deigns to spare him!'

Arabella felt the blood drain from her face. 'Cease this talk at once, Mama! I will not hear you say it.' *If only Mama knew the truth. I am guilty of all of these accusations, not Dominic.*

'I cannot, Arabella, for it needs to be said,' cried her mother. 'The spite of that man! The cruel arrogance! How you can still have a care for such a scoundrel defies logic.' Mrs Tatton was leaning forwards in her chair in full rant. 'I should have gone round to Arlesford House and given that man a piece of my mind before we left London. I should have told him exactly what I thought of him. That snake in the grass, that conniving, ill-mannered—'

Something snapped within Arabella. She could not hear her mother vilify Dominic for one minute more, blaming him for what she had done. The words blurted from her mouth,

'It was not Dominic who broke the betrothal, Mama, it was me. I did it, not Dominic.'

Silence followed her words. A great roaring loud silence.

Mrs Tatton gaped at Arabella in confusion and shock. She gave a strange little disbelieving laugh and then smiled. 'Come now, Arabella—'

'It is the truth. I told him that I did not love him and was leaving him and still he gave me this cottage and an allowance.'

The smile slipped from her mother's face. She looked as if she could not fully comprehend what Arabella was saying. 'But why would you do such a thing, Arabella? Why, when I know that you love him?'

'I do love him.' It was the first time she had admitted it aloud.

'Then why?' All vestige of colour had drained from Mrs Tatton's face. 'Why would you ruin it for yourself and for Archie?'

Arabella sat very still upon the chair; her hands lay slack. The floodgates had been opened, and there was no way to close them again. So she told her mother about Mr Smith and his threats. She told her everything, even of Miss Noir and Mrs Silver's.

'Oh, Arabella,' he mother whispered as she came to stand by her side. 'Why did you not tell me?'

'I could not risk that you would go to Dominic. Smith

will send his ruffians after him if you reveal any of
this. Dominic's life hangs in the balance. And so too
does Archie's, for Smith will publish the story and there
will be no going back from that. I have hurt them both,
terribly, but it was only to protect them from Smith.
Dominic must never know. You do understand that, do
you not?'

Her mother nodded.

'And as for Mrs Silver's, well…' Arabella fidgeted
with her fingers and could not look up to meet her
mother's gaze. 'I knew what the knowledge would do
to you, and I could not bear to burden you with such
shame.'

'I already knew, Arabella.'

Arabella glanced up at her mother. 'But how could
you know?'

'Dominic told me where he had found you, that day
he came to Curzon Street and you had taken Archie to
the park.' There were tears rolling down Mrs Tatton's
cheeks. 'You should have told me, Arabella. I would
never be ashamed of you when all you have done has
been to save those you love. You are the best of mothers
to Archie. And you are the best of daughters to me.'

Arabella got to her feet and put her arms around her
mother's shoulders, holding her and laying her cheek
upon the top of her mother's head.

'Thank you, Mama, and bless you. Bless you for all
that you have suffered because of me.'

Her mother looked drained and worried and Arabella
felt more guilty than ever.

Mrs Tatton's health was too fragile. Arabella knew
she should not have weakened and burdened her mother
with the truth. It seemed to Arabella that however hard

she tried, no matter what she did, she hurt the people she loved the most.

Dominic's voice echoed in her head. *I love you, Arabella.*

And she winced. The weight of the pain and the guilt was growing heavier with each passing day. And she wondered when Dominic would come, and she wondered how she was going to bear that meeting when eventually it happened. She felt as if she were suffocating from the weight of worry.

'Mama, I do not think that I will sleep feeling the way I do. Would you like to go for a walk along the woodland path, to help clear our heads a little?'

'I am tired, and would prefer to sit by the fire. But you go, Arabella.' Her mother took Arabella's hand in her own. 'Do not wander too far and be back before it is dark.'

'Yes, Mama.' Arabella dropped a kiss on her mother's head.

From outside she could hear the blackbirds calling and the soft rustle of leaves in the evening breeze.

Wrapping her shawl around her shoulders, Arabella slipped from the cottage out into the fresh air. She walked to straighten the thoughts in her head and to revive her resolve.

'What do you mean you are going out alone?' Hunter grumbled. 'We have not stopped all day. And we are supposed to be attending to other matters tonight, such as drinking and making merry and celebrating the joys of the bachelor life in all the most carnal of ways.'

Dominic threw his friend a speaking look.

'You are a changed man since you became reacquainted with Arabella, Dominic. A changed man, indeed.' Hunter shook his head in a sorrowful way.

'So you keep telling me. We will see how changed you are when you meet the woman you wish to marry.'

Hunter gave a disgusted snort. 'I assure you I have no plans in that direction for a good many years. And if I must eventually succumb to such a fate there will be no changing involved.'

'We shall see,' said Dominic.

'Indeed, you shall,' sniffed Hunter and helped himself to another brandy. 'All is ready for tomorrow?'

'Almost,' said Dominic and he thought again of Arabella.

'I shall be glad of the return to London. I do not know how you can stand it out here in the sticks. I bet they do not even know how to play faro or macao.'

Dominic laughed. 'I am sure they do not. Indeed, I doubt there is such an inveterate gambler as yourself within the whole village. You will have to wait for your return to London for that.'

Hunter sighed and sipped his brandy. 'Dear, dear London town, how I miss her sweet allures.'

Dominic laughed again and, gathering up his hat, gloves and riding crop, departed the Hall.

Chapter Nineteen

The evening sunlight filtered through the canopy of leaves and branches to spill in small pools and spots upon the woodland floor. There were still some patches of pale yellow primroses, although the heads of the bluebells had gone over. In their place were the tiny blue flowers of forget-me-not, bright splashes of colour amidst the earthy browns and greens of the soil and grass. A dove was cooing softly, sounding above the song of the smaller birds. Arabella walked on, small dry twigs crunching beneath her boots.

She followed the path as it curved its way around some mighty ancient oaks and then she hesitated, for there, coming closer and closer, was the shadowed figure of a horseman cantering along the pathway towards her. And there was something terribly familiar about the rider. As the seconds passed and as he came closer she recognised the dark clad man.

She stared and her heart seemed to cease beating and her lungs to cease breathing.

He was dressed impeccably in a dark tailcoat and buff-coloured riding breeches, with black highly polished top boots. His hat, gloves and riding crop were held together in one hand. The dappled sunshine touched red highlights to his hair and the breeze had stirred it to a sensual disarray.

'Dominic?' she whispered. *Was it really him? Or just a product of her own wishful mind?*

'Arabella.' His face had never looked more filled with love. There was no trace of the anger or hurt she remembered from their last meeting; he just looked glad and relieved to see her. He slipped down from his horse and came towards her, and there could be no mistake.

'Oh, Dominic!' She could not prevent herself from running into his open arms. She buried her face against his chest and he held her tight. 'Dominic.'

She heard the murmur of his voice and felt his kisses against her hair and the stroke of his hands against her back. And then she remembered. Smith. His threats. And she was suddenly desperately afraid of what she might have betrayed.

'Forgive my reaction. I was a little overcome by the shock of seeing you here.' Her voice, for all she was trying to sound sober and unaffected did not sound convincing even to herself. She made to pull back, to disengage herself from him, but Dominic's arms tightened around her so there was no escape. She dared not look at him, not trusting herself to play the role that was required to protect him.

'You have come to visit Archie.' Her throat was so tight the words sounded stilted, awkward, teetering too close to breaking down.

'I have come for *you,* Arabella.'

There was only the whisper of the wind through the green canopy of the leaves above.

Slowly, unable to fight against it any more, she raised her gaze to his. His eyes were a deep dark velvet. 'You cannot. You *must* not.' She clutched at the lapels of his tailcoat, in a silent plea. 'You do not understand!' She looked away, knowing she was handling this all wrong.

'Arabella, it is all right. I know about Smith.'

Her heart gave a flutter and fear twisted cold and hard in her stomach. 'You know?' She felt the blood drain from her face and Dominic's arms tightened around her. She looked up at him with dawning horror. 'You cannot,' she whispered. 'You cannot know. He will kill you, for pity's sake! Dominic, he will—'

But he placed a gentle hand at the nape of her neck, calming her panic and forcing her to look at him.

'Arabella, I have taken care of Smith. He will do nothing. You and Archie are safe.'

'It was not about me.'

'I know what it was about.' He stroked her hair. 'But I am safe too.'

'Thank God,' she cried and held him to her, and pressed fierce kisses to his neck, his chin, his cheek. 'I was so afraid—but how?' And the coldness of the thought that followed. 'Oh, my word, he did not publish, did he, all that he threatened?'

'He did not publish anything, Arabella, nor will he.' And then he told her. That Smith was not Smith at all, but Viscount Linwood. And why Linwood had done what he had done. He told her, and finally Arabella understood.

'You are certain?'

'Nothing can ever be certain, Arabella, but I do not

think that Linwood would risk the damage to his sister's reputation, nor Misbourne to his daughter's.'

She thought of the pretty, quietly spoken girl in the apothecary's shop in London, and this time it was sorrow that she felt for Lady Marianne. 'You would not really destroy her, would you, Dominic?'

'You know I would not. But as long as Misbourne and Linwood believe otherwise we are safe.'

She did not know how long they stood in each other's arms on that silent woodland path. Time lost all meaning. Arabella knew only that he was safe and her child was safe, and that, somehow, everything was going to be all right.

She looked into the eyes of the man that she loved and had so wounded. 'I have deceived you over so many things since that night in Mrs Silver's. And I am sorry for every one of them. I love you, Dominic.'

'I love you too, Arabella. And it is I who am sorry. I cannot forgive myself for what I did to you in Mrs Silver's, nor for what I did afterwards. I should have helped you, not made you my mistress.'

'Perhaps,' she nodded. 'But had we both chosen a different path it might not have led us to a better place. Would your father's deception ever have come to light? Would I ever have told you of Archie? We cannot know, Dominic.'

'We cannot,' he agreed and he looked at her with such tenderness that she could not doubt he loved her.

The sunlight had faded, casting the surrounding woodland in the mossy greens and deep browns of twilight. The air was growing chilled, but Arabella's heart was warm.

'The sun is sinking, Arabella. I had better get you

back to your mother before she thinks I have carried you off. She looked rather worried when I appeared at her door this evening, but she did tell me the direction you had taken.'

'Poor Mama. I am afraid I have not been very honest with her either.' And she explained the rest of it. 'So many lies.' She shook her head.

'But all are out in the open now.'

She nodded. 'No more dark secrets.' It was such a relief. She smiled. 'When did you arrive from London?'

'Late last night.'

'And you are only just come to find me?'

'There was much I had to organise this day.' He smiled in a mysterious way and then he lowered his mouth to hers and kissed her with a gentleness and care that mirrored the love in her heart.

'I have missed you so, Arabella.' His voice was low and guttural and filled with the same need that burned in her soul.

Their mouths merged, their lips revelling in the reunion. Her hand slipped beneath the lapel of his tail-coat, beneath his waistcoat to rest against his chest. Through the lawn of his shirt she could feel the warmth of his skin and the smattering of hair upon it, and she pressed her palm flat, feeling the strong steady beat of his heart. He eased back and looked into her eyes.

'I had better take you home, before I forget myself upon this woodland path and make us both the talk of the village.' His fingers brushed against Arabella's nipple and she gasped with the sensation that shivered through her.

'I fear we are already that,' she whispered. 'Everyone

has seen Archie. I fear they have guessed the truth, Dominic.'

'There is nothing to fear any more, Arabella. Everything is going to be fine.'

'Is it?' she asked.

'Yes, my love. It is.' And he kissed her again. A deep kiss. A kiss of passion and of love. A kiss that spoke of how he had missed her. She gave herself up to him, wanting to hold him for ever and never let him go, lest this all turned out to be a dream that would escape her on waking.

She felt him deepen the kiss, felt the warmth of his caress and the strength and safety of his arms. And then he stopped and looked into her eyes with such love and intensity.

'I must take you home now,' he murmured, 'or I *will* forget myself.' One swift last kiss and then he tucked her hand into the crook of his arm, grabbed the reins of his horse and began to walk her back in the direction of the cottage.

Arabella glanced down at his breeches at his obvious arousal and when she met his eyes again she was smiling.

'You, Arabella Tatton, are a very wicked woman. It is a good job you are going to church tomorrow morning,' he said and he smiled.

'Do hurry along, Archie, or we are going to be late,' Mrs Tatton scolded as they followed the woodland path the next morning in the direction of the church.

'Trojan is still eating his hay,' Archie explained to his grandmother, and gestured to his pretend horse. 'We shall soon gallop fast and overtake you.'

'Trojan?' queried Mrs Tatton to Arabella.

Arabella smiled. 'It is the name of Dominic's horse.' She smoothed down the skirt of pale blue silk and wondered if the dress was too much for the village church, but she knew Dominic would be there and she wanted to look her best for him.

Mrs Tatton smiled in return. 'I am glad you have sorted matters with Dominic.'

'I am too.' Arabella felt a warm glow of happiness.

'So, what is to happen between the two of you now?'

'In truth, I do not know, Mama. We have not yet discussed it.'

'Well, surely the betrothal will be reinstated and he will want to take you back to London?'

Arabella felt the smile fade from her face and some of the old tension was back. 'I am not so sure about that. The city does not hold such good memories for either of us. But I will do whatever it takes to be with you and Archie and Dominic.'

Her mother nodded, and as Archie galloped his imaginary Trojan past them they exchanged a smile.

There was not another soul about as they neared the church, and, indeed, the church door was closed.

'We must be very late.' Mrs Tatton took hold of Archie's hand, quickly smoothed the dark ruffle of his hair into some semblance of order again and hurried both him and Arabella towards the church.

Arabella pushed the heavy church door open and let her mother and son pass inside before her. After the bright sunshine outside it took a few moments for her eyes to adjust to the dim interior of the church porch.

'Arabella.' Reverend Martin sounded close by. 'My dear girl.' The vicar had a definite air of excitement about him and she wondered what had happened to make him so.

'Arabella!' She heard the catch in her mother's voice.

'Mama?' And then she looked through the open door into the nave where her mother was staring. The whole church was filled with flowers and greenery. At the end of every pew a large posy had been tied in place, so that the aisle was edged with flowers of pinks and purples and creams the whole way down to the altar. Garlands had been draped beneath the beautiful stained glass windows, and two massive matching floral displays stood on either side of the altar. Arabella stared in disbelief.

'What...?' she began to say and then she saw the two men dressed in their finest dark tailoring standing side by side at the front of the church. The low buzz of conversation increased as those at the back started to spread the word of her arrival and she saw the taller of the two men glance around and meet her eye.

The whole world seemed to stop. Her heart stuttered before racing off at a hundred miles an hour.

'Dominic,' she whispered and clasped her hand to her mouth as the significance of it all hit her.

'I know it is unusual, but in the absence of your dear papa and, if it is pleasing to you all, I thought that Mrs Tatton and young Archie might wish to walk you down the aisle and give your hand to the duke.' Reverend Martin was looking at her with a gentle expression of understanding upon his face.

'Thank you, Reverend,' said Mrs Tatton. 'If Arabella will have it, I would be proud to.'

'What is happening, Mama?' Archie tugged at her hand and stared up into her face.

She shook her head unable to believe this was real and not some dream.

'Mama?' Archie tugged harder.

She bent so that she might look him level in the eyes. 'Dominic is to become your papa and my husband. You are the man of the family and you must help Grandmama take me to him. Will you do that?'

'Yes, Mama. I would like Dominic to be my papa.'

Arabella smiled and she tucked her right hand into her mother's arm and took hold of Archie's little hand with her left. And with Reverend Martin following on behind them Arabella walked down the aisle.

Dominic had never seen her look more beautiful. There was such a look of wonder and surprise upon Arabella's face that he felt his heart swell with love. And when Mrs Tatton placed Arabella's trembling hand into his and stood back to leave her standing by his side, he had never felt so proud.

He knew that all of the village were filling the pews behind him. And that Reverend Martin was speaking the words of the marriage ceremony, but Dominic could think of nothing other than the woman standing so tall and beautiful by his side. He loved her completely and utterly. He had loved her since first he met her when she was a girl of fifteen. She was mother to his son, and when they left St Mary's she would be his wife.

Hunter cleared his throat and passed Dominic the wedding band to slip upon the third finger of Arabella's left hand.

'With this ring I thee wed. With my body I thee worship…' He swore his oath before God and all the village. And Arabella swore too.

'Those whom God hath joined together, let no man

put asunder…I pronounce that they be Man and Wife together.'

Arabella was smiling as he took her in his arms and kissed her.

She was his. At last.

It was such a glorious day of happiness for Arabella and it passed far too quickly. After the ceremony the villagers scattered rice over her and Dominic as they left the church, in accordance with tradition, and waiting outside were two gigs, one decorated in cream silken ribbons and pink roses and purplish-blue freesias, the other in pink and purple ribbons with white roses. Dominic lifted her up into the first gig with the cream ribbons, and she watched while Archie and her mother were helped up into the other gig. Then they were off to Shardeloes Hall, where long tables packed with food had been set out on the lawns of the front gardens and a band of musicians were already playing. A great party was just starting to which the whole of the village had been invited.

They ate and they drank and they danced, all the day through. And the sun shone from a cloudless blue sky and the breeze was gentle and soft, and the peacocks displayed the finery of their tails. And as Dominic took Arabella into his arms and waltzed her round the lawn Arabella thought there had never been a more perfect day and she told him so when he led her up the stairs to bed that night.

'Arabella,' he sat her down upon the bed. 'There is still something I must give you.'

She smiled and, taking his hands in hers, kissed his fingers. 'You have given me everything I could want—yourself and Archie. You have made me your wife. What more could I possibly want?'

He loosed his hands from hers and from a secret pocket inside his waistcoat he produced something she could not quite see, something golden that glinted in the candlelight. 'I have had it these weeks past; I always intended it to be one of my wedding gifts to you.' And then he unfastened the chain that was coiled in his hands and she saw it was the locket he had given her all those years ago. The same locket that had been stolen from the room in Flower and Dean Street and that she had never thought to see again. He moved behind her and draped it around her neck. Her skin shivered from the soft brush of his fingers against her skin as he fastened it in place.

'How on earth did you find it?' she asked.

'I hired a couple of very good thief-takers to recover it for you.' He smiled.

The golden oval lay warm against her breast. She opened it and there inside were the tiny miniature portraits of herself and of Dominic from all those years before when they had first fallen in love. And the curled lock from Archie's hair that she had placed between. The tears misted her eyes so she could no longer see the portraits properly.

'Oh, thank you, Dominic, thank you so very much.' She turned to him and kissed him.

'More tears?' he teased softly.

'I am just so happy,' she managed to say between sobs and the tears streamed all the more.

He took her face gently between his hands and wiped away the flow of tears with his thumbs, looking deeply into her eyes.

'I love you, Arabella. You are my duchess, my life, my very heartbeat. Without you there is nothing.' He kissed her so tenderly, so sweetly. She wrapped her arms around him and kissed him with all the love that was in her heart.

'I love you Dominic. I have always loved you. I will always love you, until the end of time.' She kissed him, and she knew theirs was a love that would never die. It had survived lies and mistrust and separation. Nothing would ever part them again. And when she felt his fingers against the laces of her bodice she rose to her feet and stood there while he stripped the dress and her undergarments from her body. And then slowly she teased the clothes from his body, brushing her breasts against the nakedness of his skin as she did so, delighting in the increasing harshness of his breathing and the tension that rippled throughout the toned muscles of his torso as she skimmed her fingers across it.

'Arabella...' He gasped as her fingers played with the buttons of his breeches without unfastening them. 'God help me,' he uttered and divested himself of his breeches at a speed unlike any she had seen before. And then his bare body was against hers, pressing her into the softness of the mattress. She was wet and warm and aching for him. She opened to him and felt him fill her, and she needed him to make love to her, wanted it, to complete their union of this day.

'Love me, Dominic,' she whispered to him as she nibbled at his ear lobe, and her hands slid to pull the firm muscle of his buttocks harder to her as if she would drive him deeper within her. They moved together, and he loved her and she loved him, loving and loving, their bodies worshipping each other, until they finally erupted in an exploding ecstasy of love and mutual pleasure and his seed spilled within her.

And when they had rested, they loved again—the whole night through.

A shaft of sunlight streaming through the window woke Arabella the next morning. She looked around her to make sure that yesterday and last night had not been some wonderful dream. But the heavy gold wedding band upon her finger and the large warm naked body snuggled next to hers reassured her it had been real.

'Good morning, *Wife*,' he murmured and her gaze flew to his to find the clear brown eyes awake and watching her.

'Good morning, *Husband*.' She smiled and felt his hand move upon her breast.

The sound of small running feet sounded in the passageway outside the duke's bedchamber in Shardeloes Hall.

'Mama? Where are you, Mama?' a small voice called.

Arabella laughed and rose, quickly pulling on her dressing gown that was lying across the carved wooden chest at the bottom of the bed. She threw the large dark coloured dressing gown by its side up to Dominic.

'You had best prepare yourself for your son, your Grace.' Then she hurried to the door and opened it to look out into the passageway where Archie was running. 'Here I am, little lamb, and your papa too.' She pulled him into her arms and kissed his forehead. 'Have you run away from your grandmama again?'

'Yes, Mama. I have been awake for ages and she is still snoring.'

So Archie came and climbed into the bed between Arabella and Dominic and the three of them snuggled down together.

'Are you going to let me see Trojan today?' he asked Dominic.

'Not Trojan,' said Dominic.

'Oh,' said Archie in a disappointed voice.

'I thought you might want to see Charlie instead.'

'Charlie?' Archie was staring at his father with great wide eyes. 'My Charlie, that Gemmell made for me?'

'Your Charlie, indeed, and from where do think Gemmell carved him? The real Charlie has been waiting here for you all along. He is your very own pony, Archie.'

Archie threw his arms around Dominic's neck. 'Oh, thank you, Papa! Can we go and ride him right now?'

'After breakfast,' said Dominic with a laugh and ruffled Archie's hair.

Arabella looked at her son and her husband and she knew that this truly was her happy ever after.

* * * * *

HISTORICAL

Where Love is Timeless™

HARLEQUIN® HISTORICAL

COMING NEXT MONTH
AVAILABLE DECEMBER 27, 2011

SCANDAL AT THE CAHILL SALOON
Cahill Cowboys
Carol Arens
(Western)

THE LADY CONFESSES
The Copeland Sisters
Carole Mortimer
(Regency)

CAPTURED FOR THE CAPTAIN'S PLEASURE
Ann Lethbridge
(Regency)

A DARK AND BROODING GENTLEMAN
Gentlemen of Disrepute
Margaret McPhee
(Regency)

REQUEST YOUR FREE BOOKS!

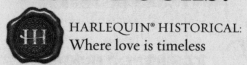

HARLEQUIN® HISTORICAL:
Where love is timeless

2 FREE NOVELS PLUS 2 FREE GIFTS!

*Brittany Grayson survived a horrible ordeal at the hands
of a serial killer known as The Professional...
who's after her now?*

*Harlequin® Romantic Suspense presents a new installment
in Carla Cassidy's reader-favorite miniseries,*
LAWMEN OF BLACK ROCK.

*Enjoy a sneak peek of
TOOL BELT DEFENDER.*

*Available January 2012
from Harlequin® Romantic Suspense.*

"**B**rittany?" His voice was deep and pleasant and made
her realize she'd been staring at him openmouthed through
the screen door.

"Yes, I'm Brittany and you must be..." Her mind suddenly went blank.

"Alex. Alex Crawford, Chad's friend. You called him
about a deck?"

As she unlocked the screen, she realized she wasn't
quite ready yet to allow a stranger inside, especially a male
stranger.

"Yes, I did. It's nice to meet you, Alex. Let's walk around
back and I'll show you what I have in mind," she said. She
frowned as she realized there was no car in her driveway.
"Did you walk here?" she asked.

His eyes were a warm blue that stood out against his
tanned face and was complemented by his slightly shaggy
dark hair. "I live three doors up." He pointed up the street to
the Walker home that had been on the market for a while.

"How long have you lived there?"

"I moved in about six weeks ago," he replied as they

walked around the side of the house.

That explained why she didn't know the Walkers had moved out and Mr. Hard Body had moved in. Six weeks ago she'd still been living at her brother Benjamin's house trying to heal from the trauma she'd lived through.

As they reached the backyard she motioned toward the broken brick patio just outside the back door. "What I'd like is a wooden deck big enough to hold a barbecue pit and an umbrella table and, of course, lots of people."

He nodded and pulled a tape measure from his tool belt. "An outdoor entertainment area," he said.

"Exactly," she replied and watched as he began to walk the site. The last thing Brittany had wanted to think about over the past eight months of her life was men. But looking at Alex Crawford definitely gave her a slight flutter of pure feminine pleasure.

Will Brittany be able to heal in the arms of Alex, her hotter-than-sin handyman...or will a second psychopath silence her forever? Find out in
TOOL BELT DEFENDER
Available January 2012
from Harlequin® Romantic Suspense
wherever books are sold.

Love Inspired HISTORICAL

Introducing a brand-new trilogy
from bestselling author

Linda Ford

The Cowboy Tutor *available January 2012*
The Cowboy Father *available February 2012*
The Cowboy Comes Home *available March 2012*

www.LoveInspiredBooks.com

Harlequin *Desire*

ALWAYS POWERFUL, PASSIONATE AND PROVOCATIVE.

USA TODAY BESTSELLING AUTHOR

KATHIE DeNOSKY

BRINGS YOU ANOTHER STORY FROM

TEXAS CATTLEMAN'S CLUB: THE SHOWDOWN

Childhood rivals Brad Price and Abigail Langley have found themselves once again in competition, this time for President of the Texas Cattleman's Club. But when Brad's plans are interrupted when his baby niece is suddenly placed under his care, he finds himself asking Abigail for help. As Election Day draws near, will Brad still be going after the Presidency or Abigail's heart? Find out in:

IN BED WITH THE OPPOSITION

Available December wherever books are sold.

HD73139

SPECIAL EDITION

Life, Love and Family

Karen Templeton

introduces

The FORTUNES *of* TEXAS: Whirlwind Romance

When a tornado destroys Red Rock, Texas, Christina Hastings finds herself trapped in the rubble with telecommunications heir Scott Fortune. He's handsome, smart and everything Christina has learned to guard herself against. As they await rescue, an unlikely attraction forms between the two and Scott soon finds himself wanting to know about this mysterious beauty. But can he catch Christina before she runs away from her true feelings?

FORTUNE'S CINDERELLA

Available December 27th wherever books are sold!

www.Harlequin.com

SSE65643